OBEYING ROWEN

CLUB ZODIAC, BOOK TWO

BECCA JAMESON

ACKNOWLEDGMENTS

I'd like to thank my editor, Christa Soule, for pushing me to be a better writer with every book. This one was rough! She went the extra mile! The finished product wouldn't be half as good without all her hard work.

I'd also like to thank my cover artist, Scott Carpenter, for digging hard to find the perfect models! He even had to swap this one out when I decided it was better suited for book two than book one!

A special thank you to my daughter, Rebecca, for proofreading this series for me during her long Christmas break. We had some fun times this month, but we also did some hard work!

ABOUT THE BOOK

She's living a lie...

She knows it. But it's easier for Faith to pretend she's a Domme or at least a switch than allow herself to feel again. To love again.

He's watching her...

Rowen can see right through Faith's false persona. But approaching her is the last thing he wants. He doesn't do switches, and he certainly doesn't do wealthy women.

She will submit to him...

When the opportunity presents itself, however, Rowen finds Faith on her knees at his bidding. There's no way he will turn down the chance to prove what he already knows—Faith is submissive. She isn't a Domme or a switch. She's the perfect submissive he's waited for his entire life.

But is it enough?

Faith has skeletons. Rowen has concerns. They both have a lot to learn about trust and second chances.

CHAPTER 1

"She's amazing, isn't she? It's like watching a moving piece of art."

Rowen didn't acknowledge Carter's statement. In fact, he wasn't sure he'd blinked in the last ten minutes. His mouth was too dry to speak.

Carter was right. The petite woman currently circling the man lying over a spanking bench was spectacular. Her thick blond hair was pulled up in a high ponytail that swayed across her back as she moved. Her skin was alabaster pale, standing out in stark contrast to the black leather skirt and corset she wore.

She wasn't tall by any stretch of the imagination, but the black heels she wore made her legs appear to go on forever.

Faith Robbins. He knew her name, but he hadn't had the pleasure of meeting her face to face yet. Subconsciously, he had to admit he'd probably steered clear of her out of self-preservation.

From his vantage point, Rowen didn't think she had a single flaw. He'd caught a glimpse of her clear blue eyes on occasion since she'd joined the club a few months ago, so he also knew a man could get lost in those orbs for days.

But none of that mattered at the moment. Not her beauty or

BECCA JAMESON

her legs or even her fucking fantastic cleavage pushed high under the corset.

What mattered right now was the way she moved, the way she held the long black flogger, and the way she kept her gaze locked on her submissive as she slowly glided around his body.

She could easily star as the Domme in any movie and make millions. Anyone watching this scene would agree in a heartbeat. But Rowen sensed something was off. He couldn't put his finger on it. But he knew.

"Is this the first time you've watched her perform?" Carter whispered from about a half a step behind Rowen.

"Yes."

"Breathtaking, isn't she?"

"Yes. I don't know the man subbing for her. Are they a couple?" he asked, trying not to sound too interested.

"That's Levi Calloway. He's also a new member. I think the two of them met recently, though. I don't think they're together." Carter nudged Rowen with his shoulder. "You interested in having her hands on you?" He chuckled softly.

"Hardly." *But I wouldn't mind getting* my *hands on* her.

"It's been months since you and Rayne broke up. Maybe you should get back out there. When was the last time you scened with someone?"

Rowen glanced at Carter, his brows raised. "What are you now, my dad?" He let his gaze roam back to Faith as she dragged her fingers across Levi's shoulder blade. They looked fantastic together. Levi's skin was dark against Faith's nearly white complexion.

Levi was resting on one cheek facing Rowen. His eyes were closed, but his mouth was open, and he licked his lips every time Faith stroked his skin. He wore nothing but a black G-string that left his butt exposed. He gripped the padded section of the bench where his fingers wrapped around the edge, and it appeared it took an incredible amount of energy for him to

2

remain still as Faith circled behind him and gripped his butt cheeks.

When her small hand smoothed down between his legs to cup his cock, Levi moaned.

Rowen almost moaned too. Luckily he managed to bite the inside of his cheek instead. Carter would never have let him live that down.

But Carter Ellis knew Rowen well. They'd been friends for years, ever since they met as enlisted men in the army when they were eighteen. Now they were business partners, each owning a share in Club Zodiac with their third partner, Lincoln Walsh.

Carter chuckled again. "Not gonna lie. She makes my dick hard too."

Rowen didn't comment. His own cock needed to be adjusted inside his jeans, but no way in hell was he going to reach around and touch his junk in front of Carter and risk hearing the man's laughter again.

Faith was a piece of art. Nothing more. Anyone would be mesmerized by her scene. Her clothing alone was mouthwatering. Lots of women wore corsets and skirts similar to hers, but none of them wore the two pieces quite like Faith. It was as if the black leather was custom made to mold to her body.

Finally, she took a step back, lifted the flogger in the air, and let it sail down to land on Levi's ass. It wasn't hard. She was warming up. But it was enough to make Levi flinch and Carter groan.

Rowen turned his head to smirk at his friend. "You gonna become a bottom now?"

Carter rolled his eyes. "Hardly. Not any more than you are. But you can't deny she's smokin' hot wielding that flogger. There's something super sexy about a confident female dominatrix. Not saying I want to be on the receiving end, but I can appreciate beauty when I see it."

Carter was not wrong.

Faith exuded a level of authority no one could dismiss. But something was still off...

"Did Lincoln say she transferred her membership from Breeze a few months ago?"

"Yes. There's a story behind that, but I don't remember what he said."

I bet there is.

Carter kept talking. "You should see the SUV she drives. That tiny ball of power drives a fucking ninety-thousand-dollar Range Rover. I saw her pull up in the parking lot."

Holy shit. Rowen's eyes widened, but he kept it to himself. Maybe the thing he was noticing about her that seemed off was simply that she was wealthy and carried herself in that manner. It would sure explain the clothing.

Rich people had a tendency to rub Rowen wrong. Or, more accurately, pretentious people. He'd met many over the years— both members of the club and clients of his accounting firm. He found that frequently the richest clients were the most entitled, nickel and diming every single cent to avoid paying their share of the taxes. And wealthy men and women who came into the club often thought they knew everything about BDSM because they googled it and had the cash to buy thousands of dollars' worth of toys.

In his experience, wealth did not make someone a good Dom. He and his partners went out of their way to ensure rich visitors didn't overstep their bounds in their exuberant desire to master the art overnight. They were statistically more likely to have a safeword called on them.

And rich submissives could be worse. Sometimes it even hindered their ability to let loose and be authentic. If they treated the lifestyle like it was a game, they also stood a higher chance of getting hurt—emotionally or physically.

But damn, Faith moved fluidly, like a seasoned Domme. She might have money, but she took her role seriously and didn't mess around.

"I didn't say that to put you on edge." Carter leaned closer. "I've seen no evidence that Faith is anything but the perfect Domme."

Rowen nodded, not glancing away from the scene.

Carter spoke again, lowering his voice. "She's not like that Brenda woman."

Rowen winced.

How did Carter remember the names of people from as far back as five or more years ago?

Brenda had come to the club while John Gilbert was still the owner. Rowen was unfortunate enough to be the one to greet her at the door. She'd flung her wealth around and demanded an "experience" as if the club were a place people paid for services.

To this day Rowen had no idea what the woman had hoped to get from her "experience," but he suspected she thought rough sex was on the menu. She was loud and belligerent and demanding. She'd disrupted the entire club before John escorted her out.

Rowen would never forget her because she was shouting that she was going to sue Zodiac for treating her unfairly. Apparently Carter hadn't forgotten either.

"Nor is she like that woman Lori. Not everyone with money is undisciplined," Carter added.

Lori. Lori had joined Zodiac soon after Lincoln bought the club. He'd been a little too lenient about vetting applicants in the early days. Lori had slipped through the process and then brought her own "Dom" one night to play.

From the moment Rowen saw the man, he'd rubbed him wrong. He was cocky, too loose, and he swung a whip around beside his leg like a crazy man would walk through a department store swinging a semi-automatic weapon while shouting about his second amendment rights.

And the unease had been warranted because Lori let the man tie her to a St. Andrew's cross and blindfold her. She'd insisted she didn't want him to go easy on her, and he did not. Within minutes she had blood running down her belly from two long cuts. Rowen had rushed forward to intervene, but he was about two seconds too late to stop the damage.

Lori had glared at Rowen with the most evil eyes he'd ever seen and blamed him for not doing a better job monitoring the scene. She had *also* threatened to sue.

Luckily neither woman had sued the club. But they had both left a sour taste in Rowen's mouth that would never fully go away.

"Rowen?" Carter interrupted his thoughts.

"Yeah?" He glanced at his friend. Had he missed a question?

Carter frowned. "You good?"

"Yep." He turned his gaze back to Faith. Carter was right. She was not Lori or Brenda. She was totally in control. Calm. Stunning.

When she lifted the flogger a second time and rained several blunt strikes over her submissive's butt cheeks, she bit the corner of her bottom lip.

Rowen's breath hitched. He watched her expression instead of her movements for several minutes. She was good. Well trained. Exacting with every strike. She took the time to soothe Levi's skin with her palms at perfect intervals. She kept him on edge by lightly grazing her nails over his cock every once in a while too.

Her perfectly manicured nails... So, not just the SUV. She literally carried herself like someone born with a silver spoon. They had a "look." The way she moved, walked, held her head, her hands. So...proper. Stilted. Or maybe that was part of her act? Was he judging her too harshly?

So what if she had money? It shouldn't bother him. She didn't belong to him. Besides, she was no slacker in the world of D/s, so Rowen needed to stuff his judgmental side down and give her a break.

Levi was in subspace within minutes. His head tipped back, elongating his neck as his body relaxed. The only time he stiffened was when Faith touched his cock through the bulging material of his G-string.

Rowen's gaze went back to her face. That lip…

He wanted to bite that damn lip. Pink. Swollen. Lush. Her perfect white teeth gleamed where they pressed into the soft flesh.

She exuded power. Except for that lip…

The room was so silent watching this piece of artistic perfection that every small noise coming from Levi echoed.

It had been nearly half an hour when Faith circled to Levi's head, set her flogger on his back, and leaned down to whisper in his ear.

Levi groaned, his torso squirming on the bench, as he rubbed his cock against the leather edge. Suddenly, he moaned loudly, arching his back as his hips thrust forward in the sharp rhythmic movements of an orgasm.

"Fuck me," Carter murmured. "I've never come on command."

Rowen hadn't either, but if Faith Robbins sauntered over to him at that moment and demanded he come too, Rowen was fairly certain he would comply instantly. He was that hard.

Carter wandered away, muttering something about needing to jerk off in private.

Rowen didn't move a muscle as he watched Faith help Levi off the bench and over to a loveseat. She wrapped a blanket around his shoulders and then squatted in front of him with her hands on his thighs and her head tipped back.

Rowen couldn't hear what she was saying, but her body language spoke volumes. When she leaned closer, her breasts rubbed against Levi's knees, but she didn't seem to notice.

People moved away to watch other scenes happening in the corners of the main play room at Zodiac. The lighting was dim. The walls and ceiling and floor were all black. But Rowen continued to watch from his vantage point partially hidden in a dark corner.

Levi nodded a few times and accepted a water bottle from

someone. After he drained half of it, Faith stood. She didn't stroke Levi's face or run a hand through his hair or caress his chest. She didn't take a seat next to him either. Instead, she waited until she was certain he was okay, and then she left.

Rowen's breath hitched again as she headed his direction. Her face lowered. She bit that lip again. And then she lifted her hands together at her waist and threaded her fingers delicately.

She didn't acknowledge Rowen as she passed. He doubted she even noticed anyone was standing there. She was in her own world. But she was not satisfied. The air around her was tense. Frustrated.

The beauty that was her dominance for the better part of the last hour had disappeared, replaced with uncertainty and...sorrow.

Faith Robbins may very well have been the best actress in the world, and her performance was breathtaking, but was it authentic? He didn't think she was a Domme. It didn't suit her. He had his doubts about her even being a switch.

He'd bet money Faith was a submissive.

If Rowen's cock could get any harder, it did. As he watched her back—shoulders squared, head tipped toward the floor, feet spread slightly farther apart then necessary—he finally gave up the battle and adjusted his dick. Not giving one solid fuck who saw him.

CHAPTER 2

"What are you still doing here?"

Rowen jerked his gaze up to find his sister, Sasha, leaning on the doorjamb at the entrance to his office. He glanced at his watch and then rubbed a hand down his face. "Shit. Is it already eleven? I'm sorry. I meant to be out of here by now."

She narrowed her gaze as she wandered deeper into the room and then leaned across his desk. "Your computer isn't even on."

He glanced at the black screen and nodded. "Yeah. I was, uh…"

A slow smile spread across her face as she righted herself, tightening the tie around her thigh-length, gray trench coat. "I saw the light on in your office. You're lucky I hadn't taken my jacket off yet."

He pushed to standing as he cringed. He didn't want to know what his sister wore or didn't wear under the coat. "My bad. I lost track of time."

They had a standing arrangement. When Sasha was going to be at Zodiac with the intention to scene with Lincoln, Rowen would take the rest of the evening off.

He could handle his best friend dating his sister. He could even handle knowing his kid sister was submissive. What he couldn't

9

handle was watching her in any state of undress. So they had an agreement. Tonight he'd broken it. He rushed to straighten up the pile of paperwork on his desk.

She tapped the top of his desk with her fingers, cocking her head to one side. "You're out of sorts. Is something wrong?"

He winced. "No. Of course not. Just wasn't paying attention to the clock is all," he repeated, tucking files into a drawer as if it were imperative he get them put away immediately.

"Hmmm. I heard you saw Faith in action tonight. I can see how that would be distracting."

Rowen winced. "Carter's a snitch."

She giggled. "She's gorgeous when she gets in the zone, isn't she?"

Rowen avoided looking directly at his sister, instead pretending to organize his desk and tuck things away that didn't need tucking. "I suppose." *She's gorgeous even when she's not in the zone.*

"Have you officially met her? I could introduce you."

"That won't be necessary."

She laughed again, the sound grating on his nerves. Sometimes he hated how well she could read him. They were close. They had always been close, but after their mother died when Sasha was only twelve, they grew even closer. Rowen was ten years older, and he practically raised her.

"It's been three months since you and Rayne broke up. It's amicable. You've both proven you can remain friends and still be members of the same club. I'm quite sure she doesn't care who you scene with."

"What does that have to do with anything?" He pushed his chair in and glanced around, completely out of ways to avoid looking Sasha in the eye. And why did he have to go and ask such an open-ended question?

"Don't be coy."

At the insult, he lifted his gaze to meet hers. "Don't you have a scene to prepare for, twerp?"

She sauntered across the room and took a seat on one of the armchairs in his sitting area. As she crossed her legs dramatically, she leaned one elbow on her knee. "So now you're going to resort to name calling?" she teased. "I must say I've never seen you this flustered over a woman."

"What are you talking about? I'm not flustered over any woman." He stepped closer and pointed at the door. "Now get out of my office so I can lock it and get home."

Making no move to leave, Sasha narrowed her gaze. "I don't get the feeling she was always a Domme, you know. As amazing as she is to watch as a top, I can only imagine how she must be as a bottom."

Okay. Now she was going too far. Rowen didn't want to picture Faith as a sub. As it was, his dick had been hard all evening. He didn't need any help. What he needed was to go home, take a long shower, and go to bed. Although admittedly that shower would include wrapping his fingers around his cock and jerking off to visions of Faith.

His palms were so sweaty he wiped them on his jeans. And then he closed the distance, grabbed his sister by the arm, and hauled her out of the chair. "Out."

She was giggling again as she let him lead her to the door. "I've gotten to know Faith a bit. I first met her when I visited Breeze a few months ago. I could talk to her," she proposed.

Rowen jerked her around to face him as they reached the hallway. "Don't. You. Dare." He narrowed his gaze at her. "I swear to God, Sasha. Do not interfere. I'm not interested in starting something with Faith Robbins. Stay out of it."

She smiled huge again. "You know her last name. How cute."

He rolled his eyes and groaned. "Sasha..." he warned.

She shrugged and turned to saunter down the hallway toward Lincoln's office, wiggling her fingers over her shoulder.

~

Rowen couldn't sleep. He'd gone through the usual nighttime motions—came home, showered, took himself in hand, had a beer. Now he was in bed staring at the ceiling. His dick was still hard, and his brain wouldn't stop the running reel of Faith.

What was wrong with him? He knew nothing about the woman other than the fact that she was sexy as hell, used to belong to Breeze, and could flog a sub's rear end like nobody's business. Oh, and she had money.

Rowen had no business letting her muddle his brain. The last thing he needed at the moment was a sub who made his dick stiffen just looking at her. He had worked hard to get himself to a place where he could separate business from pleasure.

The last woman he'd let get into his head had broken up with him and left him in a funk. He didn't need that kind of insanity again three months later.

Not that he was mad at Rayne. He couldn't blame her for moving on. They weren't compatible. She was hot. That had been what attracted Rowen to her in the first place. He hadn't even met her at the club. He'd met her in a crowded bar one night over a year ago when they'd been out with mutual friends for happy hour.

The truth was, he'd fallen hard for her because he'd been attracted to her, and then he'd let that attraction lead him by the dick for over a year before admitting it wasn't enough.

Rayne hadn't been in the lifestyle at all when he met her. He'd introduced her and slowly eased her into his world in the hopes she would become the woman he wanted her to be. And she had gradually thrived, but her kink didn't match his.

Admitting that fact took him a few more months. Finally, they'd had a heart-to-heart one night and agreed to end their sexual relationship. They were friends. He wasn't sure it would be possible, but it had worked. Rayne had joined Zodiac by then. She was comfortable in the club. She didn't want to transfer her membership elsewhere. Besides, she liked having the ability to check with Rowen, or Carter, or Lincoln before she played with anyone new.

Rowen was over her. That wasn't the problem. He could move on. He'd started doing scenes with other women weeks ago.

But no way was he going to let himself get led by the balls again over a pretty face. It never boded well. What he needed to do was find a woman whose kink matched his and *then* let the rest fall into place. As if that would ever happen.

Two key factors had held Rowen and Rayne's relationship together—she was hot, and she didn't balk at his chivalrous need to pay for everything. Even though she made plenty of money and liked nice things, she never challenged him about finances.

Admittedly, he had a deep-seated old-fashioned belief that a man should take care of his woman in every possible way— including financially. It was ingrained in him. And no matter what people said, it got under his skin when a woman he was dating wanted to split the check or pay for things. Perhaps his mother had instilled this value in him.

Or maybe his internal thought process about taking care of others had more to do with the fact that his own father had died when Rowen was young, leaving his mother without enough insurance money to care for the two of them.

And maybe his convictions were further solidified when Sasha's father took off and never came back. Rowen's ten-year-old spine had stiffened from witnessing the two examples. He had vowed he'd never leave a woman of his without the means to care for herself. And he would work his ass off to ensure she and any children they had were safe, secure, loved, fed, clothed, and housed.

Yeah, he was old-fashioned, but no one would ever be able to shake the foundation he had built. He nearly killed himself to get his degree while raising Sasha. He'd also put her through college. But he was financially secure as a result, and so was Sasha.

He'd lived beneath his means for his entire life, stashing away money as soon as he was ahead of the game. He had plenty of savings now, and he could breathe easier knowing when he met the right woman, she would never want for anything.

Unless she was rich. And she wanted things beyond his means.

Rowen was getting ahead of himself. He didn't know for sure Faith was wealthy. Maybe she simply liked nice things like Rayne. Shaking financial concerns he was totally inventing from his head, he stared at the ceiling and reminded himself once again to concentrate on the facts.

Faith was fucking gorgeous, and looks weren't everything. Looks weren't even some of the things.

Okay, looks *were* some of the things. Denying that would be a lie. But no matter what a woman looked like, if she couldn't be the kind of submissive he craved, there was no point in starting a relationship in the hopes she would change. In his experience, people were pretty much who they were. They didn't change.

Sure, they evolved and learned new things, but if he went back in his mind to a year ago, he would have to admit he'd known from the beginning that Rayne was not going to be compatible with him in the D/s realm.

Lincoln and Carter would say he was a fool and encourage him to play with a variety of women without worrying about whether or not they could be "the one." And for the most part, Rowen agreed with them. It was a fine policy. He did it often. He scened with someone at least once a week.

But not anyone who made his dick hard. He stayed away from them. The only thing that could come of that was heartache down the line. When his heart raced and his cock pulsed, it was a sure sign he was going to be disappointed at some point when he got to know the woman better.

In this case, he already knew too much without even speaking to Faith. He'd bet anything she was not strictly a Domme. Which meant she had to be a switch. He didn't do switches.

To be more precise, he didn't bottom. He could scene with just about anyone. Didn't matter to him if they were dominant with other people. But there was no sense letting his heartrate increase watching a woman top a man because chances were somewhere down the line she would want to top *him*. And Rowen didn't have any interest or inclination to do that.

Of course, watching Faith perform earlier hadn't been what made Rowen's blood pump. Nope. It was a certain something he'd been trying to put his finger on the entire time. And that certain something had been crystal clear when she finished and walked away.

He had no idea what her story was, but she was also submissive.

So, if he was honest with himself, he wasn't lying in his bed visualizing anything she'd so fluidly done in her performance that evening. Nope. He was picturing her on her knees, head bowed, blond hair cascading over her breasts. He was picturing her mouth wrapped around his cock, her hands behind her back, her alabaster skin completely bare to him.

He was imagining what her tits looked like, what color her areolas were, if her pussy was shaved. Did she scream when she came? How many orgasms could she give up to him in one evening?

Rowen groaned and flipped onto his stomach, tucking his hands under his pillow and trying to stop the rapid flash of imaginary photographs from keeping him awake.

He was in so much trouble.

CHAPTER 3

Faith woke up Saturday morning with a headache. She rolled over, glanced at the clock and groaned, burying her head in the pillow. She knew she had a pile of emails to get to, but she needed more sleep.

Playing the role of Domme always wore her out, but the effects didn't usually linger into the next day. After the stressful week she'd endured, however, it was no wonder. She was exhausted, mentally more than physically.

She loved her job working for the city as the event planner for many nonprofits, but some weeks she was slammed with events. This past week had been one of them, and she was well aware the follow-up emails would be jamming her inbox.

The good news was she hadn't run into her mother all week. If that had been the case, she would have a full-fledged migraine instead of a pounding headache. Any week that went by without that woman meddling in her business was a bonus.

Why she bothered to stay in Miami at all was a mystery. She should cut ties with her dysfunctional family and move to Seattle or someplace equally far away. The only thing keeping her in Florida these days was her job, but that was a huge magnet.

The city council loved her, and she loved them. Leaving them hanging without an event planner put a bad taste in her mouth. They counted on her. Hell, half the reason they adored her was that she kept her mother at bay. The woman stuck her nose in nearly every social event in Miami, much to the dismay of the city's employees.

She needed to get up. Coffee and some ibuprofen would hopefully eliminate the pain behind her left eye. A shower would help too. And some breakfast. She couldn't remember if she'd had dinner the night before.

As she rolled onto her back and blinked up at the ceiling. She had an appointment that afternoon with a new submissive, Brooke Madden. She was working with the shy woman on off hours when the club wasn't open.

Brooke didn't have the gumption to come into the club when it was in full swing yet, and besides, Faith found a lot of gratification in helping newbies find themselves. She suspected in the long run Brooke was going to need a lot more help than Faith could provide, but for now, she certainly didn't want to let the skittish submissive down.

Time to get up, get caffeinated, and get moving.

Rowen stepped into Carter's office two hours before opening Saturday night, surprised to find Lincoln in there with him. "Who's using a private room on the main floor if you're both up here?" He'd noticed the closed door with the lights on inside, but he hadn't wandered down the hallway in case Lincoln was in the room with Sasha.

Lincoln was lounging on the loveseat, his feet up on the coffee table. "That would be Faith Robbins."

"Faith? Why?" *And why the hell is my dick twitching at the mention of her name?*

Carter was sitting at his desk, flipping through a pile of papers. "She's working with a newbie. It's sensitive. They've been using a private room when we're not open."

Both of Rowen's brows shot up before he could stop them. Maybe he had pegged Faith wrong if she was so dedicated that she was spending that much time with a new submissive. Unless, that wasn't what Carter meant at all... "Is she training a new Domme?"

Carter chuckled. "Hardly." He lifted his gaze, brows furrowed. "You still haven't met Faith yet, have you?"

"No." Rowen lowered himself into the armchair across from Lincoln, facing both men.

Lincoln laughed now. "Are you avoiding her?"

Rowen flinched. "What? No. Why would I do that?"

Carter spoke next. "Because she's fucking hot and she makes every man's dick hard watching her, even those of us who aren't submissive. I get it. She's intimidating. She makes me question my refusal to bottom every time I see her."

"Don't be ridiculous. We simply haven't crossed paths yet." *And it would be best if we didn't.*

Lincoln leaned forward. "Faith is working with a woman. Brooke. She's skittish to say the least and most assuredly not dominant. She needs guidance, and she's not ready to make a public appearance."

Carter sighed. "She may never be."

"That's dedication," Rowen acknowledged. "How did Faith meet her if she doesn't come when we're open?"

"Here, actually," Carter said. "Brooke works for our cleaning company. She happened to be here off hours while Faith was practicing one day. They hit it off, and Faith's been working with her."

Why couldn't someone point out an inherent flaw in Faith that would make Rowen stop visualizing her as perfect every time his mind wasn't focused on work or the club? *So, in addition to not being a rich bitch who has no idea what she's doing in the BDSM world, she's also gracious and helpful?*

Awesome.

Not.

Rowen had concerns nevertheless. "And you're both sure the arrangement is safe? How well do you know these women? Either of them?"

Lincoln chuckled. "Jeez, when did you start doubting my ability to vet new members? Faith's been coming on and off for two months. I've spoken to her many times. Besides, I called Marcus Pierson at Breeze where she used to be a member to ensure she wasn't a psycho lunatic. He highly recommended her and told me I had nothing to worry about."

"And the other woman? Brooke?" Rowen asked.

Carter fielded that one. "She has signed all the paperwork. Faith explained everything to her before she ever touched a piece of equipment. They're fine."

Rowen nodded. Unease still crept up his spine, though he suspected it was due to his compelling interest in Faith more than anything.

This was perfect, really. Gave him a chance to rein in his attraction. Obviously if Faith was this dedicated to performing with a new submissive when the club wasn't open, she had to be a true Domme.

Right?

No, asshole, she could still be a switch.

And I still don't do switches.

He felt foolish that he hadn't met Faith and hadn't known a thing about Brooke. The truth was, he'd been rather scarce lately. He still kept up his end of the bargain doing the payroll and maintaining the books, but he'd been busy with the clients of his private accounting practice too and hadn't had much extra time to come into Zodiac earlier than they opened.

Perhaps it was a good thing he hadn't been around much if the mere mention of Faith Robbins had his hands sweating and his cock stiff. He wished he were a fly on the wall in that private room downstairs.

~

Four hours later, Faith's hands were shaking.

She was super glad the women's restroom had a sitting area with a few lockers so she could relax in relative privacy. She sat on the plush red armchair and leaned her head back, closing her eyes while she took deep cleansing breaths. Tucking her hands under her thighs, she focused on debriefing herself after the intensity of her recent scene.

It was always hard when she dominated someone. It took a lot out of her and left her needing aftercare almost as much as the sub. It was exhausting. So much concentration. Precision. Responsibility.

She knew she was good at it, partly because everyone told her so, but also because a crowd surrounded her scenes in hushed silence.

The door to the restroom opened, and she glanced over to find Sasha stepping inside.

"Oh, hi." Sasha smiled as she headed through the sitting area to the bathroom. After a few minutes, she returned, drying her hands on a paper towel.

She looked amazing, wearing all white. Her darker skin offset the fitted, stretchy, white dress. It wasn't as revealing as a lot of submissives wore, but it was still sexy. The tight skirt landed a few inches down her thighs and the bodice covered everything important. She even wore a bra, the lace showing through the slightly translucent material. Her heels made her seem taller than she was, and Faith pegged the two of them to be almost the same height. Five four.

Sasha started speaking almost before she was fully back in the room as she tossed her paper towel in the trash can. "I heard you did an amazing scene before I arrived. Sorry I missed it."

Faith smiled.

"You okay?"

She nodded and then took a deep breath. "It wears me out, especially when I do more than one. I did another scene earlier before Zodiac opened."

Sasha lowered herself onto the matching red armchair. "How long have you been a Domme?"

Faith took a deep breath and glanced down at her hands, trying to decide how much to reveal about herself. She'd met Sasha several times, but she had no idea if she could trust her. Suddenly, exhaustion won out over common sense, and she let her guard down. "I'm not. Not really. I mean, not all the time." Faith scrunched up her face. "I'm not making any sense." She liked Sasha. She'd met her a few months ago when she'd still been a member of Breeze and Sasha had come as a guest for her first foray into BDSM.

Sasha smiled warmly, not pushing Faith to keep speaking but waiting patiently in case Faith decided to continue.

Faith licked her lips and sighed. "I learned to top years ago when I first joined Breeze. I was young. I wanted to try everything. The entire lifestyle intrigued me. I was a sponge."

"That must have been amazing. I wish I'd had that opportunity."

"You're so young still. You have time," Faith pointed out.

Sasha chuckled. "I don't think Lincoln would be too excited if I decided I wanted to switch."

Faith narrowed her eyes. "What do *you* want?"

"Wow. Deep."

Faith waved a hand through the air. "Don't mind me. I get melancholy sometimes. I like to make sure everyone is true to themselves." *Like you're being true to yourself?*

Faith shook her own self-recrimination from her head.

21

Sasha nodded. "Even though I'm new to the scene, I'm not new to the concept. I've actually been coming to this club since I was twelve."

Faith's eyes bulged before she could stop herself from reacting so violently.

Sasha shook her head. "Don't get the wrong idea. I didn't come into the club itself before I was eighteen, and even then, only sparingly until a few months ago. My mother died when I was twelve. My father had skipped town when she got pregnant."

"I'm so sorry." Faith's chest seized. She had always been a sensitive person. Hearing something like that tugged at her heartstrings.

Sasha continued. "I was lucky. My brother, Rowen, was ten years older. He had just gotten out of the army, and he took me in. He also worked nights here at Zodiac, so the owner let me hang out upstairs in the breakroom while my brother worked."

"Lincoln?" Faith knew Lincoln was the majority owner with two other partners, but she didn't think he was old enough to have been here that long ago. Besides, somehow he was also Sasha's Dom. Faith hoped to God this story didn't start to creep her out.

Sasha shook her head. "No. John Gilbert owned the club back then. Lincoln bought it five years ago. I was seventeen. In fact, he freaked out about my age the day we met and banned me from even coming near the club for the next year. I've never been so humiliated in my life. He had a hissy in front of everyone who worked here, and I'd known them for five years. They were like siblings to me."

"Wow. How did you come to be his sub? You must have wanted to punch him in the face."

Sasha giggled. "Yeah. I did. But I also wanted to jump his bones. And it turns out he felt the same. It took us another five years to figure that out."

Faith laughed finally, relieved the story hadn't gone in a

squicky direction. "So, I guess you knew enough about the lifestyle to know what you wanted."

"Definitely. I didn't have experience because my brother and his partners didn't let me join the club, but I knew I was a sub. I knew I was Lincoln's sub, to be honest. I've never considered playing with anyone else. I didn't even date."

Faith was stunned again. "That's kinda…nice."

"It is." Sasha smiled. "What about you? You seem to be in tune with other people. Why do I get the feeling you aren't very happy yourself?"

Faith gave an exaggerated wince. "That obvious?" She sighed. It wasn't like her life was a secret. The members of Breeze knew her story. She didn't intend to go around blabbing it to everyone she met, but that was because she didn't like the way people looked at her with so much sorrow when they knew.

"You don't have to tell me anything you aren't comfortable with. I didn't mean to pry."

"No. It's not that. It's just been a while." She glanced down at her lap and pulled her fingers from under her thighs. They were still shaking, so she threaded them together. She felt comfortable with Sasha, and it had been a long time since she'd had a close friend who was in the lifestyle. Maybe it was time to open up to someone. "I was married. My husband was in the navy. He was killed in the Middle East a year and a half ago."

Sasha's eyes widened. "Oh God. I'm sorry." She covered her mouth with her fingers.

"Yeah. Me too." Faith swallowed. "I met him when I was twenty-four. At Breeze. He was on leave. We hit it off immediately and got married two months later." She didn't add the gritty details, like the fact that she hadn't told her parents about Victor until after the wedding. That she'd intentionally hidden her excitement to avoid their chastisement and disapproval.

After all, Victor wasn't nearly good enough for Faith

Davenport. He hadn't come from money. He didn't own land or businesses. He was totally unsuitable.

Faith had never exhaled freer in her life than the day she took his name and became a new person—Faith Robbins. TMI for Sasha, though. Another time.

Sasha's eyes widened farther anyway. "How romantic."

Faith chuckled. "That's not what most people said to me. Usually people looked at me like I'd lost my ever-loving mind. But I knew."

Sasha shook her head. "No. I get it. I think I felt that way about Lincoln the day he walked into Zodiac when I was seventeen. He did his best to squash my feelings, but he didn't succeed. I was head over heels before he even spoke to me."

"Then you *do* get it. It's a rare thing." *One I'll never experience again. Because I'll never allow myself to.*

"Yes, it is."

Faith took a breath and decided to steer the conversation down a less serious path. "He was all Dom. I had been dabbling in every aspect of the lifestyle for two years. When I met him, I was a switch, but I could dominate anyone, male or female. Victor put an end to that. I turned myself over to his care without blinking and never looked back."

"And now?"

"Yeah. Now. That's a conundrum. For a while I didn't come back to the club scene at all. And then I returned to Breeze, but everyone looks at me like they're going to cry when I see them. So that sucks. I haven't played much in the last eighteen months. I was the dungeon monitor the night we met at Breeze."

"Yes. I remember."

"The owner, Marcus Pierson, encouraged me to switch for a while to get back in the scene. He was probably right, but after submitting so thoroughly to Victor for so long, I'm rusty. Uncertain. Drained."

"So maybe you need to switch back to subbing? Give that a try?"

"Yeah. Maybe." Faith looked down at her lap. "Honestly, it scares the hell out of me."

Sasha's voice was gentle when she spoke again. "Submitting to another man?"

"Feeling."

Sasha pursed her lips, nodding.

Faith hadn't spoken so frankly with another woman for a long time. It felt good. Freeing. She liked Sasha. Maybe they could be friends. She suspected the two of them had a lot in common. "Anyway, Master Pierson also suggested I transfer my membership to Zodiac where less people know my story and won't look at me with so much sorrow. And here I am." She hesitated. "I'd appreciate if you'd keep my story to yourself for now. It's not like a huge secret, but it's refreshing not to have everyone staring at me with such sad eyes."

Sasha smiled warmly. "Of course. I won't utter a word to anyone. I'm glad you're here. If there's anything I can do, let me know. I'm usually here when the club is open. I don't always come downstairs, but if you ever want to talk, just ask Lincoln or Carter or Rowen and they'll find me or you can come upstairs."

"I've met Lincoln and Carter personally. I haven't met Rowen formally, but I think I know which one he is. I saw him last night after my scene. Tall? Six foot? Same brown hair, tanned skin, and green eyes as you?" *Obviously.* Now that she thought about it, the two siblings looked a lot alike.

"That's him."

"He probably thought I'd lost my mind the way I blew past him after taking care of my sub. I was exhausted. I didn't even make eye contact." *But I saw him. Lord have mercy, I saw him.*

"Yeah. He told me he watched you, but he didn't mention thinking anything particular about your escape, so I think you're good."

"He mentioned me?" Faith sat up straighter. Her heart beat faster. What the fuck?

Sasha's slow smile spoke volumes. "I think he was a bit smitten. But if you tell him I said so, I'll have to kill you."

Faith laughed. "Our secret. Does he not have a submissive currently? Girlfriend? Wife?" *Oh, great. Now I sound way way way too interested.*

"None of the above. He had a girlfriend. She's also a member. Rayne. She comes here about once a week. They split up about three months ago. Amicably. They weren't compatible."

They weren't compatible... In what way? Faith was not going to ask that question.

"His words. Not mine."

"Ah." That told her nothing.

"Anyway, we never had this conversation, but if you're interested, I can safely say the feeling is mutual. Go for it."

"I don't know. He's one of the owners. And I'm still a little...guarded."

"Well, eventually you have to put yourself back out there. You're too young to hang on to the melancholy forever. I can't imagine how you must feel. I don't think I would be as put together as you seem to be if anything happened to Lincoln." She stood and headed for the door, but at the last second she turned back around. "I meant what I said before. If you need a friend, I'm here."

"Why do you spend so much time upstairs?"

Sasha grinned. "Because my brother would have a coronary if he saw an inch of my skin or had to watch me play." She plucked the front of her dress. "Though I'm not sure how it matters since this is about the riskiest piece of clothing I own."

Faith furrowed her brow.

Sasha shrugged. "Admittedly I'm not much of an exhibitionist myself, but on top of that, Lincoln doesn't like to share even a glimpse of me. So staying away from the club while Rowen is here is kind of unnecessary, but he still doesn't like to see me play. So we trade off."

"Ah." Made sense. Not many brothers would want to see their baby sister strapped to a spanking bench. Or worse. This younger woman was intriguing. And how interesting that Lincoln was so possessive. The idea made Faith squirm. She hadn't been turned on in a long time. How could these simple words about someone else's life make her pussy wet?

Sasha kept speaking, not noticing Faith's plight. "He was supposed to already be gone when I got here tonight, but apparently he got so engrossed watching you that he lost track of time." She winked and then she was gone.

Faith flushed so hot her face burned. Surely Sasha was exaggerating. She'd noticed him the night before, but it was interesting to know he'd watched her again tonight.

She squeezed her legs together and pictured the intense look she could imagine on Lincoln Walsh's face as he told Sasha what she could and couldn't wear. Maybe it was nothing like that. But visualizing it made Faith hornier than ever.

Was Rowen that kind of Dom too? If he was...

It was easier when all she knew about Rowen was that he was hot as sin. Now he had admirable traits to go with his good looks. Dammit. The guy loved his sister and had taken care of her as a kid. That said a lot about a man's character.

CHAPTER 4

Two weeks later...

Faith arrived early at Zodiac Saturday night. She wanted to change out of her street clothes and take some time to wander around in the club before she did a scheduled scene later that evening. Lately she found her dance card completely filled with both men and women who wanted to sub for her.

She was a good Domme. She knew it. But it wasn't her passion.

For now, it was her persona, at least at Zodiac. She didn't usually see anyone who was a member of Breeze, so no one had ratted her out as an imposter.

She sighed as she changed out of her street clothes and into one of her favorite club outfits. She was hardly an imposter. It wasn't specifically a secret that she had once been a submissive. It was just that no one had asked yet, and she was enjoying the anonymity at Zodiac, riding that wave for as long as it could last.

She wasn't exactly misleading people. She was trained as a Domme. She'd been a switch for two years before she met her husband. As a way to ease back into the play scene, it was safer and less stressful to control others than to permit herself to be on the receiving end of demands.

Maybe one day she could return to subbing, but she wasn't ready yet.

As she was putting her purse in one of the small lockers in the women's room, her phone buzzed. She sighed, pulled it back out, and glanced at the screen. Her mother.

Nope. Not tonight.

Not tomorrow either. She was not going to let thoughts of her mother get under her skin while she was at Zodiac. The woman didn't belong in this world.

After stuffing her phone and the rest of her belongings into the locker, she checked the mirror, straightened her skirt, and stepped out into the dim lighting of the club. It was early, only nine, but several people were already at play in the main room. As she wandered back by the entrance, she passed Carter, the head bouncer and part owner. He smiled at her in greeting.

The next person she saw was Lincoln. He nodded at her as he walked by. She had yet to meet the elusive Rowen.

Not that she wasn't perfectly aware of who he was. It was highly possible she was subconsciously avoiding him. She'd seen him several times from a distance. He was usually serious, brooding. His brow was often furrowed in concentration or aggravation. She didn't know which.

It was unlike her to avoid someone, especially one of the owners of the club, but something about him made her aware of herself in a way she hadn't tapped into in a long time. It unnerved her to find herself aware of someone in such a carnal way. She wasn't sure she was ready for something like that. Even though Victor had been gone a year and a half, she felt a bit guilty for even entertaining the thought of another man yet. And after her conversation with Sasha, she had to suspect Rowen was paying attention to her too.

As Faith stepped into the main room, she glanced around, her eyes adjusting to the dim lighting. Zodiac took up the second floor of a strip mall above the shops. Originally a large apartment, this main room would have been the family/dining room. As a club, it had an entirely different feel. With the dark walls, floor, and ceiling, it had ambiance.

The room had a variety of apparatus—including a few spanking benches, a St. Andrew's cross, a bondage table, a massage table, and even a suspension system in the center. The walls were also lined with various means of securing a submissive.

Her gaze suddenly landed on the very man consuming her thoughts. He was helping another man with a new apparatus at one corner of the open floor. It was a spider web. She'd seen a few of them before, but this one was huge.

The web itself was made of silver chain, and it was stretched to the corners of a large wooden frame. It would allow the user to arrange a sub in any number of possible positions. The best part about it was that any submissive of any size could easily be attached to it spread wide. If this one was anything like the one they had at Breeze, it could be leaned back, leaving the sub on a bed of chain at any angle the Dominant chose.

As she watched Rowen from behind, he tugged on every section to ensure its safety. He checked the bolts all along the frame and then the frame itself. He even heaved his body off the floor, suspending by his hands from the top of the frame and swinging back and forth a few times to make sure it was well and truly safe.

A second man was helping him, adjusting the chain in several locations, removing a few links in some spots and adding a few in other places. Considering the tool belt around the man's waist and the coveralls he wore, Faith assumed he was the designer who built the new apparatus.

A woman Faith hadn't noticed before stood several feet to one side of the web, biting a nail as she watched. She glanced several times at Rowen.

An unwelcome tightness spread across Faith's chest as she wondered if Rowen was going to attach this sub to the new spider web and play with her. Jealousy reared its equally unwelcome head.

Faith would give just about anything for a man like Rowen to bind her to that web and tease her mercilessly. She didn't know him at all, so her irrational lust for him was just that, irrational. Nevertheless, he had been the focus of several masturbation scenes in her mind in the last few weeks. Each of which had been followed by an unwelcome feeling of remorse as if she had no business pondering a sexual encounter with someone who was not her husband.

Victor was gone. She knew that. And he wouldn't want her to mourn him forever. But deciding to move on was difficult. She missed him. She missed what they had. She also knew it could never be emulated. Their relationship had been one of a kind. And Faith didn't have the strength to love like that again. It hurt too bad.

Nevertheless, every time she'd seen Rowen he'd done nothing to dispel her wild imaginative musings. She'd turned him into something that was larger than life.

Tonight was no exception. His six-foot frame towered over the man next to him, and his thick brown hair lay in disarray. She wanted to run her fingers through it to see if it was as soft as it looked. It was cropped short on the sides, but the top was just long enough to give him a messy look.

She lowered her gaze to his biceps, thick and tan. He was built. She could feel the power wafting off him from across the darkened room.

With relief, Faith watched as another man came from somewhere else in the room and joined the nail biter. He pulled her finger from her mouth, reprimanded her with a shake of his head, and gripped her hands behind her back.

Faith was mesmerized by the scene, deciding to continue watching. After all, she'd come early for this very chance—to observe without commitment. When the man in coveralls was finished, he grabbed his tools and headed for the doorway that led to the main entrance.

Much to Faith's surprise, the waiting couple didn't approach the web together. Instead, the tall slender man who was clearly this woman's Dom turned his sub to face him, pulled her tight black dress over her head, and patted her bare butt to get her to move closer.

Was Rowen going to dominate this man's sub on the spider web?

Faith's mouth grew dry. She licked her lips in the nervous habit she couldn't seem to break.

The woman was curvy in a way that made Faith jealous. She was taller and had an ass and chest that would be the envy of most women. Her skin was tanned with only the thin lines of a bikini at her waist and the obscenely small white triangular patches around her nipples and her pussy. Wherever she sunbathed, Faith sincerely hoped it was in private. If anyone saw her wearing the bikini that matched those lines, they would fall into the pool and drown.

A deep voice behind Faith made her flinch. "I could get you a time slot on the web later this evening if you want?" She turned around to find Carter smiling at her. "It's enticing, isn't it?"

"Yes."

"You want me to book you? I could find you a willing submissive easily." He paused a breath and then continued. "Or a Dom if you prefer."

She glanced back again. "No. Thanks. I'll just watch this evening." It unnerved her the way he'd so blatantly proposed she might want to submit to another on that web, but then again, it was his job. He was only being cautious in not assuming anything specific.

"Let me know if you change your mind. The crowd would be mesmerized watching you."

As he walked away, she wondered what he meant by that last ambiguous statement. *Watching me top someone on it? Or watching me submit to another?* Either way, she shuddered.

Crossing her arms against a perceived chill in the room, she leaned against the wall and resumed her perusal as Rowen lifted the woman's arm above her head and secured her wrist to one corner with a cuff. He did the same to the other wrist.

After whispering something in her ear, Rowen waited until she nodded, and then he bent to secure her ankles spread apart in the same fashion. The effect was not much different from a St. Andrew's cross. Except everything changed when Rowen stepped to one side and turned a crank that caused the top of the web to slowly lean backward until the woman had no choice but to rest her weight against the chain webbing.

Faith sucked in a breath. The chain would be cold against her skin. It was dispersed enough not to be uncomfortable, but it would leave its marks.

Rowen spoke to the woman again. She said something in response, and he reached to adjust her wrist. He spoke to her once more and then grabbed her discarded dress from the floor and tucked it under her head.

Finally, she nodded, and he stepped back. He didn't go far, however, just a few feet. The slender man came forward and set his hands on his submissive's ankles. He proceeded to stroke her skin, his hands inching farther up her legs with every pass.

Faith shifted her gaze to Rowen. Apparently, he wasn't going to dominate the woman. He'd simply been setting up the scene. He crossed one arm under his chest and rested the other elbow in his palm. He gripped his chin with his free hand. Concentrating.

He stood at the perfect angle for Faith to see at least part of his expression without him noticing her.

His gaze darted around the apparatus continually, making sure everything was as it should be. He was meticulous about safety.

It made her so fucking hot, she felt the flush crawling up her chest. The room was cool so her heat stood out, considering she wore a sheer blouse and a very short skirt. She should not be hot.

Rowen never left the scene. He probably rarely blinked. He didn't interrupt except the few times the Dom motioned him over to adjust something. Otherwise, he was simply there to ensure the woman's safety.

When the scene was over, Rowen gave a few instructions to the man to teach him how to return the web back to an upright position and then lock it in place to make sure it didn't tip backward unexpectedly.

By the time Faith backed out of the main room, she noticed it was already almost ten o'clock. She only had a few minutes to prepare for her own scene. She wandered back to the women's restroom and washed her hands unnecessarily. What she really needed was to look herself in the eye, give herself a pep talk, and get herself in the right frame of mind.

Rowen had put her in a sub mode that was not easy to shake out of. But she had responsibilities, and one of those was to the man she had committed her time to. It wouldn't be fair to him for her to be anything less than on top of her game.

"You've got this, Faith. You're a great Domme. Deep breaths." She inhaled slowly, watching herself as she calmed. Rowen Easton was not going to get under her skin. Not tonight. Not ever if she could help it.

The man was dangerous to her well-being. If she gave him the chance, he could bring her to her knees. She would never give him that chance.

~

"She takes your breath away, doesn't she?"

Rowen flinched as he turned his head slightly to find Rayne standing next to him but about a half step behind.

She wasn't looking at him. She was watching Faith perform. Before he could comment, she spoke again. "I haven't ever submitted to a woman before, but I'm seriously considering asking Faith to do a scene with me. She's that good."

Rowen stared at his ex-girlfriend, half-amused, half-jealous at the idea of her having contact with Faith. He tamped down the absurd thought. "You could ask," he pointed out.

She nodded slowly, and then she turned her gaze to meet Rowen's. "You could too, you know."

Rowen cocked his head to one side. What was up with his coworkers and friends? Even his sister. It seemed like they had planned some sort of gradual intervention to gang up on him about Faith. He decided to deflect, as usual. "I don't bottom."

She rolled her eyes. "I wouldn't expect you to."

Granted, Rowen had sensed that Faith was submissive from the first time he'd seen her perform two weeks ago, but it was entirely possible his desire to top her was distorting his ability to see reason.

After all, he'd seen Faith dominate three other people in the last few weeks. Perhaps he was mistaken about her. But then why had Carter, Lincoln, Sasha, and now Rayne stopped to encourage him to scene with Faith?

Could it have anything to do with the fact that you always watch her intently with drool running down your chin?

Rowen couldn't fully put his finger on his fascination. He hadn't once seen Faith submit to anyone. He had no proof she even could. He wasn't about to submit to her. So why the interest? *Because she's sexy as hell? Because you suspect she's living inauthentically?*

"She has good taste, that's for sure," Rayne added. "I'd have to save for a month to afford those boots. And that skirt... Damn. It's like someone made it for her."

Rowen swallowed as he turned back to watch the rest of Faith's scene. Rayne had just confirmed what he'd already suspected. Faith had money. He really needed to turn around and walk away. Perhaps he was a jackass for automatically assuming she was high-maintenance or a bitch, but he had no interest in messing around with a rich woman.

Lord, dude. Who said she even wants to submit to you. Cocky much? And besides, if he admitted the truth to himself, doing a scene with her would not kill him. If he ever had the opportunity, he knew he would snatch it in a heartbeat. Personal convictions be damned.

Hell, maybe he could flush her right out of his system if he came right out and asked her to submit to him. It wasn't a bad idea. Lurking around week after week watching her only made his cock harder and his imagination more out of control.

Maybe he was reading her wrong. She was so in control as a Domme it was very possible she would top from the bottom, and he would tolerate that for about half a second before walking away.

Finding his balls and approaching her was a great plan. She would either shoot him down outright or give him the opportunity to prove to himself that looks weren't everything as he got to know her.

You're a dick. An egotistical dick. Or maybe jaded from experience.

Rayne shook him out of his pity party when she squeezed his arm and then walked away.

His attention back on Faith, he took in what Rayne had seen. Faith looked spectacular in a tight black skirt much like the one she'd been wearing the first time he saw her. Tonight she had on fishnet hose and thigh-high black leather boots. Instead of the corset he often saw her wearing, she wore a white lacy bra covered by a sheer white blouse that hid nothing.

Mesmerizing.

As usual, Faith took excellent care of her sub when she finished covering his ass, thighs, and shoulder blades with perfect pink stripes from her whip.

She had a lot of training with a whip. That was obvious. And it sent a chill down Rowen's spine. Why was he spending so much time thinking about this woman? She wasn't remotely compatible with him.

Shaking himself out of his reverie, he wandered away. He was supposed to be working the floor for the next hour as a dungeon monitor, and then he needed to go upstairs and sequester himself in his office with paperwork so Sasha and Lincoln could play.

An hour later as he climbed the stairs to the third floor where the offices and staff breakroom were located, he heard female voices coming from Lincoln's office. One voice belonged to Sasha. He wasn't sure who the other was.

The office door was open, so he headed that direction, mostly to let Sasha know he was done downstairs for the evening. When he leaned around the doorframe, his breath hitched.

Sasha was sitting on the loveseat laughing. The other woman was Faith. Her face was also lit up with mirth. Both women lifted their gazes when he cleared his throat.

"Hey," Sasha said. "Wow, is it already eleven?" Her back went straight as she crossed her ankles. She was dressed rather demurely for someone intending to play in the club tonight. Then again, that wasn't unusual. He didn't know if her choice in clothing was her own doing or if Lincoln selected her outfits for her. He also wasn't about to ask. TMI.

Tonight she wore a soft blue dress that covered everything important and could easily be worn anywhere in the city.

"Yep."

"Come on in. Have you met Faith?"

He had to concentrate hard to get his legs to follow walking orders, but somehow he managed to saunter across the floor toward the women. He smiled warmly at Faith as he held out his hand. "Rowen Easton. I've seen you perform several times. Impressive. I'm sorry we haven't had an opportunity to meet. Welcome to Club Zodiac."

She licked her lips as she rose to her feet, which made his cock stiffen. As she set her smaller hand in his, she spoke. "Thank you." Her voice was far more demure than it had been a moment ago with Sasha. "I've enjoyed every visit to your club. The members have been very gracious and welcoming." She glanced down at Sasha. "Your sister is lovely. We've been getting to know each other."

"Have you now?" Rowen glanced at Sasha, hoping his sister hadn't said anything to Faith about him, even though she'd suggested to Rowen on three occasions that he should approach Faith.

As he reluctantly released her soft fingers, he waved at the loveseat. "Sit." He lowered himself into the armchair across from them and crossed his legs, hoping he looked far calmer than he felt. This ridiculous anxiety that made him sweat every time he saw Faith unnerved him.

Faith pressed her knees together and folded her hands in her lap. She swallowed several times and licked her lips again before she spoke. "Sasha tells me you're an accountant."

He nodded. "I am. What else has Sasha told you?" He eyed his sister suspiciously.

Sasha might have submissive tendencies, and she definitely yielded control to Lincoln most of the time, but she didn't ever let Rowen think for a moment she was anything but a bossy younger sister toward him. "Nothing that would get my butt spanked if Lincoln ever found out." She shot him a fake cocky smile.

Lincoln miraculously stepped into the office on the tail end of Sasha's assertion. Lincoln was six three, broad shouldered, and formidable. "What's this about you needing a spanking?" he asked, not an ounce of mirth in his voice.

Sasha sat up straighter. "No, Sir. I was telling my brother that I would never do something to warrant you to flex those fingers of yours." She stared at Lincoln's hands as she spoke, her ass squirming on the sofa.

On that note, Rowen pushed to his feet. "That's my cue to leave. She's all yours." Rowen glanced at Lincoln. "Good luck."

Lincoln was still staring at Sasha, his brows furrowed. Yeah, Sasha probably shouldn't use that tone of sass. Ever. Even if she was telling the truth. Rowen knew he wouldn't tolerate it himself. And he knew Lincoln well enough to know Sasha was indeed going to be on the receiving end of some form of discipline in about one minute.

Lincoln didn't take his gaze off Sasha as he spoke to Rowen. "We won't be going downstairs tonight. You can have the club if you want to scene with anyone. Would you lock the door on your way out?"

"Of course." Rowen fought the urge to chuckle. He had no idea why he ever worried about Sasha getting involved in this lifestyle. She was indeed suited for it, and there was also no doubt Lincoln was firm enough to ensure she stayed in line.

Faith jumped to her feet, leaned over to kiss Sasha on the cheek, and then rushed from the room on Rowen's heels. When they were finally in the hall and Rowen had shut the door, Faith lifted her gaze to his. "Yikes. That was...hot." She smiled, but her face flushed, and then her expression sobered. "Sorry. That was your sister."

He smirked. "I'm getting used to it. They've been together for about four months now. And they probably should have been together for the last several years."

"Yeah, Sasha told me some of the story."

Rowen had no idea what possessed him, but he wrapped his hand loosely around Faith's biceps and led her to the next door down the hallway—his office. When they entered, he pointed at the brown, leather loveseat under the window along one wall of his corner office. It was dark out, but the blinds were open. He hadn't taken the time to close them when he'd popped in briefly earlier. Besides, he liked the twinkling of the city lights outside.

He opened the mini-fridge next to his desk and pulled out two bottles of water. And then he joined Faith on the small loveseat as he loosened the cap on one and handed it to her.

"Thank you," she whispered.

He took a long drink of his own water and then leaned back, setting his arm along the back of the sofa and stretching out his legs. "I saw your scene earlier. You really know how to handle a whip."

"Thank you," she repeated. She turned her body to face him more fully, but her gaze landed on his chest somewhere.

Unable to stop himself, he eased his hand from the back of the couch to toy with a thick lock of her hair absentmindedly. She wore it down tonight, long thick waves hanging halfway down her back. "Have you always been a Domme?" No sense beating around the bush. He wanted answers.

"No."

No? That's all she was going to give him?

"Care to expand?" he urged.

She pursed her lips and inhaled through her nose.

He slid his hand from her hair to her chin, nudging it upward with two fingers. When her gaze met his, her face flushed a gorgeous shade of pink. She licked her lips again as if they were permanently dry.

He set his thumb on the lower one and tugged it downward.

She opened her mouth and tipped her cheek into his palm, her eyelids lowering halfway.

Fuck me. No way in hell was he going to let her know how she affected him. "Talk to me. Tell me about yourself." He removed his hand, setting it on the back of the loveseat once again, watching how she stopped breathing and followed the retreat of his arm with her gaze.

Yeah. *Domme, my ass.* She might be capable of topping a variety of people, and she did it better than most Dominants he knew, but she would not be topping him. She would submit to him. She would do it now. Tonight. Right here.

He wished he'd shut the door of the office when they came in. It had seemed presumptuous. And in reality, he wasn't sure he cared who came into the room.

"Faith," he stated firmly to get her attention.

She jerked her gaze back to his chest.

"Look at me." His dick was so hard already it threatened to explode.

She lifted her gaze again. "I'm not sure this is a good idea. I should go."

He held her gaze, unwavering. "You're not sure *what's* a good idea? Talking to me?" He lifted both hands briefly in the air. "I'm harmless."

A soft chuckle escaped her lips as her face went from nervous fear to laughter. "Nothing about you is harmless, Master Rowen."

Damn. When she said his name, adding the title, he had to bite the inside of his cheek. "What makes you say that?" Had she heard things about him? Not that he had any secrets, but it was possible people had encouraged her to approach him the same way they had done to him.

She lowered her gaze to his lap.

"Eyes on mine," he demanded. He was testing her.

She tipped her face up again. "You make me uncomfortable." She shifted slightly on the seat, her hands fisting in her lap.

Excellent. Music to his ears. "Why is that? We just met a few minutes ago." Though he felt like he knew her much better than their acquaintance would imply.

"I've seen you in the club. You're...formidable."

"Am I now?" He lifted a brow. It was difficult to maintain a normal level of breathing.

"You always look like you're in deep concentration, or you're slightly angry."

That stunned him. "I assure you, it's not intentional. I may be frequently preoccupied, but I can't remember the last time I was angry." Even when he and Rayne broke up several months ago, he'd been more relieved than angry. Although he had been pretty livid the day he found out Lincoln and Sasha were stepping into D/s territory as a couple.

He was proud of Faith for holding his gaze when she obviously felt uncertain. Her chest rose and fell rapidly. He affected her. He also had no idea what possessed him, but he had the urge to push her. "I'll admit I don't know anything about you. But I'm going to be bold here and say that I don't think you're a Domme at all. I think you're hiding."

Her breath hitched. She licked those full pink lips again. Her skin flushed a deeper red.

She also squared her shoulders, straightening her back so that her breasts lifted. And holy mother of God, she lowered her face to his lap again.

He was not wrong about her at all.

Every ounce of her screamed submissive. Not just dabbling. She was well trained. She was also clearly not interested in sharing or revealing her story. His next move was important. And he suspected whatever he said would be as pivotal for her as it would be for him.

He took her water bottle gently from her fingers, steeled himself against possible failure, and spoke. "Faith, we can play this two ways. You can either answer my questions, or you can keep your secrets and submit to me. Right here. Now."

She might have flinched, but if she did, it was subtle. He was pretty sure she stopped breathing. Long seconds passed while she considered his request.

Not that he intended to permit her to keep her secrets forever. But he would stop badgering her tonight in exchange for her total submission. Would she do it?

Finally, without meeting his gaze or lifting her face at all, she slid to the floor in front of him and positioned herself on her knees, clasping her hands behind her back. Not a word.

Fuck. Me.

CHAPTER 5

Faith didn't have a clue what possessed her to submit to this enormous bear of a man who filled entire rooms with his presence alone.

She knew very little about him except that he was part owner of this club, Sasha's brother, and one of the most dominant people she'd ever met. He exuded dominance from his pores.

And it had been so long since she'd experienced something like this. This total submission to another person. She'd been hiding, exactly like he said, and he'd called her on it. If nothing else, she owed him respect for calling her out so blatantly and forcing her to make a decision.

He was a calm individual. She didn't expect he often lost his temper—although Sasha had told her he'd lost his marbles when he found out Lincoln was sleeping with Sasha. That only meant he was a protective brother. Was he as protective of others too? She knew the answer to that. After all, she'd watched him care for someone else's sub on the new spider web apparatus just a few hours ago.

Faith had also met his ex-girlfriend, Rayne, a few times. She was sweet and kind. She was rather new to the scene, but didn't strike Faith as being overly submissive. A fringe player.

Now that she'd seen Rowen firsthand, she could see how the two of them might not have been compatible. Part of her wanted to ask him about a dozen questions, but she held her tongue since she wasn't willing to tell him a single thing about herself. Not yet. Not tonight.

Right now she just wanted to feel. Anything. For the first time in so many months. Eighteen of them. Two years really. Her husband had been deployed for six months when he was killed.

There was no reason Faith needed to spill all her private personal secrets to a man she just met, simply to do a scene. It was enough that she'd readily submitted to someone at Zodiac. Her mind was on overload.

It was only a scene. There was no commitment here. Just a few hours with an extremely sexy, dominant man who made her panties wet and her hands shake every time she saw him. She had no reason to feel guilty for wanting to submit to him. No matter how focused she was on her latest role as a Domme, when Rowen stepped into a room, her entire body switched modes.

Did he know that? He seemed intuitive. He'd also called her out on it less than five minutes after making her acquaintance.

He squared his body with hers, setting his elbows on his knees. Inches separated them. She probably should have given herself more space, but the oval coffee table behind her prevented her from doing so.

Every breath brought his personal scent into her lungs. Clean soap. Masculine. Rowen. She fought the urge to shudder.

"Good girl." His first words to her as a Dom reached in deep and shattered any hint of the dominance she herself had exuded an hour ago in the club below them.

But they weren't in the club now. They were upstairs. The only other people upstairs were Lincoln and Sasha. It was unlikely either of them would leave the locked office next door anytime soon. It was also unlikely their third partner Carter would leave the club to come upstairs. He was working the front door that night as head bouncer.

"It's been a while since you submitted to anyone."

It wasn't a question, but she felt the need to answer anyway. "Yes, Sir."

"I won't ask you why. I won't ask you anything. Not tonight. You have my word. You made a choice, and I won't take that for granted."

"Thank you, Sir."

"Safeword?"

"Red, Sir."

"Good girl." He reached forward to cup her face gently, his actions affirming what she already suspected. He was a calm, caring Dom.

She suspected he was also firm and demanding. She prayed that was the case.

"I'm going to shut and lock the door to my office. But only because I assume you'd like your privacy protected. I don't mean to give you the impression I would never display a submissive to others, but I sense you have secrets you'd rather everyone not know at this time."

She blew out a long breath as he stood and walked to the door, shutting it and then twisting the lock with a resounding snick. "Thank you, Sir," she murmured as he returned.

Rowen lifted the coffee table behind her and moved it back several feet, and then he was behind her, gathering her loose curls in his hands. He must have kept hairbands in his pocket or something because he expertly braided her thick locks and secured the end. "I expect you to keep your gaze lowered unless instructed otherwise, but when I ask you to look me in the eye, I won't permit you to hide behind a curtain of hair."

"Yes, Sir." She shivered, unable to control the reaction. His tone was hypnotizing. Her pussy was soaking wet. It had been so long...

"I need to know what you need from this scene, Faith. I can feel the heavy desire to submit. That's clear as day. And I will do everything in my power to ensure you have a fulfilling experience tonight." His hands landed lightly on her shoulders and then trailed down her arms.

Goose bumps rose on her arms.

He continued to speak. "Here's what I can surmise from your body language. You crave the firm hand of a demanding Dom. You have denied yourself this for a long time. And you have strong submissive tendencies that are pushing to be let out."

"Yes, Sir." Was he a mind reader?

He slid in front of her until he stood with his cock inches from her face. The bulge in his black jeans was huge. She would give almost anything to have it inside her. It was too soon. Wasn't it? She didn't think she was ready to have sex with anyone yet, but if Rowen Easton continued to impress her with his intuitiveness, she might change her mind.

Rowen tucked two fingers under her chin again and gently forced her head to tip back. Her gaze traveled up his broad chest covered in a tight, black T-shirt until she reached his stern but also kind face. He hadn't shaved tonight. Perhaps not yesterday either. She'd always melted a little when a man let his facial hair grow. Not long. Just a few days' worth. It was a Saturday night. She suspected if he worked in an office, his jaw would be perfectly smooth on Monday morning. Disappointing.

His thick brown hair and green eyes matched his sister's. Though he kept his hair cut stylishly short on the sides. "What I can't guess is if you need release in the form of a good flogging," he leaned down until his face was inches from her, still holding her chin steady, "or if you need me to make you come so hard you can't see straight."

She swallowed, forcing herself to hold his gaze. "I know this might shock most people, but I don't tolerate pain well, Sir."

A slow smile spread across his face as he released her chin, slid his hand around to the back of her head, and angled her face back toward the floor with just the right amount of force that her nipples tightened.

The temperature in the room seemed too high, though she knew better.

"You're an enigma, aren't you, Faith?"

She didn't answer.

He circled her. Slowly.

She watched his feet.

He built up the intensity with his deliberately lazy moves as if they had no place to be and all the time in the world. It was working.

Pausing his perusal behind her again, his fingers danced on her shoulders. "How aroused are you. Scale of one to ten."

"Eight, Sir." No sense trying to hide it. He could very well reach his fingers down and find out for himself. How did he react when his submissives lied?

"Good girl. Honesty is the best policy with me." He leaned forward and slowly eased his hands down her arms until he circled her wrists with his long fingers. As he lifted them over her head, he whispered in her ear, "Clasp your hands behind your head."

She did as he instructed, praying to God nothing he did would trigger a memory of her husband, causing her to break down and fall apart. So far she managed to keep him out of the room, but this was her first attempt to submit to someone else. She wasn't sure she trusted herself. She wasn't sure she was ready to submit to another man.

There were few similarities between Victor and Rowen. This was a good thing. Perhaps their differences had been what attracted Faith to Rowen in the first place several weeks ago.

Victor hadn't been as tall as Rowen. Nor was he as broad. He was fit, of course. But not as large. He had dominated Faith completely when he was home on leave, but his demeanor had been different. He talked more. Perhaps he hadn't had the same level of confidence Rowen exuded? She hadn't noticed it at the time, but now that she found herself on her knees in Rowen's office...

He broke her from her mental comparison when his hands trailed around to her collarbones, and then he began unbuttoning her blouse. "This sheer material is sexy, but I've been dying to see what's under it."

She licked her lips. It was a nervous habit. She knew it. She couldn't stop it. At this rate, Rowen would be able to make her come with the timbre of his voice alone. Another rush of wetness leaked from her pussy to coat her thong.

Every move Rowen made was slow and deliberate. It took ages for him to reach the final button and tug her blouse out of her skirt. He somehow managed to do so without brushing against her bra at any point. Undoubtedly also deliberate.

He lifted the thin, barely existent material up her body, causing her hands to separate at the back of her head for a second to remove the blouse.

He trailed one finger down her back until he hit her skirt. She arched forward, a soft whimper escaping her lips. It almost annoyed her knowing she was so easily affected by him and unable to hide the fact.

When he stepped in front of her again, it was to continue trailing a finger over her skin. This time he dragged it slowly across her shoulders and then down along the V of her bra. The lace was thin. There was no way to conceal the pucker of her nipples.

She arched her chest more fully toward him.

"That's my girl." His voice was deeper. Sensual.

How had he managed to make her so hot and bothered in so

few minutes? Though if she were honest, it hadn't been a few minutes. She'd seen him in the club a number of times. Brooding. Brow furrowed in concentration. Had she been at least partially responsible?

"Stand up for me, sweet girl."

With a practiced ease she would never forget, she planted one foot and rose gracefully to her full height without swaying. Her hands remained threaded at the back of her head, shoulders back, chest high.

Rowen let out a low whistle. "My girl has done this before."

"Yes, Sir."

Luckily he didn't ask for more. He'd promised he wouldn't pressure her to speak, and so far he had not. He leaned his head down and kissed her neck at the juncture with her shoulders. "You smell fantastic."

She shivered at the unexpected gesture, although she suspected a lot about Rowen would always be unexpected. "Thank you, Sir."

"Vanilla..."

He wasn't wrong. Her body lotion had been warm vanilla that morning.

"I like it."

She made a mental note to use it next time she was with him. *Next time? Lordy.*

He chuckled. "Interesting choice for a woman who is so obviously not vanilla."

She smiled. He was right. There was no connection, though. She happened to like the scent.

He reached between her breasts without warning and popped the front clasp of her bra. Her heavy breasts sprang free as she sucked in a breath. The cool air in the room hit her nipples, making them pucker further.

Leaving the bra hanging loose from her shoulders, he cupped her with both hands and dragged his thumbs over her nipples.

She rose onto her toes at the contact.

He released her chest and stepped back. "Mmm. I need you to stay still, sweet girl. Hard rule. If you can obey that rule, I'll make you come so hard you won't remember your name."

She swallowed. Damn, his words. His tone. His entire demeanor. Victor had been a firm Dom, but nothing like this. His voice had never held this level of command. She felt another wave of guilt that she was so aroused so fast from this man who was not her husband.

He's gone. He wouldn't want you to spend your life alone. He told you so himself...

She shook Victor from her mind as Rowen backed up another step and sat on the loveseat. Shocking her. He set his arms on the back of the couch and crossed his legs. "Strip for me. Slowly. Make it sexy. I want to watch you unveil the rest of your gorgeous body for me."

She had stripped before. She could do this. It was only hard because she barely knew Rowen. It was their first scene together. He was fully clothed. She was about to totally bare herself to him.

She lowered her arms, glancing at the windows. Would anyone see?

"The glass is tinted, Faith. But it shouldn't matter. I don't want you to question my demands. Just follow them. Don't think. I know I'm pushing you, but I also know you need it worse than your next breath tonight. Am I right?"

She nodded. "Yes, Sir."

"Good girl. Then you'll obey me for the next hour without question, yes?"

"Yes, Sir."

"I'll keep track of every time you hesitate and discipline you at the moment of my choosing."

She pursed her lips. What did discipline look like to him? She had her safeword. She trusted him. He had a reputation that was unblemished in the club. Not one person had spoken an ill word against him. So far he had proven to be intuitive when it came to her needs. Eerily so.

She'd also told him she wasn't a fan of pain, so it was unlikely he intended to mark her as a form of punishment. However, it would be in her best interest to follow his instructions without hesitation to avoid finding out what his brand of discipline entailed.

"Do we have an agreement, Faith?"

"Yes, Sir."

"Then I need you to stop thinking so hard and strip for me. Now."

She let her bra fall to the floor and reached behind her waist to unzip the back of her tight black skirt. She wiggled it over her hips seductively. At least she hoped it was seductive. It had been so long she wasn't sure she still had the touch.

As she stepped out of it, he whistled low again. "You sure know how to make a man's dick hard. Turn around."

She turned her back to him, exposing her bare cheeks. The only clothing left on her body was a thin lacy black thong, her garter belts, the fishnet thigh highs, and her black boots. They weren't stilettos because those were too difficult to dominate in. She had several pairs in her closet however.

"Spread your legs wider. Bend over. Grab your ankles."

She did as he asked, trying to control her racing heartbeat.

"Your ass is like porcelain. I bet it gets pink at the slightest swat of the palm."

"Yes, Sir." It did. Every time. And it lasted longer than other people too. She hoped he wouldn't spank her too hard...if that was even something he was considering.

He read her mind. Of course. "I would never leave a mark on you, sweet girl. At least not one that lasted more than a few hours. Relax. I've spanked bottoms as pale as yours before."

She shivered at the way he said "bottom." When she heard that word, it made her slide into a more submissive role for some reason. It went with the way he also referred to her as his good girl. Sweet girl. It wasn't insulting. It didn't make her feel demeaned. It made her feel cherished. Her husband had never used diminutive words like that with her.

For so long she had feared she would not be able to submit to another Dom without thinking of *him* or welling up with tears. Perhaps it was time. Perhaps Rowen was simply not *him*.

But could she keep her heart out of this? That was the question. Letting Rowen take her to subspace and make her come was one thing. Letting herself fall for him was not possible. She would never open herself up to that level of vulnerability again.

"Pull your cheeks apart for me, little one."

She slid her palms up her legs toward her ass and then spread her cheeks. He would be able to see the hint of her tight hole, but the thong still offered her some protection.

"Do you have any idea how sexy you are?"

She didn't answer. She knew. She'd been told more times than she could count. She'd been ogled by men since she hit puberty. She was aware of her classic blond beauty. Most days it did nothing but annoy her. Tonight she felt as sexy as he insisted she was.

"Is your pussy shaved bare?" he asked, the bold question making her struggle to continue to obey him.

"No, Sir. I leave a strip." The truth was she'd let herself go over the past year. She hadn't resumed grooming the thin strip that led to her clit until recently. After she joined Zodiac. After she first saw Rowen.

She hadn't spoken to him before tonight. That didn't matter. She hadn't considered scening with him either. What she'd done was use him as inspiration when she masturbated.

Yes. She'd also started touching herself with far more frequency lately too. Letting herself feel. Letting herself live again. Letting herself experience pleasure.

Dominating at the club had given her back some of her power, but it wasn't authentic. And Rowen knew this.

"I like how obedient you are. It pleases me. Now, as sexy as those boots are, I want you totally bare to me. All of you. I find it humbles a submissive to be forced to expose herself down to her feet. Remove your boots and then your stockings and thong."

Damn, he was good. He had a way of making her pussy wet with just his words, but when he gave such detailed, well-thought-out instructions, moisture leaked to coat her thighs. There was every chance he could get her to come without touching her.

She leaned down to unzip the back of her boots and tugged them off. Stepping her feet closer together, she unhooked the garter belts. She wiggled her ass back and forth while lowering the fishnet down first one leg and then the other. It felt good to strip for this Dom. She felt sexier than she had in a long time. Appreciated.

After slowly pulling the stockings from her feet, she righted herself and lowered the garter belt and thong at the same time. The thin scraps of black lace were the last small barrier between her and Rowen. When she stepped out of them, she gave them a slight kick toward her skirt.

Like the well-trained submissive she was, she kept her back to him, but stood tall, hands clasped at her back, feet spread a foot apart, head tipped toward the floor.

Long moments passed, making her nervous. Probably his intention. Finally he stood and circled her again, spiraling around her, growing closer and closer as he moved. When he stopped in front of her, he brushed a wisp of hair from her forehead and then trailed his finger down her cheek, neck, and collarbone until he reached her breasts.

She stared at her tight nipples, willing him to touch them.

"Don't move an inch while I explore." He circled her nipple with that finger.

She watched as it grew harder. Her breasts felt too heavy.

Rowen had an amazing ability to affect her with little contact. His presence alone was so dominating that she melted under his gaze. How many women had felt this power?

When he switched to torturing the other breast in the same fashion, she shivered.

"Gorgeous." He didn't comment on her slight involuntary movement. Instead, without ever touching the spots she most craved, he glided his finger down to her belly.

She hollowed her stomach at the contact.

He continued lower, teasing the thin strip of hair she had groomed as recently as that morning. Still exploring, he rounded to her back and traced the edges of her butt cheeks before cupping them in both hands and squeezing. "Your skin is so soft and thin. Not a blemish anywhere. One spank against your bottom would leave a perfect pink handprint, wouldn't it?"

"Yes, Sir." She'd seen it before. If Rowen wanted to spank her, she would gladly admire his work later that night alone in her bathroom.

"No one has ever used a whip or a crop on you, have they?"

"No, Sir," she murmured.

He stroked his fingers up and down her back. "If they did, you would likely scar."

This was true. Besides the fact that she didn't get off on pain, she also wouldn't be able to hide any marks a Dom chose to put on her. It would take much longer for them to heal on her than other submissives.

He leaned in closer, whispering in her ear, "But you've been spanked."

Her breath hitched again. "Yes, Sir."

"For punishment or for pleasure?" he breathed.

"Both, Sir."

"I thought so. The idea makes you wet."

She whimpered. He hadn't asked a question.

He stepped even closer until his torso lined up with hers, his

T-shirt and jeans grazing her skin from her shoulders to her shins. His lips remained millimeters from her ear as he danced his fingers up and down her spine and then her butt and then her thighs. "Softest skin I've ever seen. So lovely to touch and to look at."

"Thank you, Sir."

When he dragged one finger slowly down the crack between her cheeks, she lifted slightly onto her toes. "Flat feet, Faith. That's two."

She swallowed hard as she forced her heels to the floor.

"Good girl. Stand still." He set his free palm on her belly, fingers spread so wide they reached from the underside of her breasts to the strip of groomed hair. Was his intention to help steady her?

He boldly tapped her tight rear hole, testing her ability to stay still? And then he continued downward until his finger stroked lightly over her swollen outer lips.

"So fucking soft," he whispered. "I can't wait to set my mouth here."

She licked her lips. He couldn't see her face directly, so she figured she could make nearly any expression she wanted.

With two fingers, he eased her lips apart and then held them open while his middle finger dipped into her wetness. "Oh yeah. My sweet girl is so wet."

Her breaths came faster as her mind swam with the need to come. *Please, God, don't let him drag this out much longer.*

He swirled his finger through the moisture at the entrance and then pressed it slowly into her. "Damn, you're tight. It's been a while."

Two years... But she didn't tell him that. She hadn't told him anything about her husband or how she hadn't seen him for six months when he'd been killed. From the comments Rowen made, she didn't think his sister had filled him in on anything Faith had divulged to her either. That spoke volumes about her bourgeoning friendship with Sasha.

Rowen eased his finger out of her channel and circled her clit with it. "I wonder if you're a screamer," he mused against her ear. "I wonder how many times you can come before you call for mercy." He licked her earlobe. "I wonder if you gush when you experience a G-spot orgasm."

She shivered, which was apparently acceptable because again he didn't comment on the slight movement. She was also grateful he didn't make her answer those queries. The reality was she couldn't answer any of them with specificity.

Screaming was a state of mind. Sometimes she could be loud. It depended on how fucking horny she was and how far into her mind she went. Sometimes, if she was in deep enough subspace, she'd been told she screamed.

As for how many orgasms she could have, the record was three before she grew too sensitive. She had never been in a position to call for mercy.

And the G-spot orgasm? Well, it had eluded her until now. She wasn't concerned. Lots of women never had one.

"I intend to find out the answer to all of those questions. Not necessarily today, but soon," he promised.

She opened her mouth to argue and then thought better of it. This was a one-time scene. Wasn't it? When Rowen had suggested she submit to him, he hadn't mentioned anything other than tonight in his office. Although, of course he wouldn't have. They'd just met.

In Faith's mind, there would be no more scenes after this one. He was tearing down her walls so rapidly she couldn't even hang on to the semblance of a fence anymore. No one had been permitted inside. Not in eighteen months. And no one ever would again. She had barely survived the loss of her husband. She didn't have the strength to care that much for another human being.

She trembled as he continued to circle her clit. He was getting to her, seeping through her barriers so easily when no one had managed anything even remotely similar in so long. It made her nervous. And she tensed.

He inched closer to her, his palm pressing firmly against her belly. "Relax your body. I've got you."

Her nervousness wasn't something she could control, but she didn't bother to explain.

He thrust his finger into her channel again, and she forgot her tension as a gasp left her lips. "That's a girl. Stay out of your brain. Concentrate on how good I'm gonna make you feel." His finger swirled around inside her, pressing the walls of her sex.

She closed her eyes, taking deep breaths.

When a second finger joined the first, she whimpered again.

"Yeah. That's it. Just you and me. Feel my touch. Let it go. Don't fight it."

She nodded.

"It's been a long time since you've let yourself go. Give it to me." Still whispering. So intuitive. So damn sweet.

She squeezed her hands together tighter at her lower back, pulling her shoulders back farther. She wanted to please him. If she broke form, he would reprimand her, and right now she wanted to feel everything his voice promised with none of the punishment that would come later.

While he slowly fucked her with those two fingers, his other hand eased down her belly and angled toward the floor until his middle finger stroked her clit.

A noise escaped her lips. Not loud. Not quiet either.

"Oh, yeah. So responsive." He kissed her earlobe. His tongue danced around the edges, teasing, tempting, taunting. And then he whispered again, "I'm going to get my first wish, aren't I?"

First wish… She had no idea what he was referring to, but she didn't care. She couldn't think. All her concentration was focused on her pussy.

Suddenly, he pinched her clit at the same time he angled his other two fingers to stroke over her G-spot, fucking her hard and fast.

She shattered, the orgasm taking her by surprise and sucking the breath out of her...right after she screamed out his name.

While she rode the waves of pleasure, Rowen continued to fuck her with those fingers and flick two others over her clit. It wasn't until she slumped slightly forward that he jerked his hand back up her belly to steady her. "I've got you, sweet girl." He removed his fingers from her channel and lifted her into his arms.

Before she could protest, he was seated on the sofa, cradling her against his chest and wrapping a soft blanket around her body. "That's a good girl. Just relax." He stroked his hand up and down her back while he continued to whisper.

CHAPTER 6

Rowen had no idea what just happened. He'd driven right off the road and into a ditch. What possessed him to claim this woman so thoroughly? He knew nothing about her.

When he'd given her that ultimatum a while ago, he hadn't expected her to submit to him. He'd expected her to turn him down. Maybe choose to talk to him. Open up. Apparently her secrets were guarded tightly, though. Either that or she had been desperate to have someone top her. Probably a little of both.

Never in his life had he so totally connected with a woman like this. He realized it was a fluke and couldn't be repeated, but he was ruined anyway.

Faith's soft breaths against his neck told him she was slowly relaxing, perhaps even asleep. He would hold her for ten hours if that was what she needed. In fact, he wouldn't move a muscle if it meant she remained asleep in his arms.

She was so dainty. Almost fragile. And yet so strong at the same time. Nothing that happened in his office resembled the Domme he'd watched several times in the club the last few weeks. It was like she had two different personalities. He could easily guess which one was authentic.

Why was she hiding from herself?

He sensed it was monumental that he'd broken down her walls, no matter how temporarily, and forced her to be herself for an evening. It had been forever since she'd submitted to anyone. He was reasonably certain she'd been shocked by her ability to do so.

Every tiny noise, every whimper, every lick across her lip, every inhalation... All of those things were permanently imbedded in his mind now. And then there was the way she screamed. Not just an outburst of emotion. No. Faith had screamed his name.

His cock was still hard at the memory. He closed his eyes, set his chin on the top of her head, and forced himself to breathe.

Unexpectedly, this wisp of a woman had gotten to him, slammed through several of his roadblocks, and left him reeling. For one thing, she showed no sign of being tainted by whatever wealth she possessed. She wasn't haughty or superior in any way. For another thing, she did not top him from the bottom. Since she was accustomed to the role of Domme lately, he'd been unsure she could so totally turn the tables.

Rowen guarded his heart, however. He liked her, of that there was no doubt. But he needed to rein in his emotions. He'd fallen for women before. Hell, most recently he'd fallen for Rayne. Just because he liked Faith and they had one scene of fantastic submission didn't mean she was "the one." He also knew nothing about her, and she'd kept her secrets close.

She squirmed.

He held her tighter. "Relax, sweet girl." For this moment, this hour, she was his.

"I should go," she murmured.

"Not yet." Holding her with the arm wrapped around her waist, he reached with his other hand to grab the bottle of water she'd sipped from earlier. He tucked his finger under her chin to tip her head back and held the bottle to her lips. "Take a sip."

She obeyed, parting her pink lips for him and letting the cool water into her mouth. As she swallowed, she moaned.

"Good girl." Lord, she was an angel.

She wiped her lips with the back of her hand and snuggled closer into him, tucking her chin down so he could no longer see her face.

He decided it was time to say a few things, though he honestly had no idea where to begin or what his objective was. "That was beautiful, Faith. You're a natural submissive."

"Thank you, Sir." Her voice was weak as though she didn't want to admit his words were true. Not to him. And certainly not to herself.

He stroked his hand up her back and then cupped her head. "I don't know why you've been moonlighting as a Domme, but it's obvious to me your true nature is as a sub."

She didn't move or speak.

"I'm not going to ask you why. I promised I wouldn't, and I won't. Not tonight. But I want you to do something for me."

He barely heard her response. "What, Sir?"

He inhaled slowly, staring at her. Was he out of his mind? "Don't let this exploration end here. Submit to me this week."

She stiffened.

He smoothed his hand down to massage her neck muscles. "I'll make it easy for you. I won't see you this week, not even once. I'm asking you to submit to me from wherever you are. One week. From your home or work or wherever you go. Baby steps. On your honor. Ease back into the life. No one will know but you and me." The words tumbled from his mouth as if they were rehearsed, when in reality, he was shocked by his own suggestion.

She didn't respond except to press her hand into his chest. At least she was considering his proposal.

He was making this up on the fly, but the more he spoke, the better the idea sounded. "We'll communicate through text, email, and phone. You'll do as I say without question or hesitation. You won't have the pressure of submitting to a Dom in person."

Her body softened slightly. He was reaching her. She was softening to his plan.

"You come to me Saturday night one week from today and we take your pulse. What do you have to lose?"

Time stood still while he let her ponder his suggestion. Seconds ticked by interminably before she finally spoke. "I have a private appointment with a submissive on Wednesday."

"With Brooke?" He remembered her name from Lincoln and Carter. He also remembered that Faith was working with her when the club wasn't open.

She nodded.

"Can you reschedule it? I'd rather you focused solely on submitting this week. It would be confusing to switch in the middle of the week."

She thought for a moment before nodding again. "Okay, Sir."

"Good girl. I know that was a hard decision for you." He slid his hands to her shoulders and pushed her small frame a few inches from his chest. The blanket fell to her lap, baring her fantastic tits. He kept his gaze on her face. "Look at me."

She lifted her eyes. Fear consumed her.

"As your Dom for the week, I'll expect you to obey me implicitly without question when it comes to my demands on your body. In addition, I'll ask you questions throughout the week in attempt to get to know you better. You reserve the right to answer them or not. I'll permit you to hold on to your privacy on any subject you want for the entire week.

"You may also question me about my personal life. I'll answer you as often as I can unless your question seems counterintuitive to my objectives."

"What are your objectives, Sir?" Her eyes were wide, the deep blue orbs baring more of her soul than she would probably like.

"To guide you back to your authentic self. You've told me very little, but I know from watching you the past few weeks and from the way you responded to me tonight that you've been under the care of a strong Dom before. You know too much. I can't imagine what happened to break that bond, but it destroyed you on a level you've been unwilling to face.

"You've been dabbling as a switch, trying to make it as a Domme in order to fulfill at least a fraction of what you truly crave. It provides some relief, but it leaves you unfulfilled. Your eyes remain sad. At least do me the favor of admitting all of this is true before we proceed."

She stared into his eyes for so long he thought he might have totally missed the mark. But then a tear slid down her cheek, and she licked her sweet lips. "Yes."

She didn't add *Sir*. It was difficult for her to utter even that one small word. He wouldn't point out the omission. He pulled her back against his chest, tucking her head under his chin. "Good girl. I'm proud of you. We'll work on the rest gradually."

"Yes, Sir." Her voice was stronger.

"How did you get here tonight?"

"Uber, Sir. Sometimes I'm too drained to drive home," she told his chest.

He chuckled. "I can imagine. Tonight more than others."

"Yes, Sir." Her breath hitched. She had something else to say.

"What is it, sweet girl?"

"Could we keep this between us...for now? I mean, I don't mind if Sasha knows or Lincoln or whatever, but maybe not the entire club."

"Of course. Done." Oh yeah, Faith was hiding. From herself? He didn't need to make more out of her request than the obvious. People in the club knew her as a Domme. It was up to her to reveal what she wanted them to know—on her own timetable. If she ever wanted them to know. Whatever she was hiding from could be insurmountable—for her or for him.

"Thank you, Sir."

"Let's get you dressed. I'm going to take you home. When we get there, I'll give you some instructions. I'll start easy and add to my requests during the week."

She leaned back. "I can just take Uber home, Sir."

He stared at her a moment. Half of him thought it might be best to let her have her way on this topic, but the other half reminded him she was defying him already. He narrowed his gaze. "I don't believe I was making a suggestion."

She lowered her gaze and her voice. "Yes, Sir. Sorry, Sir."

He patted her perfect bottom. "You owe me two swats of my hand for hesitating when I gave you an order and lifting onto your toes when I told you to remain still." He needed to make sure she understood he didn't forget any infraction and wouldn't hesitate to discipline her. In addition, he needed to assess how she would react to his statement.

She pushed herself to sitting, straightening her spine, her head tipped toward her lap. "I'm ready, Sir."

Fuck. Me.

She was amazing. If his cock wasn't already stiff to the point of exploding, it would have pushed right out of his jeans at her words. Ignoring his plight, he lifted her by her waist to standing. The blanket that had pooled in her lap fell to the floor as he scooted forward a few inches and guided her to the side of his thigh.

Without a word, he angled her over his lap, clasped both her wrists at the small of her back, and set his palm on her bottom. "Why am I going to spank you, Faith?"

Her voice wobbled slightly as she responded. "Because I hesitated when you gave me an order and then moved when you told me to remain still, Sir."

"I have a good memory, Faith. It would serve you well to keep that in mind. Two swats of my palm to your bottom. I'll be quick. It will hurt." He lifted his hand, flattened his palm, and spanked her twice in rapid succession low on her cheeks. Normally he

65

reserved that spot for pleasure, but since she was only going to get two swats, he relished the idea of possibly leaving her slightly needy.

She only flinched briefly between each slap, and then she relaxed when it was over as he palmed her bottom, massaging the pinkened skin.

"That's a good girl. I'm proud of you." When he thought she was okay to stand, he released her wrists and helped her up. He guided her to stand in front of him between his legs, clasping her hands and gripping them at her sides. "Look at me."

She met his gaze, her eyes slightly watery, her face a deep pink.

"You're not a fan of punishment."

"No, Sir." Her words were barely audible.

"I can tell. Then you won't disobey me often, will you?"

"No, Sir." Her lips were slightly swollen as if she'd been kissed senseless when he hadn't even tasted them yet. He intentionally forced himself not to kiss her for fear he would lose control and take this thing too far. Their puffiness indicated she had been holding them between her teeth.

"I'm not an unreasonable Dom. You don't have to worry about that. I'll never ask you to do anything I don't believe you can handle. However, on the flip side, I expect you to obey me without question in all things."

"Yes, Sir." This woman, standing before him, head bowed, naked, nipples puckered, pussy wet, a slight tremble—she was the hottest submissive he'd ever seen. It was time to get out of his office before he did something he might regret.

He released her hands. "Get dressed. Slowly. While I watch." He leaned back against the couch and crossed his legs, mostly because there was no way he could move without wincing at the stiffness of his cock. He needed a few moments to pull his shit together.

Instructing her to tease him while dressing had not been his best-laid plan, however. Watching her pull on her thong and then garter belt made him grit his teeth. She was a professional tease.

He wondered if it came naturally or if she had training stripping and dressing for a Dom. He hoped any instructional assistance she'd been given had been from a seasoned Dom. The thought of her having stripped for an audience at some point in her life made him shudder with a strange protectiveness.

She perched her ass on the coffee table to roll her stockings up her legs. The entire time she kept her thighs parted enough for him to see between them. Teasing him. Not meeting his gaze. Pretending she was simply doing as she'd been told.

He didn't comment.

When she lifted her lacy white bra and stuck her arms through the straps, he noticed the juxtaposition of her innocent white top half against her naughty black bottom half. Pure white lacy bra. White sheer blouse. Black thong and garter and stockings and skirt and boots. The contrast was stunning.

All too soon she was dressed. She clasped her hands at her back, spread her feet, and faced the floor without a word.

She was nearly perfect.

And until she divulged a bit about herself, she would remain that way.

Part of Rowen wanted her to tell him something horrifying about her past to break the veil of perfection he had draped around her. Instead, he forced himself to stand, headed over to his desk, and grabbed his phone and keys. "Where are your things?" he asked. "I assume you have a purse somewhere."

"In the women's room, Sir. I'll need to change into my street clothes."

He stepped back to face her and tipped her chin up. "I realize you just showed me a side of you no one in this club has seen. I respect that. I'm going to release you to go gather your things. Meet me out front. I'll pull the car up and pick you up. White Toyota 86. Wait inside the door with Carter until I'm there."

"Thank you, Sir."

He slid his hand around to her cheek and held her gaze. What he wanted to do was kiss her until her knees buckled. What he did instead was gently set his lips on hers for the briefest second. Just enough to make him want more and hopefully have the same effect on her.

Two minutes later, he was heading toward the entrance, his gaze locked on Carter as he approached.

Carter stepped out of hearing distance from anyone near the entrance. "What's up?" he whispered. They knew each other well.

"I'm taking Faith home. Gonna pull the car around. Would you see her down the stairs to the door?" The club was located on the second story above a strip mall with a discreet entrance on the first floor. The offices were on the third floor above the club. Most passersby wouldn't ever realize there was a business above the shops.

"Of course." Carter's brow was furrowed, but his lips were lifted slightly in an incongruent grin.

"Carter..."

He shook his head. "Never saw you. Never spoke to you. Never saw Faith leave."

"Thank you." Of course, Rowen would tell Lincoln about his chance meeting with Faith later, but he knew his third partner would also remain discreet. What he didn't want was for the rest of the patrons to know about his encounter with Faith. Or any future encounter either. Unless and until she agreed.

What was he thinking? This was a temporary arrangement. A favor. He was helping another human being find her way back to her true self.

It didn't hurt that she was sexy as hell and made his dick ache to be inside her, but he would never take advantage of his role. She needed a firm Dom to guide her back to authenticity.

What he didn't need was to dwell on the possibility that things might actually work out between the two of them. That was so far in the distance it was unfair to ponder. He wouldn't even let himself hope for something more. The last time he attempted to forge the sort of relationship he craved with a woman had been Rayne. And he'd fallen on his face in the attempt.

The level of commitment he'd wanted from Rayne hadn't jibed with the level of submission she'd been willing to surrender. He had tried hard not to ask more of her than she was able to give, but in the end it hadn't been enough. He'd *wanted* more. He would have been miserable in the long run if he'd settled.

He'd never regretted the decision to throw in the towel, and in fact he was relieved, especially tonight. After a lengthy reminder of what he craved in a submissive, he was even more certain he and Rayne had made the right decision four months ago.

There weren't a lot of women out there who could give themselves to a Dom as fully as Rowen desired. Very, very few, he reminded himself. He shouldn't even be thinking of such a thing with Faith after one single evening.

His current goals were clear. He needed to shove the future where it belonged—in the future. To do otherwise would disappoint him. Just because she demonstrated a propensity for a level of submission he craved meant nothing by itself. He couldn't know she would submit like that again. Nor did he know a damn thing about her other than that she was fucking sexy and had a lot of money.

No, scratch that. Just because someone wore expensive clothes and drove nice cars still didn't mean they had money. Some people were simply pretentious.

As Rowen turned to head down the stairs, he paused and looked back at Carter. "By the way, Lincoln is with Sasha in his office."

Carter smirked. "Her mouth get her in trouble again?"

"You could say that." Rowen smiled as he took the stairs two at a time. His sister was a handful. No way would Rowen ever want to train a submissive like her. Of course, it was his fault—all three of their faults actually—that she was so innocent. Neither Rowen nor his partners had permitted her to join the club. At twenty-two she was eager and green.

She was also apparently perfect for Lincoln who thrived on the challenge.

Rowen shuddered at the thought of disciplining and training a woman like his sister.

His mind wandered back to Faith as he folded into his car. She was the exact opposite. Seasoned. Trained. Demure. Obedient. All things he loved in a submissive.

As he pulled up to the entrance, he popped the locks on the passenger door of his car and waited while Faith slid into the seat. He normally would have rounded the hood and helped her inside, but she would have tensed at the idea of stretching out the likelihood they would be seen, and besides, Carter was there to help her into the car and shut the door.

Seconds later they were off.

"Thank you. For the ride, I mean. Sir." She sat straight. Stiff. Hands in her lap. Facing the window as he sped toward the exit to the parking lot. She had changed into street clothes and carried a bag. No change of clothing would ever convince anyone she was a regular person, however. The white crop pants she wore were pressed and fit her perfectly. The blue blouse tied beneath her breasts and matched her flats. Ordinary enough clothing for some people. But not Faith.

"Of course. My pleasure." He handed her his cell phone. "Put your address into my GPS. And then add your contact information to my list. Cell and email."

She did as he instructed, her fingers trembling.

"Relax, sweet girl. Nothing is going to happen. I'm just taking you home."

"I know. I just… It's been a while since I've brought someone home."

He set the phone on his thigh and reached for her hand, threading their fingers together and squeezing. "You're safe."

She nodded, lowering her gaze to their entwined fingers in her lap. Nerves made her stiff. He recognized the signs. He needed to tread carefully. She obviously needed this. She needed to let go of some past hurt and move on. But it was hard for her. And he had to keep that in mind every step of the way. His suggestion that she submit to him from a distance all week was the best possible arrangement.

It could also backfire. It was possible she would use the distance to dig a wedge between them and lose focus on the objective. Only time would tell.

When he pulled up to a nice apartment complex several miles away in a swanky section of Miami, he was impressed. Not shocked. Impressed.

She pointed at a spot in the street. "You can park there."

He parallel parked along the side of the street. At least she didn't insist on jumping out and fleeing him at the door. Smart girl. He gave her hand a final squeeze. "Hang tight. I'll come help you out."

As he climbed from the car and rounded the hood, he took a deep breath. The air shifted around him. There was something monumental about this agreement. He could feel it.

Whatever they were about to embark on was going to change both their lives. He just hoped it was for the better. For both of them.

CHAPTER 7

Faith was shaking as she led Rowen to the elevator and pressed the button for the tenth floor. Every step from the car to the lobby to the elevator and then down her hallway felt increasingly more difficult.

She didn't bring men to her apartment. Ever. Rowen was the first.

She'd lived here a year now, and she rarely had guests. Never men. And certainly not Doms.

She was nervous as hell and prayed to God she wasn't making a mistake.

Rowen had shown no signs he meant to accomplish anything except exactly what he'd suggested in his office. He intended to see her home, give her some instructions, and leave her alone for a week. Physically, at least.

Her stomach was in knots at the thought of submitting to him. It unnerved her to so willingly accept his proposal and to allow herself to feel as intensely as she had from the moment he led her to his office.

Perhaps she'd lost her mind, but she steeled herself to go with the flow. It felt good. It felt right. There was no need to sabotage things by retreating into her head and reminding herself how far south things could go if she let someone into her fortress.

When they reached her door, she pulled her keys out of her purse, but her hands were shaking so badly she fumbled them.

Rowen eased them from her hand and pressed into her from behind, crowding her against the door while he spoke softly into her ear. "Relax, sweet girl."

"It's not that simple. I don't bring men home."

"I'm glad to hear it." He chuckled lightly. "And you won't start now either. But tonight, it's just me." He slid a hand up her back and tugged on her braid until she tilted her face up.

She forced herself to look at him. His concerned expression gave her strength. "This is my sanctuary."

"Okay."

"Will you still honor your earlier promise not to ask questions? Just for tonight."

He furrowed his brow. "Promise me two things."

"Maybe."

"You aren't married, and you aren't involved in anything illegal."

"Swear."

"Then I won't ask questions. Not tonight."

"Thank you...Sir."

He held her gaze for another moment and then released her to unlock her door. When it swung inward, she led him into her personal space. He shut the door behind him as she took her keys from him and dropped them on the small table next to the door where she also left her bag. For now. She'd put it away later.

He stepped farther into her living room as she leaned against the front door and tried to see things through his eyes. There was no way to hide the fact she had money. Her apartment was upscale, spacious, and modern. It was more than she needed, but she hadn't chosen it. She flinched at the reminder. *Please don't let him ask.*

"You're tidy to the point of anal." He turned to smile at her and held out his hands. "Just an observation. Not a question."

She smiled. He wasn't wrong. If he delved any deeper, he would find out just how anal she was. Her closet was organized by colors and styles. The irony was that she hadn't always been this obsessive. It was a new trait she acquired after Victor died. It kept her occupied at times when she thought she might go stark raving mad. After a while, the new habits stuck.

Rowen meandered around in her living room. When he came to her built-in shelves, she held her breath. Of course he would hone in on her photos. He didn't touch any of them, but he did lean forward to examine each one. At the last one, he paused.

She lowered her gaze, hoping he would keep his promise. He would have to guess she had been married, but she didn't have the energy to talk about it tonight. After performing as a Domme earlier and then submitting to him so thoroughly, she was wiped out. She needed sleep. Explaining her relationship with Victor would bring her to tears.

He said nothing, and she blew out a breath in relief.

"Sasha knows some of your story," he stated.

"Yes."

"I won't ask her anything. You'll tell me in your own time."

"Thank you, Sir."

She followed his gaze around her space, taking in what he saw. Her built-in and the cabinets in her attached kitchen were white. Her appliances stainless steel. Her kitchen table and chairs were also white. Her sofa, white leather. She had a glass coffee table and two glass end tables. The two armchairs were the blue-green color of the sea, and a variety of throw pillows were in shades of blue and green. The rug under her coffee table was a swirl of blues and greens. The rest of the floor was hardwood.

Would he realize her furniture was top of the line and expensive? Her apartment looked like a model home, not a place where someone actually lived. Even the pictures on the wall were of abstract art that had little actual sentimental meaning to her.

Her mother had joined forces with her sister to get her into this new apartment and decorate it for her. Faith had contributed nothing.

"Can I get you anything to drink?" she finally asked, shaking herself into hostess mode.

"No, sweet girl. I'm fine. Come here." He stood in the middle of the room, not moving.

She shuffled toward him, stopping when she got within a foot of him, dipping her head and clasping her hands behind her back. It had been a long time since she'd assumed positions of submission for anyone, but it came naturally like riding a bike. Probably because he had such a strong air of authority.

He cupped the back of her neck and squeezed. His voice was calm and level when he spoke. "I want you to go to your room and get ready for bed like you would any other night, except remain naked. Come back to me when you're done."

She pursed her lips but didn't hesitate to leave the room. She could take a breath and pause in her bathroom, not in front of him. And she did exactly that, leaning against the white vanity and staring at her reflection in the mirror. Who was the woman looking back at her?

She stared for several minutes, wondering if the woman in the mirror was the authentic version of Faith making a comeback or an imposter forcing her way in to take away some of the pain. Did it matter?

She pondered those two possibilities as she stripped off her clothes and dropped them in the hamper. The pain she felt no longer could be placed solely on the loss of her husband. It was more than that. It was the loss of a way of life.

And Rowen Easton was standing in her living room offering her at least a week of what she craved. Could she give herself to him so completely?

Could she not?

She removed her makeup, baring herself to him completely. If he didn't like what he saw without mascara and blush and eyeliner and lip gloss, she might as well know it now.

She brushed her teeth, leaving her hair in the braid.

With a deep fortifying breath, she returned to find him standing in the exact spot where she'd left him. She had her hands clasped at the small of her back, her shoulders straighter, and her face tipped toward the floor. When she stepped in front of him this time, she spread her feet slightly.

There was no denying the way her body reacted to him. She was wet. Her nipples were stiff. Perhaps partly a reaction to the cool air conditioning, but mostly from standing naked in front of this huge Dom who had not removed a stitch of clothing for her at any point yet.

He closed the distance between them, tilted her head back with a finger under her chin—as seemed to be his custom—and searched her face. A slow smile spread. "You're so beautiful. I like to see a woman without all that makeup on."

She didn't speak. As a general rule, there were a lot of things she would do to submit behind closed doors, but she would draw the line at any man who asked her to leave her home without makeup. A flush rushed up her cheeks.

He brushed his thumb over the warmth. "I especially love the way you blush for mysterious reasons."

He reached with his other hand to circle a nipple, his gaze remaining on her face, amazing her with his super peripheral vision skills. "I want you to sleep in the nude this week. Every night."

It was hard to concentrate with him touching her like he was, but she nodded.

"I want you to shave your pussy bare tomorrow morning and every morning from now on."

"Yes, Sir."

"You're permitted to touch yourself, but do not come without permission."

"Yes, Sir." She shifted her weight from one foot to the other.

He smiled. "I expect you to text me first thing every morning before you get out of bed and last thing every night before you slide between the sheets. During the day, I'll touch base with you between clients."

She realized she knew very little about what he did. He was an accountant. That was it. Did he work for a firm? She didn't ask since she wasn't willing to tell him what she did either. It wasn't that her job was such a secret. Who cared that she was the events coordinator for the city. That part wasn't a big deal. The amount of money she made doing the job and what she did with it was the part she'd rather he didn't know.

"If you have questions, email me or text. I'll answer as soon as I can. If you need to come, call me and I'll consider your request." He lifted a brow.

"Yes, Sir."

"I'm a fair Dom. You won't need to worry about being disciplined as long as you obey my instructions. Are we clear?"

"Yes, Sir." Seemed simple enough. He hadn't given her more than she could handle. So far.

"Turn around and bend over so I can see your bottom."

Her breath hitched at the unexpected request before she remembered he had spanked her and probably wanted to inspect it. Not surprising. Comforting even. She did as he requested, grabbing her ankles and parting her legs farther.

He stroked her cheeks, leaning down to examine them. "Pink but not too bad. I don't see my handprints. I don't ever want to bruise you. That's never going to be my intention. In the past, how much have you been able to tolerate?"

"I, uh…"

He helped her stand and turned her to face him. "Never mind. I won't be spanking you this week anyway."

Thank God. Not that it was a difficult question, but discussing how she'd been spanked in the past and the results was slightly mortifying.

"It's late. I'm going to leave. You should go to bed. Text me when you wake up."

"Okay, Sir." She followed him to the door and locked it behind him. The moment he was gone, she leaned against it and sucked in deep breaths as if she hadn't gotten enough oxygen in several hours. She was light-headed.

When she was certain she could make it to her bedroom, she grabbed her cell phone from her purse, padded that way, slid under the sheets, and turned off the light next to her bed.

Sleep alluded her while she stared at the ceiling, piecing together the events of the last several hours.

Holy shit.

Had she really submitted to Rowen Easton?

She slapped a hand over her forehead. She was certifiable. Closing her eyes, she considered the implications. It wasn't the submission that bothered her. She was relieved actually to have finally taken the steps to get back in the saddle. And she was glad it had gone well. She hadn't flubbed it up or broken down in tears or made a fool of herself.

The problem was she'd liked it too much. She'd liked *Rowen* too much. He was the perfect Dom. So far. He needed flaws. If he didn't come up with any soon, she was doomed. Her objective was to remain aloof, enjoy the ride with a capable Dom, and get out before feelings got involved.

Feelings for Rowen had existed even before she met him. Submitting to him had been a bad idea. She needed to keep her wits and not let herself get invested.

Never again would she let herself love another human being as fiercely as she'd loved Victor. For one thing, she was unwilling to fully let go of his memory. Not for the first time, she felt a twinge of guilt for even considering letting another man dominate her.

The fact that she had so easily submitted to Rowen tonight was unsettling. For another thing, she wouldn't live through the pain of another loss like Victor. Life was too fragile. People died every day. They got into accidents. They had cancer. They were killed in battle. They left...

Victor wasn't the first man to leave her. He was the first man to leave her against his will. But he was *not* the first. She shuddered, shaking thoughts of her college boyfriend out of her head.

She understood the adage that it was better to have loved and lost than to never have loved at all. And theoretically she agreed. She couldn't imagine not having known Victor's love and devotion. Every moment she had with him had been a blessing. But losing him had hardened her. She wouldn't go through something like that again.

Her phone vibrated on the end table, and she reached for it, wondering who would text this late and already smiling before she looked. It would be Rowen.

Thank you for the honor of submitting to me tonight, sweet girl. Sleep well.

She held the phone to her chest for a long time, smiling, heart pounding.

Ignoring the fortifying pep talk she'd just had with herself.

CHAPTER 8

Rowen was exhausted when he got to his apartment about ten minutes from Faith's. He dropped his keys on the kitchen table, kicked off his shoes, and grabbed a beer from the fridge. As he sank onto his sofa and set his feet on the coffee table, he glanced around the room.

Faith would lose her shit the first time she saw his place—if there ever was a first time. There were no guarantees.

Where her place was all white and feminine, his was all dark and masculine. His cabinets and furniture were black. His leather couch was black. Even the armchair was black. His feet rested on a black coffee table, and he would eventually set his empty beer bottle on the black end table. Except for the beige paint on the walls and the beige area rug on his black hardwood floors, he was as gloomy as a person could get. How had he never noticed?

Faith had not responded to his text, but that was okay. He hadn't required her to. In fact, she might have already been asleep when he sent it.

He stared at the ceiling and thought back on his time with her. She made his blood pump with a force no woman, submissive or otherwise, had ever accomplished. More important was the fact that she was indeed submissive in every possible way.

She had secrets. A pile of them apparently. She'd been married. He had nearly gasped when he saw the wedding photo. Her husband had worn his navy white uniform. Was she divorced? He doubted that. If she'd been divorced, she wouldn't have his picture displayed on her shelf.

Which meant he had undoubtedly died. Rowen blew out a long breath, aching for the woman he'd dominated all evening. How long ago had he passed away? Was it in combat? Was he a Dom? Was Faith over him?

Other observations filtered into his mind. She was a perfectionist. Over the top. So anal her books were lined up and the pillows on her couch were perfectly placed. He'd been afraid to mess up the lines on the carpet from her vacuum cleaner.

He had no idea what she did for a living, but whatever it was, it paid well. Her apartment was upscale. She had nice things. Very nice things. If he wasn't mistaken, some of the artwork in her living room was original. Her clothing was expensive. She carried a Kate Spade bag and a Michael Kors purse. Maybe most men wouldn't notice such things or even know about them, but Rayne was a fashionista. He'd learned more than he ever wanted to know about top-of-the-line clothing and accessories in their time together.

What if Faith made a lot of money? He inhaled long and slow. He hated to lump her in the same basket with other rich women who had visited Zodiac in the past. At least she hadn't shown any signs of acting like an entitled bitch, so he owed her the benefit of the doubt. It wasn't as though he was going to marry her. This was a temporary arrangement. Finite.

Half of Rowen was curious enough to google Faith Robbins and dig around in her social media until he knew her better, but that would be cheating.

He'd promised she could tell him about herself on her terms, and he would give her that. Delving into her private life behind her back seemed unfair. Besides, he'd said he would dominate her this week from afar. If he prematurely discovered things about her that didn't suit him, it would be difficult to keep up the charade.

He was enjoying himself. She was an amazing submissive. He would take that on face value and guide her back into the life. She needed it as badly as she needed her next breath.

Working with Faith was not going to be a hardship.

It was nine in the morning when Rowen got the first text from Faith. He smiled as he glanced at the screen. *So, not an early riser...*

Faith: Good morning, Sir.

Rowen: Good morning, sunshine. Did you sleep well?

Faith: Yes. Thank you, Sir.

Rowen: What are your plans for the day?

He didn't want to pressure her, but he did intend to slowly ask her questions until he knew her better. It was a Sunday. What did Faith do on Sundays?

Faith: I'm going to go for a run and then catch up on things around the house.

A run? Nice. A woman who liked to exercise. But taking care of things around her apartment made him chuckle.

Rowen: Laundry been piling up on you?

He was teasing and hoped she could figure that out.

Faith: Are you making fun of me, Sir?

Rowen: Yes. You stepped right into it.

Faith: I probably deserve it.

He laughed again.

Rowen: Listen, I sent you an email. Check it now before you do anything else.

Faith: Okay, Sir.

His computer was open on his lap where he sat on his sofa scrolling through his own emails and his appointment calendar. He opened the email he sent her to read it again.

Faith,

I'm sending you two lists. The first one is instructions I want you to follow. If there is anything on the list you can't comply with or would prefer to discuss, let me know. We'll negotiate.

The second part is a list of questions. I want you to answer my questions in any order, but I want two answers a day. That's fourteen answers before I see you next Saturday night. I've come up with more than fourteen questions. You can pick the ones you're most comfortable with.

This week is a trial of sorts. A chance for us to get to know each other and feel each other out. It's not threatening because we won't be seeing each other face to face. We can dabble in our arrangement this week, and then on Saturday we can evaluate where we both stand and how we feel and decide if we would like to continue our agreement or terminate it. If I'm going to work with you, I need to know you better.

Likewise, I encourage you to send me a list of questions, and I'll extend the same courtesy. Whatever you'd like to know about me, ask.

Sincerely,

Rowen

Rowen realized one leg was shaking as he stared at the computer. Would she balk at his demands and his personal questions?

His phone buzzed a few minutes later. His hand was shaking when he picked it up. It unnerved him that this woman was under his skin.

Faith: Got your email, Sir.

That's it. Damn. He set the phone back down without responding. He needed to come up with a pile of patience to work with this submissive. She was skittish, and he had no doubt her reasons were legitimate.

When his phone rang a few minutes later, he grabbed it off the couch so fast he nearly dropped it, and then he sighed when he saw the caller. "Hey, Sasha."

"Wow, sounds like you're having a bad day. How many things could possibly go wrong in the life of Rowen before ten a.m.?"

He rubbed his temples with his free hand. "Nothing. What's up?"

"I just wanted to say hi."

Uh-huh. "Sure you did. I'm thinking you were feeling nosy."

"Me?" She gave a fake gasp.

"Does Lincoln know you called me?"

"No," she snapped. "Lincoln doesn't keep tabs on my phone calls, Rowen. Don't be ridiculous."

Rowen laughed. "Sure."

"Fine. How did it go with Faith? You left the office with her. Did you two talk?"

"I'm not going to talk to you about Faith. But I need you to do me a favor."

"Sure." She sounded hopeful.

He realized he'd given her the wrong idea. "I'd like you not to mention her to me for the next week. Not a word. And if you talk to her or see her, don't speak of me."

"What? Why?"

"Sasha, just do it." Rowen didn't have the kind of rein over his sister to command her like Lincoln did. She was his sister. In all her twenty-two years she'd rarely acquiesced to anything he suggested without an argument.

She sighed.

He decided to throw her a bone to keep her from spending the next week mulling over his intentions. "Listen, I spoke to her. We're...talking. This week, I mean. But she holds her privacy close. And I want to respect that. So, I don't want you to stick your nose in it. She'll tell me what she wants me to know when she's ready."

"Oh. My. God. What... Like, what happened last night?" Now she was way too damn excited.

"Sasha. That's enough. I'm not discussing this with you."

"I'm your sister. You should be able to discuss your relationships with your sister." Her inflection was still playful.

"How about this. You tell me what you were doing from eleven p.m. until one a.m. last night, and then I'll tell you. Sound good?"

She sighed. "You're right. I see your point."

"I thought so. Now, tell me how things are going with you."

"Things are great. I've never been happier."

"I want you to be happy. You know I'll always be here for you if you ever need me, right?"

"Of course." Her voice was lower, serious. But that was good. He wanted to be sure she took him seriously. She was his only family member. He would always worry about her no matter what. Even though one of his best friends in the world also had her best interests in mind.

"Good. Now put Lincoln on the phone, you little minx." He let his voice lift in a tease, breaking the serious moment.

"Are you going to tell him I was pushy? Because if that's your plan, I'm just going to hang up."

"Wouldn't you like to know?" With a firmer, solid voice he said, "Put Lincoln on the phone, Sasha."

There was some shuffling and then Lincoln's voice came through. "Hey, man. What's up?"

"I'll be at the club Wednesday night, but I'm not scheduling any scenes. I'll fill in for some of the dungeon monitor slots."

"Okay. Sasha could have told me that."

"Yep. And that was my plan. Until your sub got mouthy with me."

Lincoln chuckled.

"I'm not going to tell you what we discussed, but do me a favor and reinforce that I meant what I said. She needs to contain herself this week and stay out of my business."

"Consider it done. I'm pretty sure she'll be tied up this week."

This time Rowen laughed. "TMI. See you later." He ended the call, still smiling. If his sister wanted to play hardball with him, she would find herself in a world of trouble with her own Dom. Rowen didn't have to chastise her himself. She needed to remember that Lincoln was one of his best friends.

Rowen set his computer aside and pushed up from the couch. He needed to get a workout in and run a few errands himself. He'd been up for several hours before Faith texted him. In addition to the email he'd sent, he'd also made several plans for the week. He wasn't going to see her in person, but that didn't mean he didn't intend to ensure she kept him in the front of her mind several times a day.

It was time to put his plans into action.

CHAPTER 9

Faith's run was long and hard and did nothing to calm her nerves. She'd hoped if she went farther and pushed herself, she might be able to shove Rowen to the back of her mind and gather her wits. Alas, no.

After she showered and put moisturizer on her face, she pulled her hair back in a messy bun and glanced down at her body. She had decisions to make. And she needed to make them now. She had two choices—commit to following Rowen's demands or bow out gracefully. Lying wasn't her style. She'd never been the sort of person to lie about anything.

She padded back into the bedroom and opened her computer on top of her bed to remind herself what Rowen's demands entailed—as if there was any way she would forget them.

What's expected of the submissive for the period of seven days:

The submissive is expected to shave every morning, including her entire pussy.

The submissive is not permitted to use a vibrator or any other electrical stimulant on her body.

The submissive is not permitted to wear panties or thongs.

The submissive will wear dresses or skirts when she leaves the house except to work out.

The submissive will finger herself at least four times a day for a period of five minutes without allowing herself to reach orgasm.

If the submissive feels the need to orgasm at any time, she is expected to call and ask for permission. The call may or may not be answered, and permission may or may not be granted.

The submissive will remain naked at all times when she is at home.

She found it interesting that he referred to her in the third person as if this were a contract he made with all sorts of people. She shuddered, wondering if that were possible, and if so, how many women had submitted to him like this before?

She would be sure to ask when she shot her own list of personal questions back at him.

Faith fidgeted while she read the list several times. The truth was, there was nothing on the list she couldn't comply with. Rowen had made it simple enough to serve one objective—keep her aroused all week without relief.

She wondered if she ever called and asked permission to orgasm, would he grant it?

She had shaved the small landing strip of hair in the shower, leaving herself bare for the first time in her life. She wasn't currently wearing anything, but she wasn't sure she could wander around her apartment butt naked all week.

She wasn't a prude, but she'd also never had this request before, so she had no idea how it would make her feel. At the moment, a ball of need was forming in her belly at the thought of working from her home office, watching television, reading, cooking, or cleaning naked.

She was turned on. Shit.

As for not wearing pants, though it was true she frequently wore more pantsuits than dresses and skirts, she had plenty of them in her closet, and she wore them often enough that no one would think twice about it.

She was super clear that Rowen wanted her to be aware of her naked pussy at all times.

Faith had no idea if she could commit to this list all week. Nor was she certain she wanted to. Deeply buried feelings were coming to the surface. She hadn't been this aroused for this long in eighteen months. It felt good. It scared her to death at the same time. It felt like a betrayal to Victor's memory to so easily find herself under the spell of another man. It didn't matter that Victor would have wanted her to move on and enjoy life again. It still made her uncomfortable.

She needed to remain detached from Rowen and keep her head screwed on straight.

Every time she thought of him, her nipples jumped to attention. This had not started last night. It had been true for several weeks. What were the chances the first man in years who could turn her insides to mush would also approach her and offer her a D/s arrangement?

It's only for one week, she reminded herself. *One week. It feels good. It's healthy. You're hurting no one. No one even needs to know. You can do it.*

Could she, though? She worried she was kidding herself if she thought she could submit to Rowen for seven days and then walk away. She could already tell there was something about him that called to her soul.

But her soul was not available. It would never be available again. It was permanently damaged. Irreparable. No longer open to hurt.

Seven days. I can do seven days. Especially without contact with the Dom.

Finally, she took a deep breath and knew one thing for certain —she could definitely do one day. Tomorrow she could commit to tomorrow.

With that settled, she glanced down at his list of questions.

She read the entire list again, mentally tallying how many of the questions she was willing to answer and which two she was willing to answer *now*.

1. *What do you do for a living?*
2. *What family do you have nearby?*
3. *Why did you transfer your membership from Breeze to Zodiac?*
4. *What happened to your husband?*
5. *Do you have OCD?*
6. *Do your close friends and family know you're in the lifestyle?*
7. *When did you first know you were submissive?*
8. *When did you enter the lifestyle?*
9. *Has anyone ever drawn blood on your body?*
10. *What D/s arrangement did you have with your husband?*
11. *Do you consider yourself a sadist?*
12. *Have you ever been in a 24/7 relationship?*
13. *Do you get aroused when you dominate others?*
14. *Do you get aroused when you submit to others?*
15. *How do you feel about public exposure?*
16. *How do you feel about humiliation?*
17. *Do you consider yourself a service submissive?*
18. *Do you consider yourself a switch?*
19. *Do you need to dominate to feel whole?*
20. *Do you see yourself dabbling, or committing to something more permanent in the future.*

With a smile, knowing full well she was going to frustrate Rowen, she pulled the computer to the edge of the bed, leaned over, and typed her first response.

I've chosen two questions to answer for you, Sir.

No. No one has ever drawn blood on my body. If they did, I would cut off their balls and feed them to them.

I also do not consider myself a sadist. I can strike people in whatever way they need or request, but it's not something I crave or need to feel whole.

Realizing she needed to add a list of personal questions, she got down on her knees to make it easier to type and continued the email with a list of twenty questions similar to his with a few variations.

She was pretty proud of herself when she hit send. And then she closed the computer and went about her day.

Naked.

Very naked after shaving.

She ate lunch, cleaned up the kitchen, started a load of laundry, and folded the shirts in her T-shirt drawer. Anything to avoid thinking about Rowen and the fact she was naked.

She sent a text to Brooke to let her know she needed to cancel their appointment for Wednesday, feeling irrationally guilty. She knew better than anyone how much Brooke needed someone she could trust to help her break through the thick walls she'd spent a lifetime erecting.

With that task accomplished, Faith paced for a while and then sat on the corner of her couch and opened a book she'd been meaning to read. After reading the first page several times, she slapped it shut and turned on the television. Channel surfing was not her thing either, though.

She was relieved when her cell phone pinged, letting her know she had a text. But she frowned when she saw it was her mother. Again. Twice in two days. No way was she going to engage her mother in any sort of conversation. Not by text or phone. Not this week. She ignored the text and took a deep breath.

Faith had a precarious relationship with both her parents, but at least her father left her alone for the most part. Her mother insisted on attempting to contact her at least a few times a month. She was undaunted by the frequent lack of response.

To say their relationship was strained would be an understatement. It wasn't something she liked to think about, and it certainly wasn't something she liked to discuss.

Rowen wanted to know her story. He'd made that clear. He also hadn't pushed. There was no compelling reason why she needed to tell him yet, so she wouldn't. After all, this was a week-long arrangement. Not a lifetime. Even if they continued to explore their chemistry for longer than the week, she still didn't need to divulge her insane life secrets.

It drained her to discuss her parents. Literally sucked the life out of her.

What Rowen didn't know wouldn't hurt him. And he had no reason to even know she *had* parents, let alone encourage her to speak of them.

When her phone pinged again, she glanced at it with apprehension and then smiled when she saw it was from Rowen.

I answered your questions, sweet girl. Check your email.

Finally, something exciting. After shoving off the sofa, she made her way to her bedroom, situated herself on the bed, leaning against the headboard, and opened her computer.

It would probably take two seconds to read the answers to two of her questions, but she was intrigued to find out which ones he chose.

When she opened the email, she gasped. He'd answered all the questions. Every. Single. One.

1. *Why did you and Rayne break up three months ago? (And don't just say it was because you're incompatible)—Rayne is relatively new to the lifestyle. In fact, I introduced her. She likes to play, but it's not important to her, and she has no*

interest in devoting as much time to it as I would like in a
permanent submissive.

2. *Are you prone to losing your temper?*—I'm a pretty even guy.
Rarely do I lose my temper. If Sasha told you I punched a hole
in Lincoln's kitchen wall a few months ago, that is correct.
But you would have to know all the extenuating
circumstances that led up to that to understand. Trust me. It
was warranted. And no one faulted me.

3. *When did you enter the lifestyle?*—I joined Club Zodiac when
I was eighteen, but then I joined the army soon afterward.
(Yes, I was in the service. I served four years.) I was twenty-
two when I started my next four years of Individual Ready
Reserve while attending college. I took a job at Zodiac to
defray some of my costs. A few months later, my mother died,
leaving Sasha (twelve at the time) without a parent. I raised
her. Out of desperation, she came to work with me three
nights a week and waited for me in the breakroom on the
third floor of Zodiac while I worked. So, to answer your
question, I've been going to Zodiac as both an employee,
player, and now owner for fourteen years.

4. *When did you first know you were dominant?*—I figured out
I was dominant when I heard some of the guys talking about
BDSM in the locker room in high school. They were just
joking around. I was intrigued. So I researched it and joined
Zodiac. Then I met Carter when I joined the army. He
already knew he was a Dom. He taught me a lot before I came
back to the States.

5. *How many women have you sent this list of demands to?*—
None. You are the first.

6. *Have you entered into an arrangement similar to this one
before? One where you didn't have physical contact with the
submissive for seven days?*—I've never had an arrangement
like this where I expected a submissive to follow my orders
without seeing her for this long. (Yes, all of my submissives

have been women, though I have done scenes with submissive men at the club on occasion.)

7. *Have you been in a 24/7 relationship?*—Not for any length of time. I have made attempts with a few women, including Rayne, but was never able to negotiate an agreement that was suitable for both parties.

8. *What sort of D/s arrangement are you looking for?*—In the long run, I'd like to find a submissive who's interested in a full-time arrangement that meets both our needs.

9. *Have you ever submitted to a Domme or a Dom?*—Only for the purposes of learning.

10. *Have you ever drawn blood on a submissive?*—No.

11. *How important is striking your submissives to you?*—That's a difficult question. If you're asking me if I get restless without flogging or whipping a submissive, the answer is no. If you're asking if I frequently use spanking as both a means of punishment and for pleasure, the answer is yes. Is it a deal breaker? Probably not. There are many other aspects of D/s that fulfill me. The highest compliment from a submissive is having her relinquish control to me, trusting that I will make decisions for her that will demonstrate she is cherished, cared for, and happier than she would ever be otherwise.

12. *Do you get aroused when you dominate others?*—Another loaded question. In general, no. Doing random scenes at the club with strangers, no. When I need to concentrate because I'm using a tool to strike a sub, no. When I'm in a defined negotiated relationship, yes.

13. *Is sex an integral part of BDSM for you?*—Same answers as number twelve above. And let me add that in a long-term relationship with a woman, I would expect to have sex often. I would expect her to orgasm more frequently than me. A goal of mine is to find the woman who can learn to orgasm at my command.

14. *How do you feel about exposing your submissives?*—It's

negotiable. Not a deal breaker. There are occasions and locations when it can be hot. In the general public outside of the club? No.

15. *How do you feel about humiliating your submissives?—Humiliation is not my thing. Belittling a sub doesn't do it for me. If that's something a submissive needs, she should find another Dom.*

16. *How do you feel about restraining your submissives?—I enjoy restraints. They're pivotal to the lifestyle for me. Immobilizing a sub and making her crazy with the need to come makes my blood pump. I'm well-trained with rope bondage. Not to say I'm excellent at Shibari, but I am knowledgeable enough to maintain 100 percent safety in a way that never causes my submissives to be fearful.*

17. *Do you enjoy the company of a service submissive?—I can't truthfully answer that. I've never had a service submissive. It would require a tremendous amount of negotiation to delve into the motives of the submissive. If a woman clearly derived pleasure from taking care of me and our environment, I suppose I might acquiesce. But I would tread carefully into that territory.*

18. *Do you enjoy gagging your submissives?—On occasion. Again, taking away a submissive's ability to speak requires careful planning and negotiation. There are safety factors. Have I used ball gags? Yes. Bits? Yes. I've also used bandanas. Again, not a deal breaker.*

19. *Do you need to dominate to feel whole?—After fourteen years, I can safely say yes. After a year trying to make things work with Rayne, I know my heart is not full without a pretty intense level of D/s in my relationship.*

20. *Do you see yourself dabbling, or committing to someone on a permanent basis?—If I ever meet that woman, I will never let her go.*

CHAPTER 10

Faith's chest was pounding. Sweat had built up on her brow. Her pussy was so swollen and wet she was shaking with desire. Every word. Every thought. Every sentence. Holy shit.

She snapped the computer closed, set it aside, and slid beneath her covers to curl up on her side. Her body was warm, but she still shook.

How had this man come into her life at this time? More importantly, what was she going to do?

Rowen held nothing back. He didn't tease her with a trickle of information as she'd conspired to do to him. He'd given her everything in one fell swoop. His life story. He'd bared his soul to her. What did it mean? If she was reading him correctly, he was definitely interested in her after one evening together.

Okay, that wasn't entirely fair. He'd watched her from the fringe for several weeks. She'd also watched him.

How much did he really know about her, though? It wasn't as if she had giant secrets with regard to her husband or how she'd come to switch to a Domme. Her story was easy to piece together on that front.

But that was only one side of her. She had other secrets.

Secrets she would have to reveal to anyone she made plans with that lasted beyond a few dates—or in this case, scenes.

She forced herself to roll onto her back and take deep breaths. There was no reason to panic. One day at a time. She wasn't even going to see him until Saturday. What harm could it do to play along with him and see where things led?

Closing her eyes, she visualized him standing over her last night. The serious expression he had when he commanded her. The way he looked at her like she was the most gorgeous woman alive while she stood naked before him.

She shivered, goose bumps rising on her body as she absorbed the fact that twice she had stripped for him. He had not even taken off his shirt, and yet she had readily removed everything—including the strip of hair above her clit this morning. And it turned her on to please him.

She squirmed, squeezing her legs together and then toying with her stiff nipple. Without thinking, she slid her other hand down her belly and over her mons. When she dragged one finger between her lips to gather the wetness, she moaned.

She tipped her head back, exposing her neck and arching her chest forward. Suddenly too hot for the covers, she kicked them to the foot of the bed and lifted her knees. Digging her heels into the mattress, she let her thighs fall open. To anyone watching, she knew she would look wanton and greedy. But no one was watching.

She bit down on her bottom lip as she got closer to the edge. And then she froze, yanking her fingers away from her throbbing clit and gasping for air. "Fuck," she muttered into the silence.

She twisted to one side, grabbed her phone from the bedside table, and typed a text to Rowen.

Permission to come. Please, Sir.

She stared at the screen, knees shaking, body tight, fingers gently stroking her outer lips to keep the momentum going without risk of orgasm.

Seconds ticked by. No dots appeared to indicate he was returning the text.

And then the blessed phone rang, making her flush with embarrassment. Sure enough, his name showed up on the screen. She answered, "Sir."

"Did my email make you so horny you can't keep your fingers to yourself?" His voice was light, fun, but serious at the same time. The clear command he always maintained was underneath everything else.

"Sir... I..."

"Faith..." he warned. "Stop touching yourself."

She froze and lifted her fingers.

"Where are you?" His voice was so sexy there was a chance she would come anyway.

Her own voice squeaked as she responded. "On my bed, Sir."

"Are you naked?"

"Yes, Sir."

"Did you shave this morning?"

"Yes, Sir."

"And you read my email."

"Yes, Sir."

His voice deepened. "Spread your legs wider. Don't touch yourself."

She slid her heels out farther, opening her pussy to the point that her lips parted on their own. She moaned.

"Faith," he demanded, "where are your hands?"

She whimpered, her eyes sliding shut. Did he not realize it didn't matter? "Holding the phone, and, uh, gripping the sheets at my side."

"Good girl. Deep breaths."

She tried to follow his instructions. In. Out. In. Out.

"Good girl. Bring it under control. I have not given you permission to come. Let's talk."

Talk? Was he crazy?

"Yes, talk. Keep your fingers off your body."

"Yes, Sir." She whimpered. *Whimpered?*

"So, here's what I know about you. If anyone dares split your skin open with an implement or their hand, they can expect to feast on their own balls that night. And you've been in the lifestyle since you were twenty-two. How old are you now?"

"That's an extra question, Sir. You didn't list it." She bit her lip to keep her voice from letting him know she was grinning.

"Faith," he warned.

"Twenty-eight, Sir."

"Good girl. See, that wasn't so hard, was it?"

"No, Sir." *But stop asking me questions before you get to the hard ones.*

"There's a delivery on its way to your apartment. It'll be there any minute. I'll make you a deal."

She moaned.

"If you can make yourself come before the doorbell rings, you can have this one. If not, you will stop, put on a robe, and go meet the delivery man."

"Thank you, Sir." She breathed out a sigh of relief as she released the sheets and thrust two fingers into her pussy so fast she started panting.

"That's my girl. Reach deep inside. Are you wet, sweet girl?"

"Yes, Sir." It was hard to speak. Her words were choppy.

"Pull your fingers out and flick your clit, Faith."

She did as he instructed.

"I bet your little nub is swollen and pink. Sensitive. You're being such a good girl. I'm proud of you."

She half tuned him out, concerned she needed to speed thing up. She flicked her fingers over her clit rapidly, her mouth falling open and her legs shaking. The phone slid from her fingers to land next to her head.

She had no idea if Rowen was still speaking because all her energy was concentrated on getting off, and fast. She thrust two fingers from her free hand inside her and pressed them upward to hit her G-spot. And then she pinched her clit just enough to send herself over the edge.

A sharp scream echoed in the room as she crested the peak and then rode the waves of pleasure. As she came back to earth, removing her fingers from her pussy and relaxing her legs, she realized she'd dropped the phone.

Hastily, she grabbed for the cell and brought it to her ear. "Sorry, Sir. I dropped the phone."

He chuckled. Deep. Making her shudder. "I gathered. I need you to get up now. Do you have a robe you can put on? Something thick and long. Not some sort of silky kimono."

She pushed herself to sitting, her body not fully recovered enough to accept orders. Her legs weren't responding yet to commands from her brain.

"Robe, sweet girl."

"Right. I'm getting there, Sir." She slid to the floor and gingerly padded toward the closet. Shoving the bulk of her clothes to one side of the rack, she was relieved to find a thick navy robe behind everything else. She had no idea why she still had the thing. It was too warm for Miami, and she didn't think she'd ever worn it.

If she remembered correctly, it had been a gift from some great aunt. Or maybe her grandmother. Why she hadn't donated it to charity by now was a mystery. She managed to tug it off the hanger and shrug into it with one hand just as the doorbell rang.

"Go to the door, sweet girl."

Right. Okay. I can do this.

If the delivery man was under the age of ninety and not blind, he would never be able to overlook the fact that she had just been fucked hard. Never mind she had this flush strictly from masturbating. The idea that he might figure it out was mortifying.

Still holding the phone to her ear, she checked the peephole and then opened the door. The only thing she could see at first was an enormous bouquet of red roses. Two dozen she guessed.

The person behind the spray of roses, held them out. "Delivery for Ms. Faith Robbins."

"That's me." She set the phone on the small table next to the door without explaining the situation to Rowen. He'd ordered the massive arrangement. He had to realize she would need two hands to handle it.

"Just a second," she murmured to the still-unseen man as she claimed the vase and rushed to set the bouquet on her coffee table. Rowen didn't mess around.

She hurried back to the door, tugging the belt of her robe tighter as she went. The man standing in the threshold was indeed older. Not ninety, but at least seventy. He held out a clipboard. "Would you sign here, ma'am." He gave no indication he thought it was odd she was wearing a robe, nor did he make enough eye contact to absorb her flushed cheeks.

"Thank you," she managed as she shut the door and reached for the phone. "Rowen, they're beautiful."

"I'm glad you like them."

She stared at the bouquet as she lowered herself onto the sofa.

"Faith. I want to see what you're wearing. Take a picture. Text it to me."

She glanced down. Lordy. "This is truly the least attractive thing I own, Sir. I don't think it's going to earn me any points."

He chuckled. "If it's that unseemly, it will earn you all the points because it will mean you followed my instructions."

"Okay then. But remember, you asked." She lifted the phone from her ear and touched the screen until she came to the camera. Two seconds later, she had a selfie of her torso, intentionally cutting off her head. She sent it. "Sent, Sir."

"Good girl." His voice grew distant as she imagined him looking at his phone. And then he laughed. "Aren't you funny?"

"What? I sent what you asked for," she taunted.

"Is that sass I hear in your voice?"

"Maybe..."

"Excuse me?"

"Maybe, Sir." She gulped. This went south in a hurry.

"I'm going to give you two points for doing as you were told, but I'd say you're in a deficit for intentionally trying to goad me by leaving out your face and then getting snarky."

"Yes, Sir." She sobered at the tone of his voice she was coming to realize could and would command her any place any time. Instantly. The last thing she wanted was for him to figure that out.

"Take the robe off now, Faith. Drape it near the door in case you need it again during the week."

She stood at his demand and headed across the floor while she shrugged out of the thick cotton and then hooked it on the doorknob.

"Are you still wet, sweet girl?" His voice changed that fast. Gone was the hard Dom. Back was the man who could melt her.

Who was she kidding? Both sides of Rowen made her knees weak. "Yes, Sir." *It's a permanent affliction.*

"Good. Occupy yourself. Text me when you're going to bed. I'll talk to you later." He ended the call before she could respond.

CHAPTER 11

By the time Rowen received Faith's text that night, he was completely unfocused. He'd been out of sorts the entire day. He'd sent several emails to confirm appointments for the coming week and did some accounting for Zodiac, but after all that was accomplished, he ran out of ways to occupy his mind.

He imagined Faith had a similar day. Only she spent it naked.

He grinned at her text.

Faith: Going to bed, Sir.

Short. Sweet. Informative.

He responded similarly.

Rowen: Sleep tight, sweet girl.

He had almost as many questions as he'd started with. No. He had even more questions. Faith was an enigma. He had absolutely no idea where she worked or even what profession she was in. He had no idea what time she would get up Monday morning or where she would go. He had no idea if she had family in the area or even friends.

He *was*, however, intrigued, which also managed to annoy him.

He didn't expect her to answer all his questions today. That wasn't why he'd answered all of hers. He'd done so to prove he was an open book. Something about her suggested she needed that in a Dom. Her past haunted her. He could see it in her eyes. And it made him want to chase away her demons. He could only hope it was possible. It was hard to chase down an unknown enemy.

On Monday, he got her text at eight. He was at the gym at the time, but he responded with a simple *good morning*. He wanted to ask about a thousand questions, but he didn't. He needed to be patient. He'd asked for two answers a day. He would wait for them. If he pushed her, she might run.

It was hard enough knowing how difficult it could be to keep her mind focused on him without seeing her. He hoped to God giving her the space he promised would work in his favor.

Rowen ran his own accounting firm, and he did so from his apartment. He had a home office right inside the front door, which meant he only needed to keep the great room presentable. He had a cleaning lady who came once a week to keep him from looking like a slob.

When his nine o'clock appointment left, he found an email from Faith.

My husband's name was Victor. He was in the navy. He died eighteen months ago in combat. I hadn't seen him in six months. I didn't have OCD until after he died. I think it was a new nervous habit that kept me too busy to think about the loss at first, and I just never stopped.

Rowen stared at her words for a long time, reading them over and over again. She had given him something. He knew it was hard for her. He also noted she had skipped questions one and two again. Intentionally?

It didn't matter. Any question she answered he would appreciate.

Thank you for sharing, sweet girl. I hope you're having a good day.

He sent that short message after deliberating for a while. He could have written two pages, but decided after the lengthy email he'd sent Sunday, less was more.

Taking a risk, seeing as he had no idea what her sweet tooth looked like, he had a box of dark chocolates delivered later that evening. At ten o'clock he got a text.

The chocolates were wonderful, Sir. Thank you. If you keep sending deliveries to my apartment, I'll get a reputation among delivery drivers all over the city as the woman who always opens the door in a ridiculous thick robe. This is Miami. I look suspicious.

He plopped down on the couch with a smile and called her. He'd been patient all day. He couldn't go another moment without hearing her voice.

He was still grinning when she answered.

"Hey, sweet girl. You think delivery people all over Miami have a secret society and compare notes?" he teased.

She giggled, the sound going straight to his cock. "Maybe. If it spreads around social media, we'll know."

"That would be bad. You have a point."

"It could be worse," she added hesitantly.

"Sweet girl, it could be so much worse."

"I appreciate the gesture, Sir."

He loved it when she spoke to him in that tone and called him *Sir*. His cock grew stiffer, and he had to adjust it. "Trust me, I wouldn't share your body with random strangers at the door."

"Noted, Sir."

"How was your day?" Innocuous enough question.

"Busy, Sir. I'm sliding into bed now. That's why I texted."

"You sound tired."

"I didn't sleep much last night."

"Sorry to hear that. Can I do anything to help?"

She giggled again. "I'm pretty sure you caused my lack of sleep, Sir. So, no. Unless you can arrange for my brain to shut down and stop pondering the implications of submitting to you, I don't think you can help."

Damn. He considered his next words carefully, unzipping his jeans to release his straining cock. "Is submitting to me, even from a distance, adding stress to your life?"

She sighed. "Not going to lie. Yes. But that doesn't mean it's a bad thing. I need to do this. It's time. It's past time."

"Submit to a new Dom, you mean," he stated gently.

"Yes. And Rowen..." She stopped speaking mid-thought.

"You can say anything to me, Faith. I'm listening."

"Yeah, that's the problem. You're too...perfect."

He swallowed. Was this an it's-not-you-it's-me speech?

"That came out wrong."

"Sweet girl, it's not my intention to add stress to your life. That's why I suggested this week of separation. You need to ease back into the lifestyle. I don't want you to feel pressure from me."

"I don't, Sir. Really, I don't. It might be easier if I *did* feel pressured." A soft chuckle that held no trace of humor followed those words before she continued. "It's easy for me to follow orders. It comes naturally. And it's been so long and it feels so good. Too good. Scary good."

"Take your time. Let yourself feel. There's no rush."

"I'm not being fair to you."

"Let me worry about what's fair to me. I suggested this arrangement, and I'm still one hundred percent committed. It doesn't matter the outcome. I'm here to help."

There was a long pause, only her deep breaths filling the silence. "There's so much you don't know about me."

"And you'll fill me in when you're ready."

"It's not all sunshine and roses."

"No one's closet is, sweet girl."

"Yours is. Your closet is damn near empty. Whatever was on the shelves, you handed to me on a silver platter and left the door open."

He rubbed his forehead with his thumb and middle finger. "I can't deny you have a point. It's not like my life was filled with balloons. But I don't have secrets. My dad died when I was very young. When I was ten, my mom got pregnant with a man who freaked out, took off, and never came back.

"I became the man of the house when Sasha was born. I grew up too early. I was forced to grow up even faster twelve years later when my mom dropped dead from an aneurysm. I was twenty-two. I had just gotten out of the service. I had four years of college ahead of me, two jobs, and a young girl to raise.

"My life isn't pretty, but it isn't something I keep secret either. I'm an open book. I have no reason not to be. I don't say these things so you'll feel sorry for me. I say them so you'll understand where I come from.

"I've been in charge of my surroundings for two-thirds of my life. Falling into a role of Dom was a no-brainer. I enjoy ensuring the women in my charge are taken care of. It started with my mom and moved to my sister. Sasha doesn't need me anymore. She's a grown woman. She has a Dom of her own. I'm sure she much prefers taking orders from him than she did me." He chuckled to lighten his speech.

He could tell by her breathing that she was still on the line and listening closely. "That must have been hard, Rowen. I've never known that kind of financial hardship." There it was. A small piece of Faith. A piece he'd already suspected but now had confirmed.

"It was all I knew. I never thought about any season of my life as being hard at the time. It just was. I made it work. I was never homeless or went without food. I was able to go to college, and I'm part owner of a business. Sasha is well-rounded. She has a degree. She's happy. I did okay. We had everything we needed. I wouldn't have wanted it any other way."

"You did amazing. I'm not sure I would have had the strength to survive everything life threw at you. Sometimes I think I'm weak. Perhaps that's why I hide behind submission."

"Whoa. Stop right there. Only the strongest individuals are submissive. You know that. You didn't enter this lifestyle last weekend."

She sighed. "Yeah, people say that. But I'm not sure it's true for me. I think I use submission as an excuse. It's easier for me than facing... Well, it's just easier."

He'd been making headway, and then she'd caught herself and cut herself off. "Faith, stop. Think about what you're saying. You know better. I've seen you in action at the club. You obviously have a dominant controlled side. I'm going to assume whatever you do in your real life entails you being in charge. I bet you step out into the world with your head high and your game face intact. Am I wrong?"

"No." Her voice was barely audible.

"Then you know good and well that the people in the highest stress jobs who spend their days taking care of the rest of the world are the ones most likely to come home at night and turn that power willingly over to someone else."

"Yeah, I know."

"And you don't think that applies to you?" He leaned forward, setting his elbows on his knees. Was he reaching her?

"Maybe. Though I'm not sure I deserve it."

He winced. "Sweet girl, we all deserve to have whatever we need. If it helps you restore your energy and calm your mind to submit, then that's what's right for you. But I think you already know this. I think you've been in this kind of committed relationship before. I'd even bet it was with your husband. Which means you're afraid to put yourself back out there again. And that's understandable."

She said nothing. He knew he had gotten to her on some level.

"Faith, you're being too hard on yourself. This is a huge step. Take some deep breaths. Slow down. No one's pressuring you."

Her next whispered words were so soft he had to hold his breath to hear her. "What if I want someone to pressure me? What if I don't like slow? What if I'm feeling like there's too much silence in my life and I need to hear someone else's voice to help me go on?"

Rowen pushed to standing, his heart racing. He needed to be careful. She was vulnerable.

Who the fuck was he kidding? *He* was vulnerable too.

"I need you to be sure what you're asking for, Faith. I can be inside your apartment in ten minutes giving you what you need. But I'm worried you aren't as ready as you'd like to be, and you'll be traumatized if you jump back in too soon."

"It's not just that. If I were a selfish bitch, I would tell you to take the wheel that controls my life and steer it anywhere you see fit, but you know nothing about me. So that's not fair. You gave me all of you in two days. Over and over in so many ways. I've given you nothing."

"Then you're not ready. You have your answer. Faith, I'll be honest with you. I like you. A lot. More than I should. But you're right about one thing. It's not fair for you to hold back relevant pieces of yourself when and if you give yourself to a new Dom."

He needed to rein this in a bit. He was overstepping his bounds. She was not his. Chances were, she could never be his. If he pushed her, he might hurt her. Hell, he might get hurt too. Wishful thinking was not going to make her the perfect submissive his mind had managed to conjure.

Step back, Rowen. Arm's length.

"I'm not saying that Dom is me. I'm just suggesting you allow yourself to open up and reenter the world. There's another Dom out there for you. You can live again. I know it must seem impossible right now, but you will get there."

His hands were shaking. His voice was too. She was so raw and open. He wanted to claim her. Force her to see how well they clicked. This magnetism between them was unlike anything he'd ever felt. He wanted to own her.

But that was absurd. And he knew it. *She* knew it. He knew nothing about her, and whatever she was withholding was important enough that she guarded her secrets close to her chest.

This was nothing more than a long scene. A Dom helping a submissive back into the lifestyle. He needed to keep reminding himself of that fact.

They'd met two days ago. *Two days, Rowen.*

While he listened to her breathe, he ran a hand through his hair and closed his eyes. Even the first night he'd watched her perform, he'd known he wanted her. His cock had been so hard he'd locked himself in his office to relieve the pressure.

Her breaths grew heavier. What was she thinking?

He continued, rounding the couch and gripping the top of it with his fingers. "Here's what we're going to do."

"Sir?"

Damn that voice. Damn the way she slid back into a submissive role and gripped his aching cock with one syllable. "You do not stray from this week's plan, understood?"

"Yes, Sir."

"Follow my orders every day. Text me in the morning and at night. Answer as many of my questions as you can manage each day. Ask me anything that comes to mind that fills a hole in what you'd like to know about me."

"Yes, Sir."

Perhaps he wasn't being fair, but he didn't give a solid fuck. He was in the fight of his life against an unknown enemy. He wanted to own her. Possess her. He wanted her to give herself to him freely and without hesitation. All of herself. Until she could do that, they were simply playing around in the fringe of the lifestyle.

She moaned, shocking him. Had she slipped her fingers into her pussy as soon as he'd taken control again?

"Faith," he stated sharply.

"Yes, Sir." Her voice was too dreamy.

"Fingers off your pussy. Now."

"Yes, Sir." The deflation in her voice made his pulse pick up.

"Have I made myself clear?"

"Yes, Sir."

Maybe he needed to pick things up a bit. Toss a larger bone her way to lure her in. The odds were stacked against him without seeing her, but he needed to stay strong and play this out. Not just for her well-being, but his own.

But, no one said he had to fight fair. He simply had to fight from a distance. "I'm going to send you some new toys tomorrow. Do not open anything without permission. Be prepared to face a few challenges, mental and physical."

"Yes, Sir." Breathy. Sexy. *Yes.*

"What hours of the day will you be home?"

"I'll be here until noon and then won't return until late, Sir."

What the living hell did this woman do with her time? "Perfect. Expect a delivery at ten. Call me when it arrives. Don't open anything without permission."

"Yes, Sir."

"Do not touch yourself again tonight. You don't have permission to come. Go to sleep, Faith."

"Yes, Sir." Deflation. Also sexy. *Yes.*

He smiled. "Good night, Faith." And then he ended the call. He couldn't have gone another second. He needed to catch his breath as if he'd been fighting a real actual battle with his fists.

He had to pull himself together. He had some planning to do before morning.

CHAPTER 12

Faith didn't fall asleep for a long time, but when she did, she slept hard. She woke up at eight, refreshed. After a quick text to let Rowen know she was awake, she grabbed her computer, propped against the headboard, and stared at his list of questions while she held her thumbnail between her teeth.

She needed to answer some of them. Give him more of herself. Not just two, but several. In good faith. To show she took him seriously and was still invested in this experiment.

Was she using him?

Damn, it felt good to be with someone who understood her. It seemed Rowen understood her from the moment he first saw her. Eerie in a way.

How much could she give him?

I was probably twelve when I realized I was submissive. That may sound crazy, but I was an avid reader. I read everything I could get my hands on. My parents had a cleaning woman who always had books with her. One day she flipped out when she caught me reading one of them. I thought she was going to have a heart attack, until I made her a deal. I swore I would never tell anyone she let me read her books if she would get me new ones every week. That was the end of my innocence.

When I was twenty-two, I discovered there were clubs for people like me. I had just graduated from college. Until that point, I had never met another person who openly admitted they were interested in BDSM. The first time I went to Breeze, I was shaking so badly it's a wonder I didn't pass out.

I observed for weeks, always worried someone inside the club would think I was an imposter. Always worried someone I knew outside Breeze would find me out. None of my family members know I'm in the lifestyle. Eventually, I relaxed and learned to trust that people at Breeze would never out me.

Although I had fantasized for ten years about being dominated, that wasn't the path I took. It scared the hell out of me to allow someone to top me. I had done my research. I understood conceptually it was a power exchange. But I couldn't bring myself to bottom for anyone.

So I learned how to be a Domme. I was good at it. People complimented me. I knew I fulfilled people's fantasies. Just not my own.

I also learned how to submit by default of course. But until I met Victor two years later, I never did more than one scene with any one Dom. Just enough to understand how a particular instrument or apparatus felt on the receiving end.

Victor was eight years older than me. He seemed ancient at the time. Thirty-two. He was in the navy. I didn't know anyone in the military. He approached me and convinced me to do a scene with him. I never went back to dominating.

Until after he died.

Faith hit send on the email and then closed her computer, slid off the bed, and headed for the shower. Day three and it was already second nature to shave herself bare. After she set the razor down, she flattened one palm on the tile wall and stroked through her folds with her other hand.

Five minutes was a long time when the objective was to get

horny but not tip over the edge. She had to remove her fingers several times to stop the momentum. Before this week, she had never managed to come so quickly. Not even with her husband. She squeezed her eyes closed at the memory. If he'd never died... If she'd never met Rowen... Would she have been missing out on something?

It hurt. She hated letting her mind go there. Her relationship with Victor had been amazing. She'd never wanted more. Another wave of guilt slammed into her. It felt wrong to not only find another Dom but then to compare him and find he had qualities even Victor hadn't demonstrated.

Rowen had a hold on her that was not like any other relationship she'd ever been in. It felt as if he were in the room, watching, staring, ensuring she didn't cross the line he set.

And she did not. Lying wasn't her strong suit. Disappointing him gave her the chills.

Did he realize what a grip he had on her?

Today was going to be a test of her sanity. Yesterday she had worked from home, taking calls, making arrangements. Today she had to leave the house. In a skirt. Without panties. Her pussy bare and wet and wanting.

It was going to be a challenge.

As she finished drying with one of her favorite luxuries—a towel that cost enough to make most people cringe—her phone buzzed on the counter.

She snagged it to see Rowen had texted.

Rowen: *I'm proud of you, sweet girl. You worked hard this morning.*

Faith: *Thank you, Sir.*

Rowen: *Delivery at ten. Does that still work for you?*

Faith: *Yes, Sir.*

She glanced at the time. She could still get coffee and a bagel before the latest mystery delivery person arrived.

Sure enough, she was licking the last of the cream cheese from her finger when the doorbell rang. She wiped her hands and hurried across the floor to shrug into her robe and open the door.

This time the delivery person was a woman. Barely twenty-one. She smiled and held out a large black bag. She had gorgeous blond hair with the ends dyed fuchsia. She also had an eyebrow piercing and a tattoo that ran down her right arm. It was an intricate row of colorful flowers like someone might arrange across the middle of a table.

Faith wished she had been born into a different life. One in which her parents wouldn't have disinherited her for coming home with a tattoo. Of course, she was a grown woman now. What was stopping her from getting a tattoo or a nose piercing?

The woman glanced down at Faith's body and giggled. "Nice robe. You being punished or something?"

Faith's face flushed. The robe. Good grief.

The woman's word choice was interesting. Was she in the lifestyle?

Before she could respond, the woman spoke again as she handed Faith the giant bag. "Someone really likes you," she said as she winked. "Enjoy." And then she was off.

Faith closed the door, locked it, and hauled the heavy bag to the kitchen table where she set it on the surface. As soon as she shrugged the stupid robe off, she picked up her phone and texted Rowen.

This is a really heavy bag.

Two seconds later, her phone rang.

"Hey," she whispered.

"Hey, yourself."

"You don't want me to open anything? What is all this?"

"The packages are numbered. I'll tell you which ones to open and when."

"Okay, Sir." A rush of excitement made her giddy. Like it was her birthday and all the guests had brought her gifts. Except she doubted there was anything in the black bag she would open in front of people even at a bridal shower.

"Put me on speaker and find the box numbered one."

She tapped the screen, set the phone on the table, and rummaged through the large discreet bag for the package labeled *One*. There were eight items in total, each wrapped in black paper that made her reconsider the bridal shower and go with a fiftieth birthday instead. "Got it," she declared before she could stop herself from sounding like a kid at Christmas. It was the size of a shoebox.

Rowen chuckled. "If I had known it would be this easy to get you excited…"

"Sir, I've been excited from the first moment I saw you," she blurted out, also without thinking.

"I like that." His voice was lower, sexy, deep. "I wonder when that was?" he mused.

She shivered and hurried to change the subject. "You, uh, want me to open this?"

"Yes, sweet girl. I do."

Her fingers shook as she ripped into the paper to reveal a box. Also plain and black. Geez. Finally, she managed to open the box itself to expose a blue padded compartment. The item in the center made her stop breathing.

"I take it you got the box open," he teased.

She pursed her lips as she stared at the very real-looking dildo. It was shaped exactly like a penis. It was even flesh colored. She swallowed as she picked it up. The base had a suction cup.

Faith was not a prude. Far from it. However, she didn't own a dildo. Not like this one. She had several vibrators, which she used externally, but nothing like this that wasn't electronic.

"Sweet girl?"

"I'm here, Sir."

"Where are you, exactly?"

"Kitchen table, Sir."

"Good. Attach it to a chair, right in the center of the seat."

He had to be kidding...

Of course he was not kidding. She pulled out the chair she'd recently sat in to eat breakfast and pressed the base of the cock right in the center. Nerves crawled up her spine.

"Faith..."

"Yes, Sir."

"Find box number two."

"Okay." She was far less excited than she'd been five minutes ago. Who knew what box number two held? At least it was significantly smaller and not nearly as heavy. "I have it, Sir."

"Open it, sweet girl." The tone he was using was new. Playful Rowen. Amused.

She opened it with much less enthusiasm, relieved to find a bottle of lube.

"How wet is your pussy, Faith?"

It had been wet. It had been wet for days. It had been wetter from the moment she heard his voice. But as soon as he asked her that specific personal question, it went from wet to soaking. "Pretty wet, Sir."

"Good. Nevertheless, I want you to squirt some of the lube on your hand and grip the cock just like you would a man's, jerking it off to coat it."

She popped the lid, but her nerves had a hold on her. Obviously he intended for her to fuck this dildo while he listened. The concept was kinda hot, but she'd never done such a thing. As she spread the lube onto the dildo, she commented, "This gives new meaning to the term phone sex."

"I so wish you had me on video."

"You are *so* never going to get me to do something like that."

No way would she risk pics or videos that portrayed her naked, and certainly not fucking a dildo in her kitchen.

"Sweet girl, wipe the lube off your hand."

He thought of everything.

She headed to the kitchen and grabbed a paper towel, returning a moment later.

"Faith, this isn't going to go down the way you're imagining."

"Okay..."

"Straddle the seat of the chair, sweet girl."

She took a deep breath and did as he asked, lining the tip of the cock up with her entrance. "It's kinda large, Sir. And I haven't had sex in two years."

He groaned. "You're killing me."

"Just pointing out the incongruences, Sir. Tight hole. Large cock."

"Faith, that's enough. I don't need a commentary. Hold your tongue. Stick to answering direct questions."

"Yes, Sir." Damn him and his tones. Commanding Rowen made her hotter than any of his other voices.

"Ease onto it. I don't want you to bounce. Don't lift back off at all. Just slowly lower your pussy until you're fully seated."

Seriously? She gripped her thighs with her hands and did as instructed, holding her breath as the slick girth forced its way up inside her. She closed her eyes as she felt the stretch, panting when she finally rested on her butt.

It wasn't particularly large. She was certain Rowen was larger. Besides, he was unlikely to purchase a dildo bigger than himself. Though from a sadistic standpoint, anything was possible.

"Deep breaths." Soft, gentle, sexy Rowen. "Are you comfortable?"

"I guess." *If you don't mind having your legs spread wide and your pussy stretched indecently.*

"Faith..." he warned. "Be more specific."

"It's very full." She gritted her teeth, trying to acclimate to the intense pressure. What she wanted to do was lift off and slam back down.

"Play with your nipples, sweet girl."

She did as instructed, making matters worse. Could she come like this? From nipple stimulation and a rubber dildo inserted?

Her clit demanded attention. It was touching nothing. He knew that. Rowen knew everything.

"Squeeze them for me, Faith. I want you to make them stiff."

She pinched both tips between her thumbs and forefingers and arched her back into the slight pain. Her pussy gripped the dildo. She had to lift her feet up to keep from succumbing to the urge to fuck herself hard.

The slight whimper had nothing to do with her nipples and everything to do with the frustration of not having contact with her clit. "Sir…"

"Don't come. If touching your nipples is too much, I want you to stop."

She released them, not entirely certain she wouldn't come at any moment. In fact, she gripped the edge of the table and leaned forward. Her clit still made contact with nothing.

"Tell me how it feels, sweet girl."

"Full. It feels so full, Sir." There was no way to hide the arousal in her voice. "I need to move, Sir."

"I'm sure you do, but you need to obey me instead."

"Yes, Sir." Damn, but he was right.

"Stay still. I'm timing you. I want you to keep that thick cock in you for ten minutes."

Ten minutes? That was an eternity.

"I'm proud of you for sending me such a long email, Faith. I wasn't sure how you were feeling after our talk last night."

She squeezed her eyes closed and pursed her lips, not responding.

"Don't move," he crooned.

She nodded, not giving a shit how ridiculous the gesture was.

The insane part was that under ordinary circumstances, she would never be this aroused from holding something inside her. No matter how large it was. Without the friction, she had no idea what was driving her so close to the edge.

She knew the answer. Rowen's voice. His demands. His presence on the phone.

"Five more minutes, sweet one."

Five minutes? Lordy.

"Feel the stretch…"

How the fuck could she do otherwise?

"Imagine it's my cock inside you…"

Did he think that was helping?

"Do you normally come from penetration alone, sweet girl?"

She swallowed, prying her lips apart. "No, Sir." Her voice was weak. It belonged to someone else.

"Where are your hands?"

"Gripping the edge of the table, Sir."

"Good girl. Leave them there." He lowered his voice. "Do you know what I would do if I was there with you?"

"No, Sir." She whimpered.

"I would stand behind you, cup your breasts, and flick my fingers over your nipples. Can you feel my touch?"

"Yes, Sir." Absurdly, yes.

"Are your nipples hard?"

"Very, Sir." She curled her toes. Every word he spoke made things worse.

"Feel my hand sliding down your belly to reach for your clit."

She moaned. It was as if his fingers were actually on her clit.

"The little bundle of nerves is so sensitive and wet…"

"Yes…"

"Don't forget your manners, sweet girl."

She almost cried. Manners? Fuck manners? She was about to come.

"Faith…" he warned.

"I'm sorry, Sir."

"Your ten minutes is over. Should I make you lift off the dildo without relief? Or should I let you come while I listen?"

She responded with the hardest words she'd ever spoken. "Whatever you think is best, Sir."

"That's my good girl. Plant your feet. Keep your hands on the table. Fuck the cock as hard and as fast as you want. But do it without touching your clit."

She gritted her teeth and followed his instructions. It took about three lifts from the seat of the chair for her to moan. On the forth, she came. Hard. Her pussy gripping the rubber cock with every pulse. She cried out, though she had no idea if it was intelligible.

A final whimper escaped her lips as she lifted all the way off the dildo and stood next to the chair on wobbly legs. "I can't believe I did that, Sir." She panted.

"It was so sexy, sweet girl. So very sexy. My dick is so hard I'm going to have to finish myself off when we hang up."

"I could listen, Sir." Suddenly she wanted to hear him masturbate more than anything in the world.

"I bet you'd like that, but alas, no. Another time."

She sighed.

"You need to get ready for wherever you're going at noon, sweet girl." He said that matter-of-factly, not a hint of annoyance in his voice, which made her wince out of guilt. "Did you already shower?"

"Yes, Sir."

"Then I don't want you to clean up. Leave your arousal and the lube on your thighs. Wear a tight skirt for me, sweet girl. I want a selfie."

"Yes, Sir."

"Text me tonight."

"Okay, Sir."

He ended the call so fast her head was still spinning. She'd just masturbated on a dildo in her kitchen. Naked. For a man. On the phone. A Dom. A Dom she was coming to concede was her own Dom, which was something she never believed she would feel about anyone again.

And she had told him nothing...

CHAPTER 13

It was hot in the ballroom when Faith walked inside. She cringed and spun around to march back out with the intention of locating someone who could fix this problem ASAP.

She ran right into the hotel manager. How he'd snuck up behind her without her knowing was a mystery, but luckily he grabbed her by the shoulders to keep her from falling. "Sorry, Faith."

She stepped back. "What's wrong with the A/C?"

"It broke down in the night. A crew is on their way. It will be running within the hour. Promise."

"Mr. Lauderman, five hundred guests are going to show up in formal attire in about six hours. They aren't going to feel very charitable if it's stifling hot in here, especially the men in full suits." She had worked with Mr. Lauderman many times, often using his hotel conference room for charity events. She'd never been as curt with him as she was this afternoon.

Tonight's event was being hosted by the local Boys & Girls Club. They usually had a full house and typically netted a sizable portion of their annual budget from this event. If it was too hot in the room, people would leave early and feel less inclined to donate.

"I understand." He nodded. "And I'm doing everything I can. I'm confident the A/C will be running in time."

"Meanwhile a dozen people are going to be here any minute to set up in this furnace," she mumbled as she pulled out her phone and flipped through her contacts. She needed to let the staff know they should come appropriately dressed for the heat or they were going to swelter.

After sending three texts, she returned her gaze to Mr. Lauderman. It wasn't his fault, and she usually wasn't so snippy, but she also wasn't ordinarily under the influence of a Dom who had her totally tied in knots, which both irritated her and intrigued her.

As if she'd conjured him out of thin air, she suddenly had a text from Rowen.

Hope you made it on time, sweet girl. I didn't mean to make you late.

Guilt crawled up her spine. He so eloquently worded everything he said to emphasize the fact that he trusted her.

He should not.

She returned his text.

I made it. Thank you, Sir.

Pocketing the phone, she faced Mr. Lauderman again and blew out a breath. "What time did you say the A/C people are going to arrive?"

A voice she knew better than her own called out from behind her, making her back stiffen. She closed her eyes as she counted to ten, waiting for the grating pitch to get closer. "Darling. Faith. You're here."

She'd known there was a possibility she would run into her

mother at some point today, but she had hoped it would be later, brief, and after about two dozen other people filled the room.

Alas, the Boys & Girls Club was her mother's favorite charity event, and every year she managed to weasel her way into the venue at some point during the day under the pretense that she wanted to either "make sure everything was perfect," "drop something important off before the event started," or "say hello to her daughter." Which would it be today?

Faith was dressed to kill. She was always dressed to kill. She wore an expensive, perfectly tailored, gray pencil skirt, a relatively modest, sheer, but tasteful soft pink blouse, and her favorite matching pink pumps. She had put her hair up in a sweeping knot. Thank God because it was going to be a long, hot day.

Jane Davenport, no matter what the occasion, always outdid Faith. Faith was convinced her mother got up every morning of her life with the main goal of ensuring she outshined her daughter just in case she might come upon her at some point.

Miami was a large enough city that Faith managed to avoid her mother nearly every single day. In fact, it had been weeks since she last saw her. And that had also been at a charity event.

Jane knew what Faith did. She knew where she could find her on any given day. Faith was, after all, an event planner. Her schedule was public information because she worked for the city. Faith organized nearly all of Miami's largest charity events.

So, it would be easy to find her. Any day. Any time. Any place.

But Jane planned her moments with extreme precision. And an agenda.

Pasting on a smile she didn't feel, she turned around. "Mother."

Jane winced, her hand at her throat. "What are you wearing, dear?"

Of course...

Her mother's gaze wandered to the blouse. "Your shirt is so wrinkly, dear. You really need to speak to your dry cleaner."

"My shirt is fine, Mother. It's hot in here. I have a lot to do. Did you need something?" Faith walked away, taking quick strides to get to the table where she'd dropped her binder. She would do anything to pretend she was urgently busy.

Jane followed, her footfalls resounding louder than reasonable on the carpet. She looked far younger than her fifty-two years, and she carried herself as if she were the queen of a large country. Today she wore an off-white pencil skirt and matching jacket with a pale green blouse underneath. Even though it was too hot in the room, she made no move to take off her jacket—probably because her stupid fake boobs were delicately arranged to look best with the entire outfit in place.

Her pointy spiked heels were the same green as her shirt as if they were made to match. Her bleach blond hair had probably been arranged in a perfect coif at the hairdresser five minutes ago. "I'll be at the fundraiser tonight of course, with your father, but I knew you would be busy, so I thought we could talk now before things get crazy."

"Things already are crazy, Mother. If you haven't noticed, the A/C is broken, and I have a dozen people showing up any minute to set up in his heat." Faith glanced up to find Mr. Lauderman and three of his staff carrying in huge fans. *Thank God.*

Jane pulled out a chair and lowered herself onto it across from Faith as if she were royalty. She even picked up a piece of loose paper from Faith's binder to fan herself with. "I texted you several times this week. You haven't responded."

"I've been busy, mother." It definitely hadn't escaped her notice that her mother had been persistent though.

"I want you to come to dinner. It's been a long time. Sunday night. Your sister is coming. With her boyfriend."

Faith lifted her gaze. "Hope has a boyfriend?" She felt a twinge of sadness that she didn't even know this about her sister. They weren't close. Hope was four years younger, twenty-four, and found that she was rather fond of money and appearances. Hope wasn't rude to Faith, nor did she treat her with the same level of disdain as their mother, but she also didn't call to chat.

Obviously, since Faith had no idea she was dating someone seriously enough to bring him to dinner.

"Can't, Mother. I have plans." *Washing my hair... Balancing my checkbook... Submitting to a Dom at a BDSM club...*

"Well, cancel them. I think this relationship is serious. You need to meet Hope's boyfriend. It's embarrassing that you never join us for dinner. He's going to start thinking you're the black sheep of the family or something." She tipped her head back and closed her eyes as she fanned herself harder.

"Mother, I am the black sheep," Faith deadpanned.

Jane jerked her gaze to the front again. "Don't be ridiculous. You went through a rough patch. You're back on your feet now. It's time to come back into the fold. Claim your spot in society."

A rough patch? Those were the words Jane chose to describe Faith's entire marriage. Faith's face burned with a deep flush. She didn't have time for this today.

Luckily, two of her employees came through the door, saving her. "We're not discussing this right now, Mother," she murmured as she walked away.

The encounter stuck with Faith all day, however. Annoying her to death. Making it difficult to concentrate, especially in the heat.

When her phone buzzed in her purse at five, she pulled it out to see a text from Rowen. A smile spread across her lips. She needed the distraction.

Rowen: Hey, sweet girl. Just wanted you to know I'm thinking about you. Hope your day is going well.

She typed a response.

Faith: My day has been a shitstorm actually, but you have brightened it. Thank you.

Rowen: So sorry to hear that. Anything I can do to help?

If only it were that simple. If only Faith had a partner she could confide in and complain to. When Victor was alive, she could vent her frustration at him and he would listen. It had been a long time since she'd had someone like that to confide in. Her arrangement with Rowen was far too superficial for Faith to dump her dirty laundry on his lap. *It's your own fault the relationship isn't more*, she reminded herself.

Faith: Thank you for asking. That's very kind. Nothing I can't handle.

Rowen: I'm sure you can handle anything, sweet girl. You're a strong woman. Formidable.

As an afterthought, Faith decided to take a quick selfie and send it to Rowen. He'd asked for one that morning, and she'd yet to comply. Discretely as possible, she snapped a picture of herself with the phone angled downward to ensure he got her skirt and blouse.

Not waiting for his response, Faith tucked her phone back into her purse and took a deep breath. At least the second half of her day would look brighter after that brief text exchange.

Rowen was staring blindly at his computer later that night, absently rubbing his chin with two fingers. He had done everything imaginable to occupy his mind, but his thoughts kept wandering back to Faith.

He was too involved. This was supposed to be a simple arrangement for *her*. To help her get back in the game. He shouldn't have let his heart get involved.

But the truth was, he liked her. And he was stuck. He had no choice but to remain patient and let her call the shots. If she wasn't willing to open up to him about her personal life, he needed to hold her at arm's length.

As the clock ticked, he grew frustratingly impatient. Where was she? She hadn't texted. What did it mean? Was she home in bed asleep and she hadn't remembered to text? Or was she intentionally avoiding him because she had changed her mind and wanted to sever their relationship?

He forced himself to flip his phone around in his hand but not text or call her. The ball was in her court. She had been instructed to text him last thing every night.

Finally, just before midnight, the text pinged. He jerked the cell up to read her words.

Sorry, Sir. I know it's late. I hope I didn't wake you. I just got home. I'm exhausted. Crawling into bed now.

He needed to hear her voice. If it made him sound desperate, he didn't care. He called her.

"Hey..." Her voice was soft. "I hope I didn't wake you." She sounded as exhausted as she claimed. In fact, a long exhale escaped her mouth as he imagined her lowering into bed.

"No. Of course not. I was waiting for you."

"That's... I don't even know what to say. It's been a while since anyone has waited up for me."

"And I'm not even in the same home," he joked, nervously pacing his living room floor.

"If you were, I would be horrible company. I can hardly hold the phone to my ear at this point."

What the hell had she done all day? *Her job must be taxing.* Whatever it was, she had worn a skirt, though… Hmm…

He deepened his voice intentionally. "I guarantee you if I were there with you, you would find a second wind."

"Mmm. I believe you. Just the idea makes me tingle."

He smiled. *Good.*

"Sir, I have a confession. I didn't touch myself again today after this morning. I didn't manage four times. There wasn't an opportunity."

"That's okay, sweet girl. Sometimes life gets in the way. The fact that you were honest about it is what matters. How does tomorrow look for you? I hope your day isn't as jam-packed."

"No. I'll probably sleep late and then work from home."

Doing what? Why didn't she just tell him? This was getting crazier by the day. "That sounds like a good plan. Text me when you wake?"

"Of course, Sir. First thing. Thank you."

"Sleep, sweet girl."

"Good night, Sir." Her voice was already trailing off as she said those last words, and then she was gone.

Rowen made his way to his bedroom and climbed into bed. He stared at the ceiling for a long time. He didn't know enough about Faith Robbins. He had nothing except the bones she'd thrown at him in the last few days. And he needed to hold his shit together and give her more days. She had his list of questions. She would answer the ones she felt comfortable with in her own time.

And what if she didn't? He needed to be prepared for that eventuality. Either that or the possibility he wouldn't be able to live with the answers. No matter how hard he tried to imagine what secrets she could possibly have that would turn someone away, he came up blank. Nevertheless, she must have thought her private life was too horrifying to share. And that alone should give him pause. It *did* give him pause.

There were too many holes. He reminded himself that he knew several things about her—she had been married to a Dom, she'd started her foray into BDSM as a Domme, she was sexy, and she could submit like an angel. There were still many variables.

CHAPTER 14

It was ten in the morning before Rowen got a text from Faith, and he was with a client, so he could do nothing more than glance at it.

When his client left, he sat back down at his desk and took a deep breath. There was an email from her also. It had come in about thirty minutes after the text. He was anxious to read it. Which questions would she have answered this morning?

I'm feeling generous today. Lucky you:

I don't need to dominate to feel whole. You've probably figured that out by now. I don't need to dominate at all. I've used domination as a way to scratch an itch at times in my life when I've been too scared to bottom for anyone.

I'm not really a switch either. I can be. But honestly I would say my life has been divided into three phases of practice: dominating before I met Victor, submitting to Victor, and dominating after his death. Until this week.

I'm sorry to repeatedly bring up my husband, but if you want to know the answers to these questions, he was an integral part of who I am. There's no way to avoid it. Don't mistake my mentioning him as me not being over him. I've made peace with my loss. I didn't return to Breeze until I had. It took more than a year.

On that note, I did service my husband in many ways. We had a unique relationship that had to change and evolve when he was deployed. It was easy to take care of our home when he was stateside because I was used to doing it anyway. He hardly knew where anything was.

That being said, it was an arrangement that worked for us. I can't say it would necessarily work for me if I were ever in a long-term relationship again.

Public exposure—Victor insisted I was the sexiest woman alive, and he liked to show me off at the club. I think he wanted to make other people jealous. He never shared me or let anyone else touch me. (And, for the record, I would never want to be shared either.)

All of this was circumstantial, mind you. I had been a member of Breeze for a long time. I had seen nearly everyone who belongs to Breeze naked at some point in time. I might not feel the same way about Zodiac for a while. My comfort level isn't there. Besides, if I showed up at Zodiac as a submissive right now, all heads would turn in confusion. Lol.

Humiliation—it has its place. Within an agreed-upon scene it can be integrated. Would I want to be shouted at in public? Fuck no.

Rowen was stunned by everything she'd given him. He was also more than aware of everything she did not give him.

Perhaps she didn't have much to tell about her family and friends, making mentioning them seem unnecessary. But her job. That was another story. Nope. She was intentionally withholding those two huge elephants.

He also found it curious that she insisted she was over her husband, vehemently, as if she needed to convince herself instead of him. He suspected she still carried a lot of emotional baggage when it came to Victor. And there was nothing wrong with that. It was completely understandable. They hadn't divorced. He'd died and left her mid-relationship.

It was only natural she would still have feelings for him. She might even be angry at him for leaving her. Or, she might feel guilt for moving on. Rowen's only concern with regard to those possibilities was that Faith's perspective was perhaps skewed. If she was still beating herself up over lingering feelings for him, that could pose a problem.

He picked up his phone and called her.

She was out of breath when she answered. "Hey. Sorry. I was jogging. Just got back to my apartment."

"Do you want to call me back?"

"No." She dragged in a deep breath. "I'm okay. Really. I...like talking to you...Sir."

He smiled. Every time she gave him an inch, it warmed his heart. He felt like he was on a pogo stick bouncing up and down over and over between convincing himself she was not interested in him enough to divulge personal information and then rethinking his doubts when she said things like that.

"Fuck," she muttered under her breath.

"What's the matter?" He hadn't heard her explode like that yet, and what caused her mood to switch so suddenly?

"My damn mother is at the door," she whispered. "Thank God I still have my workout clothes on. Gotta call you back." She hung up.

Leaving him stunned. He was shocked at the first mention of a family member. But more importantly he was reeling at the way she referred to her mother. *My damn mother...* Who spoke that way about their mom?

He had to shake himself out of his stupor because his next client was at the door.

After another hour of dealing with one of his wealthiest

clients, he was even more frazzled. He'd spent the entire time listening to the older gentleman discuss the merits of hiding his money in an offshore bank to avoid paying his fair share of taxes.

The man was rich. His type was responsible for the bile that often rose in Rowen's throat when he encountered rich people. When a client like that came to his office and arrogantly discussed how to hoard his money, it made Rowen sick and reinforced his disgust with the wealthy. What was wrong with people? He hated the reminder. It put him in a bad mood.

As soon as the man left, Rowen sank back in his desk chair and ran a hand over his face. His mood didn't lighten as he remembered Faith's words. And her tone. *My damn mother...*

It was like a mantra that never stopped running over and over again. It left a bad taste in his mouth. Did Faith have no respect for her parents? Hell, he still didn't know if she had a father. If her father was no longer living or if he was out of the picture, even worse. That kind of loss should make a person appreciate their other parent even more.

What he'd heard was a total lack of respect oozing from Faith's wealthy, disgruntled lips. And he didn't like it. He didn't want anything to do with it.

He shoved from his desk and stomped to the kitchen to grab a beer. Fuck the fact that it was barely noon. He needed something to calm him down. A beer or two always helped.

He'd told Faith he never lost his temper. At the moment, his fuse was so short, he was afraid he might have lied. He opened his patio door and stepped out onto the balcony. The air was hot and muggy, as usual for Miami, but it at least felt real. It hit him in the face, bringing his awareness back to earth.

Settling on one of the two patio chairs that flanked a small table, he leaned back, took another swig of his beer, and sighed.

My damn mother...

Was he reading too much into things? Judging Faith without

having all the facts? He ran a hand through his hair and reminded himself of the very facts he *did* know.

She had money. She hadn't discussed it with him. She had a mysterious job she also had avoided discussing. She hadn't mentioned a single family member except to finally berate one. Her mother at that.

Perhaps Faith had been less than authentic with him for the last few days. She'd seemed so genuine. But maybe she was just another rich woman who didn't value the blessings she had in life.

He wanted to shake some sense into her. But he wouldn't. It wasn't worth it. She was a grown woman. If she wanted to guard her secrets and talk shit about her mom, who was he to stand in the way?

Of course, that also meant he didn't want to stand anywhere near her. He'd left his phone on his desk where it had sat upside down during his meeting and remained in that spot still. He was afraid to see if she had called or texted. Ignorance was his current last measure of bliss.

Whatever she divulged to him next would change everything.

When he finally had himself talked down from the ledge enough to take several deep breaths and act like a rational human being, he went back inside, dropped the empty bottle in the recycling bin, and trailed back to his office.

There were two texts from Faith.

Sorry, Sir, for cutting you off before.

And an hour after that one:

Have I done something wrong, Sir?

Her texts didn't soothe him. They got under his skin. His entire spine stiffened. Perhaps he never should have taken her under his wing. The truth was she was probably a spoiled rich girl he would want nothing to do with in the long run.

He needed more time to calm down before he contacted her. If he called or texted her now, he would likely lash out and be unable to give her the benefit of the doubt. But what could she say to fix *my damn mother?*

It was Wednesday. He had filled several of the dungeon monitor time slots for later that night. Since he didn't have any more clients to see, he decided to head to the club. He had accounting to do there anyway. And payroll. Getting out of the house would do him good.

~

Several hours later, Lincoln stepped into his office, sauntered really, hands in his pockets. "You're here early."

Rowen glanced up from his computer screen, knowing his brow was furrowed in frustration. "I needed to do payroll."

"And the numbers aren't adding up? You look like you're ready to launch the computer across the room."

Rowen sighed, leaning back and running a hand through his hair. "The payroll is fine. It's done."

Lincoln lowered himself onto the chair across from Rowen's desk. "Then something else is bothering you."

"What are you, my shrink?" There was no need to get his hackles up, but he couldn't stop himself. At Lincoln's raised eyebrow, Rowen rolled his neck. "I made some bad decisions."

"Okay. I'm going to assume your choices aren't related to the stock market, but rather one very powerful small woman with long blond hair."

"Yep."

"I gathered from Sasha that you were involved with Faith."

"Sasha has a big mouth."

"Sasha is my woman. We don't keep secrets." Lincoln leaned forward, elbows on his knees.

Rowen nodded. "You're right. I'm being a dick. Ignore me. This isn't about Sasha."

"I didn't think so." Lincoln didn't move an inch. Rowen knew him well enough to realize this subject was not closed and wouldn't be as long as Rowen continued to hold his tongue.

"When we left your office Saturday night, I made the mistake of inviting Faith to my office. What I should have done was keep my distance and walk away."

Lincoln leaned back in his chair. "Why was it a mistake?" Was he grinning?

"I'll be honest. I'm attracted to her. Physically. Hell, emotionally too. I thought I could dominate her and help bring her back to submission."

"How did you know she was submissive?" Now Lincoln was full-on smirking.

Rowen rolled his eyes. "Don't pretend you didn't see the same signs."

Lincoln chuckled. "You're right. I was aware she was at least a switch. She can dominate anyone like nobody's business, but when she isn't playing the role of Domme, she carries herself like a seasoned submissive."

"Exactly."

"So, what happened? Were we both wrong?"

"Fuck no. We were right. That's half the problem. She's the consummate submissive. I've probably done more harm than good for her this week. After bringing her to her knees right here in my office, I had the bright idea to make an arrangement with her to *help* her get back to her authentic self." He realized his voice oozed sarcasm.

"And..."

"I proposed she submit to me for the entire week by phone. I haven't had any physical contact with her. Unfortunately, there were red flags from the beginning. I knew it even while I made the proposition. I thought I could keep my heart out of the arrangement and simply give her what she needed."

"Your heart." Lincoln sat up straighter. "This is serious." He wasn't laughing.

"It would be ridiculous to argue otherwise. If I didn't care about her, it wouldn't hurt so badly." He felt like he was giving up his man card by having this conversation with Lincoln. They were close friends. The best. But this was more personal than they usually went.

"What are the red flags?"

"First of all, she's wealthy." Rowen held out a hand to keep Lincoln from interrupting. "And before you say anything, remember who you're talking to. I hate money. It gets under my skin and rubs me wrong. I could tell by her clothing and the way she handles herself that she has money.

"I keep telling myself it doesn't matter because this arrangement is temporary. But it grates on me anyway. I keep thinking at any moment she's going to say or do something to reinforce my beliefs about rich people. They usually can't help themselves."

Lincoln sighed. "Not all people with money are assholes."

"That may be true, but I can't say I have a pile of good examples to the contrary. Which is why I'm hesitant. And frustrated."

"Because you like her."

Rowen's shoulders fell. "Right. Anyway, there's another issue, and that's her family."

Lincoln winced. "Strike two with Rowen Easton. Do. Not. Mess. With. Family." He grinned. Lincoln knew him well. Rowen was fierce about family, especially since his only living relative was his sister. Both his parents were gone, and he had no other extended family members.

"Honestly, the red flags exist because Faith won't discuss either subject. She hasn't mentioned money or even told me where she works. She also hasn't mentioned her family. Until this morning when she hung up with me because, and I quote, 'my damn mother is at the door.'"

Lincoln cringed. "Okay, but maybe you don't know all the details."

"Oh, that's for sure. How the fuck could I know the details? She keeps her lips pursed together on both subjects at all times, leaving me with no choice but to assume the worst."

"Have you asked her?"

Rowen smirked. "Oh, yes. That was part of our arrangement. I sent her a list of questions Sunday morning with instructions to answer two of them a day. She has covered nearly the entire list while leaving out the first two questions entirely. Family and job."

"Yikes. Okay, instead of freaking out and assuming the absolute worst, I think you need to talk to her. If she still won't provide info, cut her loose. That would bother anyone. Not just you."

Rowen nodded. "I know. You're right." Perhaps that was why he had avoided her all day. He knew his next step had to be to push those two issues. And if she failed, it was over. He was dragging his feet.

Movement at the door made Rowen lift his gaze just as Sasha stepped in. "Hey. There you are. I was wondering where everyone was." She strolled across the room and set her hands on Lincoln's shoulders, leaning over to kiss his cheek. "Everything okay?"

Rowen knew he was still frowning, so when Sasha lifted a brow and met his gaze, he didn't have time to school it.

Lincoln pushed to standing and cupped Sasha's face. "I have some things to take care of before we open. How about you pull your brother out of his funk and I'll see you in a bit?" He gave her a quick peck on the lips and left the office.

Sasha tipped her head to one side and slid onto the seat Lincoln had vacated. "What's up?"

Rowen leaned back and tapped his desk with his fingers, staring at them. His mind wandered back in time. After a long silence, which his sister graciously granted, he spoke. "Remember when Mom used to make you wear that orange beanie to school in the winter?"

Sasha laughed. "God, yes. It was awful. That thing was so ugly. This is Miami for heaven's sake. No one needed a knit cap even in the winter. She thought I would catch cold. What I caught was a lot of flak from the other kids."

Rowen smiled. "You never put up much of a fight with her," he pointed out.

She shook her head. "It wasn't worth it. Would have hurt her feelings and caused a fight. Instead, I just rolled my eyes, wore the darn hat, and then pulled it off when I got out of sight. I don't think she ever found out."

"Yeah, that's how I remembered it. She may have been a single parent, but she commanded respect."

"She sure did. It never would have occurred to me to openly defy her."

"She was a great mom," he whispered, glancing away, his eyes watering.

"The best." Sasha sighed. "You okay? What brought this on?"

He shrugged. "I was just thinking about the value of family." He leaned forward, knowing he was about to get overly sentimental. "You know I love you, right?"

"Yeesss…" She furrowed her brow. "You have never let me go a day without making sure I knew I was loved. Even though you were too young to take on a twelve-year-old girl, you did it anyway. And I love you for it."

He swallowed, holding his breath.

"Rowen?"

"Yeah." He glanced at her, forcing a small smile.

"Is everything okay? You haven't answered me. You seem off."

He took a sharp breath in and sat up straight, pushing his

sentimentality to the side and facing her head on. "Everything is great."

"You're sure?" She didn't look convinced.

"Positive."

CHAPTER 15

Faith was extremely nervous as she stepped out of the Uber at Club Zodiac and headed for the entrance. Tonight she was already dressed for the role she intended to play, wearing a lightweight rain coat over her clothes to avoid shocking the Uber driver.

Perhaps less conspicuous was the black bag she carried by her side. This night could go one of two ways. In either case, she needed the contents of the shopping bag.

When she stepped inside, Carter smiled at her. She didn't waste any time. There was no point in pretending she was there for any other reason. "Hi, Carter. Is Rowen here?" She held her breath while she waited for him to answer. She figured her chances were good. The club was only open Wednesdays, Fridays, and Saturdays. But maybe he didn't come in every night they were open.

"I think so. I haven't seen him, but Lincoln said he was upstairs. I'll call him for you." Carter reached for his cell.

But Lincoln suddenly approached and stopped him. "It's okay. I'll escort Faith upstairs."

Faith's shaky hands started to sweat, so she stuck them in her coat pockets. What did Lincoln know? Or was she reading too much into this?

As Lincoln opened the door that led upstairs for her, she prayed silently she wasn't making a mistake. She and Rowen had agreed not to see each other this week. But that was before he stopped talking to her earlier.

She was uneasy about the abrupt ghosting. He'd never gone more than about an hour without responding to her by text or email or phone. She understood he had clients to see and jobs to do, but this was unlike him. And she honestly didn't think he would be pissed simply because she had to hang up with him to answer the door. That was uncharacteristic.

Her heartrate increased as she got closer to Rowen's open office door.

Finally, Lincoln announced her as they rounded the corner. "You have a guest."

Rowen stood facing the windows, but he spun around when Lincoln spoke. "Hey." He looked genuinely surprised. "Come in."

She took two more steps forward, and then flinched when Lincoln shut the door behind her, leaving her alone with Rowen. "Hi." Her voice was too soft. She was downright scared, and she hadn't felt this way for a long time.

Breathe.

For a moment, they stared at each other. And then Rowen shook himself out of his apparent trance and motioned her forward. "Come. Sit." He rounded to the loveseat and sat on one end, patting the other side.

His gaze wandered to the bag she held at her side as she lowered it to the floor and left it there before following his instructions.

Nerves made her grateful she was no longer standing. She held her coat around her though, also grateful for its existence. If things went badly, he never needed to know what she wore under the barrier.

144

He angled his body to face her more fully, but he didn't speak. He was waiting for her to speak first.

She licked her lips. "I assume I did something to upset you, Sir."

He nodded.

"I'm afraid I can't properly apologize because I don't know what I did. Are you mad that I hung up with you to answer the door?" If that was the case, this experiment was over. She could submit in many ways to a Dom, but not being permitted to open the front door to her mother was going too far.

His head jerked back and his frown deepened. "Of course not. I'm not that unreasonable, Faith. My concerns are much bigger than that. You simply reinforced everything I've been worrying about when your mother arrived."

She swallowed. She still didn't know what he was talking about, but goose bumps crawled up her spine in warning. She had secrets. She was super clear she'd intentionally not shared many things with him. But why had he suddenly taken such a firm response to her silence after days of patience?

"Faith, your unwillingness to share personal details is more than I can tolerate. I thought I could handle it. I thought if I gave you time, you would come clean on your own. I thought if I proved to you that I'm trustworthy, you would open up. But that hasn't happened. Maybe I shouldn't give a single solid fuck. But I do, and that makes all the difference."

He cares… She licked her lips again, unable to come up with the right words. She didn't even know where to start. But she sure didn't want to sabotage this potential relationship with her stupid silence.

When she didn't utter a word, he continued. "My patience ran out, Faith. I'm sorry. I know I said I would let you have this entire week, but it turns out I lied. Your time is up."

"Why?" What was the rush?

He pushed to his feet and paced the room, running a hand

through his thick hair. "When I proposed this arrangement to you Saturday night, my intentions were to help guide you back to your authentic self. I could see in your stance, your demeanor, even your eyes, that you needed a firm Dom to help get you back on track. I lied to myself. I lied to you. For that I apologize."

She didn't move an inch, but tears welled up in her eyes. "What do you mean?"

He grabbed the chair across from his desk and set it facing her on the other side of the coffee table. Instead of sitting in it however, he stood behind it, gripped the back of it, and leaned forward. His own barrier between them.

"This isn't a game for me, Faith. I knew that from the moment I first saw you in the club weeks ago. It's not just a series of scenes. You know it. I know it. We click. There's a magnetism between us I've never felt with another woman before. I've been kidding myself for days, denying how I felt.

"I want you, Faith. All of you. I don't care that we didn't officially meet until Saturday and our entire relationship comprises hardly more than a two-hour scene together. My cock was so hard for you the first time I watched you as a Domme I had to jerk myself off just to resume breathing normally."

She inhaled sharply. Her heart thudded. She pulled her hands from her pockets and gripped her thighs. "Sir..."

He held up a palm. "Don't. Don't submit to me right now. I'm not done." He spun around, pacing again, worrying her with his silence. Finally, he resumed. "I tried, Faith. Believe me. I tried. I wanted to give you space. I wanted you to come to me on your own time with whatever secrets you keep so buried you can't utter a word, but I'm just not that man. I need more. I need your truth, whatever you're hiding. It's holding us back, keeping us from happening. Keeping this from turning into something real. If you can't give me that, then please walk out the door."

She nodded slowly as realization dawned. And he had a right

to everything he was asking for. She had to come clean or lose him. And losing him wasn't an option.

He waited, hands on his hips, gaze locked to hers.

"I'll tell you everything. But may I ask one question first?"

"Go ahead." He spoke those two words condescendingly as if to say, *why the fuck not?*

"What happened earlier to push you over the edge?"

"The way you spoke of your mother with such disrespect."

She flinched. "What did I say?" She couldn't imagine saying anything nice about her mother ever. But she also didn't remember her exact words.

"'My damn mother is at the door.'"

She nodded again. "Yeah, that sounds like me." She took a deep breath. "Rowen, my mother is a conniving bitch. There's no easy way to put it. That's being kind, actually. And half the reason I don't like to speak of her."

He jerked. "She's your mother." His eyes widened in horror. "Do you have any idea what I would give for two more minutes with my mother?"

Oh... It all made more sense now. Faith sat up straighter. "I'm so sorry about your mom, Rowen. It sucks. I can't imagine your pain. But not all mothers are kind and loving. Mine is not."

He gripped the back of the chair again. At least he was facing her and standing closer. Though he was towering over her. He also didn't speak.

"My parents are William and Jane Davenport."

"As in Congressman William Davenport?"

"That's the one." She forced a smile.

"But your name is Robbins." He slapped his forehead. "Of course your name is Robbins. That was your husband's surname, wasn't it?"

"Yes."

"Go on. Make me see this through your eyes."

Suddenly, she wasn't sure that was even possible. Her spine

stiffened. She wasn't about to let her stupid closet full of shit spill into the room if in the end he was going to be an asshole about it and cross his arms and show her the door anyway. "You know, your stance is not making me feel chatty, Rowen. How about you sit in that chair, stop glaring at me like I murdered half the town, and give me the benefit of the doubt for a minute. I deserve at least that."

He hesitated, but finally he rounded the chair and lowered himself onto it. "I'm not trying to be a dick. Sorry."

"You are *exactly* trying to be a dick. You're trying to intimidate me, and I don't like it. So stop it, or I'm going to leave. It's hard enough for me to talk about my personal life, Rowen. I guard it close. It's embarrassing, and I prefer not to think about it. Don't judge me prematurely for things you know nothing about."

A flash of sympathy crossed his face. He pushed to standing, rounded the coffee table, and sat next to her. After taking her hands in his and squeezing them, he met her gaze. "Forgive me."

"Oh, I think in the end, you're going to want to forgive me. Now shut up and let me explain."

Half his mouth tipped up in a grin. "Bossy."

"When it's necessary, yes."

He tucked a loose hair behind her ear and leaned forward, setting his forehead against hers for a moment. "Stop being sexy while you rant."

That had the effect of calming her. She smiled. "Can't help it. I'm just naturally sexy."

He sat back, releasing her hands and leaning his shoulder against the back of the couch.

"I'm super clear you've been waiting to hear two specific pieces of information about me. Let's start with my job."

He nodded, his arm going from the back of the sofa to play with a lock of her hair. "I'm listening."

"My job by itself isn't disturbing. I have a public relations degree from the University of Miami. I work for the city as the event planner for many different nonprofits. I plan and organize parties where many organizations do most of their fundraising, gaining donor support."

He watched her intently. "That must be so fulfilling. Why is it a secret?"

"It's not. What I left out is that I work for very little money, and I donate all of my earnings to charity. Because the truth is I don't need the money. I have a large enough trust fund from my maternal grandparents to last me a lifetime."

He nodded slowly. "And why is *that* a secret?"

"You seriously have to ask that? Rowen, I want people to see me for *me*. When I meet people, I never have any way of knowing if they actually like me or they just like money. It's a pain in the ass."

She knew she was about to lose her shit explaining herself. In fact, she pulled free of him and stood. She needed to move while she ranted. If he thought she was insane when she was finished, so be it. Her turn to pace.

"I don't trust people. They fail me time and again. I wanted you to get to know who I was inside without the cloud of money hanging over us. I wanted you to like me for me. If I told you who my parents were or where I worked or any number of things about me, you would see me differently. When people find out I have money, they automatically treat me differently."

"You can't know that for sure. Not everyone is an asshole."

She cocked her head and set her hands on her hips. "In my experience, most people are assholes, and I get hurt every single time. I just wanted a normal relationship for one week—if you can even call this arrangement a relationship. I wanted one week where I could be myself and not have to deal with my fucking money at every turn."

"That's ironic considering I think money turns people into assholes too. I've had few positive experiences with wealthy people. It forces me to be hesitant with you. Every woman who has come into this club with dollar signs has proven to be a pain in the ass. Every client I have with piles of money pisses me off with their unwillingness to share with the less fortunate or even pay what they owe in taxes."

"So you overgeneralize and assume every woman with money is a bitch?" Her voice rose.

"Yes," he admitted. "I'm sorry. I didn't say it was fair. I'm just pointing out how leery money makes me. I hate it. And, for the record, you weren't hiding your wealth, Faith. It's not possible."

She nodded. "I figured, but at least give me the chance to show you who I am."

He nodded. "Point well made. You've given me no reason to believe you think you're better than anyone else. It's hard for me to trust that in people, but I've tried not to judge you."

"Apparently you didn't google me. I appreciate that."

"You asked me to give you a week. I... Well, I tried. I didn't google you. I never asked Sasha about you either."

"I never told Sasha any of this anyway. She knows about my husband, but that's about it."

"The other problem is I've got some strange old-fashioned beliefs that I can't shake. I've been taking care of myself, my mother, and my sister since I was ten. It's ingrained in me to take care of my women. I don't let my dates pay for their meals or split costs for anything. It emasculates me in a way that may sound ridiculous to others, but it's who I am.

"In that same respect, I like to take care of my submissives. It's important to me."

"But you don't know I won't let you take care of me. You've never given me a chance. You judged me and then turned it into a problem in your mind, assumed I would not fit your mold, and then reacted," she pointed out.

He sighed. "You're right."

She approached him again and lowered to the couch next to him. "I can't change the fact that I have money. I do. It will always be there. And I won't apologize to anyone for it either. I'm not overly frivolous, but if I want something, I buy it."

He grabbed her hands. "I get that. And frankly I don't care how you spend your money. That doesn't bother me. I've dated women who liked nice things and bought them. Doesn't make me flinch. As long as they don't try to take care of *me*. That unmans me.

"So, you're right, I could see by your clothing, your purses, your shoes, even the way you carry yourself that you came from money. I shouldn't have judged you, or else I should have walked away. But instead, I let my emotions get in the way. I wanted you so badly that I ignored reason and took what I wanted."

She wasn't sure which way this conversation was going. From one minute to the next it seemed to go in and out of her favor. "You didn't take anything, Rowen," she said calmly. "You can't take from a submissive. They have to freely give. And I did. Knowing full well I was withholding information."

"You're right. I worded that badly. My apologies. The entire reason I was attracted to you in the first place was because you were an obviously strong woman. When you slid to your knees on the floor right here Saturday night, my heart skipped a beat. You gave that to me. It was probably the hardest thing you ever did, and yet you did it."

She held her breath, willing the tears not to fall. She was not done. "I did. And I was scared out of my mind, but I also never wanted to submit to a man more than I did that night. I prayed to God I had not judged you wrong."

He winced. "And now you find out I'm exactly the kind of asshole you abhor."

"On the contrary. You have never once treated me differently because of my money. Deep inside, I knew I wasn't hiding it well. But you said nothing."

"Until tonight."

"Well, there is that." She forced a small smile.

He leaned forward, setting his elbows on his knees and

rubbing his hands together. He looked so fucking good in his faded blue jeans and black, button-down shirt. She'd wanted to flatten her hands on his chest from the moment she'd arrived. "Tell me about your relationship with your parents."

"Yeah, that's sticky. I don't see them. Not if I can help it. To the outside world they might look like kind, ordinary, loving parents, but to me they're evil. So, I keep my distance most of the time. If it wasn't for my work for the city, I would have moved to Seattle by now. But I love my job, so I tolerate my family infrequently in order to keep up appearances. I haven't even spoken to my sister for so long I didn't know she had a boyfriend. My mother seems to think they're serious."

Rowen's brow was furrowed. He clearly didn't understand.

"My mother wanted me to marry a nice, appropriate, rich man and claim my rightful place in society. She managed to get my sister to date such a man, but not me."

"Was your husband rich? Did they approve of him?"

She laughed. "No. And my mother hated him. She chose to ignore the entire relationship, reemerging in my life after he died to pretend to pick up the pieces and bring me back into the fold. That is my mother's life goal. I'm sure she fist-pumped when Victor died, seeing an opportunity to lure in her wayward daughter. At least he was in the navy, so she can speak of him to her friends as if she respected his service. In reality, she never looked him in the eye."

"Jesus. Are you serious?"

She rounded back to sit next to him and took both his hands. "Rowen, I have loved two men in my life. The first I met in college, and my mother used her influence to threaten his full-ride scholarship. He didn't fight for me, and he shouldn't have had to either. The second was Victor. I married him two months after we met without introducing him to my family. That way no one could interfere."

His eyes went wide. "You have to be kidding."

"No." She held his gaze. "Are you starting to understand? I don't trust men. I don't trust anyone really, but certainly not love interests. Twice I lost. Letting my guard down is not easy. Telling you all this is beyond difficult."

"What about your father? You keep mentioning your mother. Does he agree with her?"

Faith sighed. "That's an entire new level of complicated. I think my father is a good man deep inside. He does good things as a congressman. I agree with his politics, and I'd hate to do anything to jeopardize his position.

"The problem is he's a pushover. He lets my mother run their lives. So, although I resent that and I'll never forgive him for not having a spine, I also don't want to mess up his position as congressman. If it weren't for that, I wouldn't hesitate to publically humiliate my parents and walk away, cutting ties."

"So, you never see them? Doesn't that raise suspicion to the public eye?"

She shook her head. "I see them when it's necessary. About once a year I make an appearance at a public function with my entire family for my father's sake. Now that I'm a grown adult with a life, the world doesn't suspect anything just because I'm not available for photo ops most of the time."

"Damn. That is complicated."

"It's a constant juggle. I hate it."

He flipped his hands over, grasped hers, and hauled her into his embrace. With his arms securely around her, he whispered into her hair, "I'm so sorry, sweet girl."

And there it was. The first indication he understood.

CHAPTER 16

Rowen's mind was spinning. He had no idea how to internalize all the information Faith had just dumped in his lap. But he did know she was hurting, and telling him her secrets had cost her dearly.

He wasn't an ass. She needed to be held. He held her tight. He had no idea what would happen next in their relationship, but he had been a big enough dick that day. It was time to man up and stop acting like an asshole.

Maybe he wouldn't be able to deal with her skeletons when push came to shove, but for this moment tonight, he could put his feelings about money and family aside and take care of her.

He slid a hand up into her hair and tugged enough to pull her face back. Her eyes were watery, but she held the emotion at bay.

"Not gonna lie. That's a lot of information. It's gonna take me some time to process it."

"I know," she whispered.

"I'm at least as weird about family as I am about money. I'd give anything to spend another hour with my mother and father. It's inconceivable to me that anyone would let that slip out of their hands."

"I understand."

"What did your mother want when she came by today?"

"She wanted me to come to dinner Sunday. She hunted me down yesterday at the fundraiser I was organizing, and I blew her off. So she showed up at my stupid apartment today to nag me again. She thinks my sister is going to get engaged soon, and it embarrasses her that I haven't met Hope's boyfriend."

"What did you tell her?"

"Fuck no."

He tried not to wince, but it was hard. He probably didn't hide his expression. "Would it kill you to sit through dinner at your parents' house at least to support your sister?"

She chuckled sardonically. "It's entirely possible."

"Perhaps I'm being naïve, but I can't imagine the situation at all."

"If you think I'm lying, you *are* being naïve."

"I don't mean to imply you aren't telling me the truth. I simply can't stomach the idea that parents exist who don't love their children unconditionally. It hurts my heart." He intentionally held her close still, not wanting to make her feel like he wasn't supporting her.

"Well, dinner with my parents would cure you of that sunny belief in fifteen minutes. Trust me."

He searched her face. "Would you go? If I went with you?"

Her eyes went wide. "You would go with me to dinner Sunday night at my parents' house? Have you lost your marbles?"

"Are you too embarrassed to be seen with me?" he teased, hoping to lighten the mood.

She rolled her eyes. "Oh, baby. You have no idea what you're asking. I'd be seen with you anywhere. You have more decency than most human beings. More couth. More respect. More common sense. You're real. Not a fake bone in your body. It's sexy." She flushed.

His cock stiffened. For the first time since she entered the room, he felt the electricity that pulsed between them. But he wasn't going to let this go. "So you'll do it?"

"Dinner? You're serious?"

"As a heartbeat."

"Okay, but don't say I didn't warn you."

He kissed her forehead. "Tell me more about your mom. Was she always so difficult?"

She set her chin on his shoulder and sighed. With a finger, she circled the buttons on his shirt absentmindedly. "We've never been close. She's never been a real mother. I had a better relationship with the woman I told you about who brought me books. Cecily." He could hear the smile in her voice even though she was hiding her face.

He didn't interrupt.

"When I was sick, Cecily took care of me. My mother wouldn't even come in the room because she didn't want my germs. When I was a teenager, Cecily taught me about my period and how to use a tampon. When I went to college, I never got a phone call or a letter from my mother. It was like she couldn't be bothered with me."

He couldn't move. His heart was seizing.

"And then I graduated, and everything suddenly changed. It took me a while to realize the only reason she started paying attention to me was because she needed to marry me off to the richest man she could find in order to look good to her friends and make connections. I didn't play the game right. I was hurt. Angry. Frustrated."

"Sweet girl, I'm so sorry." He held her tighter, wondering how anyone could have been raised in such an environment. It wasn't that he didn't believe her, but he hoped to God she had misinterpreted her mother's lack of love somehow. He needed to meet this woman. Maybe with a little help, they could mend their rift.

"The best years of my life were the ones I spent with Victor.

She gave up mostly and left me alone. I suppose I was a lost cause. But then he died, and she swooped back in to save me and bring me back into the fold like the prodigal child."

She lifted her face finally and met his gaze. "I'm sure more details will leak out if you give me the chance to show my cards. Over time. If you'll still have me."

His breath hitched. "Sweet girl, I've never wanted anything more."

She gripped his shirt with both fists, holding on to him as if she might fall off a cliff if she let go.

It felt good. It felt right. But she'd dumped a lot of information at his feet tonight. And it was still early. The club didn't open for another hour. "Faith, I can't make promises about the future. All we can do is forge ahead and see how things pan out."

"I understand, Sir." Her voice was soft.

"I'm breaking my own rules here, but would you submit to me? Now. Here. I have to work later, but I have time now. I think it would help you relax if you turn yourself over to me for a while. You're so stiff."

"Thank you, Sir." She blew out a long breath as though he'd just offered her a lifeline.

He glanced across the room. "What's in the bag?" His lips lifted in a coy smile.

"I have no idea. You tell me."

He grinned. "Why did you bring it here?"

"I figured there were two possible outcomes this evening. Either we agreed to walk away—in which case the contents of that bag needed to be returned to you—or we agreed to continue our arrangement—in which case I was hoping you might use a few items from the bag." She bit her lower lip as a flush covered her cheeks.

He loved it when she was embarrassed. It didn't happen often, but it was adorable. And damn but he was glad she had brought the black bag of mystery toys.

He grabbed her waist and stood her on her feet in front of him. And then he unbuttoned her coat. As he slid it down her arms, he stopped breathing. She had come prepared to submit.

He dropped her coat on the floor and stroked his fingers up her bare arms. There was often subtle or no difference between what a woman might wear to Domme or submit. Plenty of women wore the same thing for either position. Black was often the preferred color. Heels. Corsets. Tight, short skirts. A woman walking into the club wearing that standard outfit would give no indication from her attire which side she intended to assume on any given evening.

But Faith was not dressed to dominate tonight. No wonder she had come to the club in the jacket and left it securely fastened around her body for the last hour.

Faith was wearing a tiny, white baby-doll top with a matching lace thong. Her pink nipples showed through the transparent lace at her breasts. He'd never seen her wearing anything like it, nor had he expected her to own something so revealing and provocative.

As he let his gaze slide down her legs, he found she also wore silver strappy heels he had not paid any attention to since her arrival. Though how he avoided them was a mystery since they made her shapely legs look divine.

She looked like an angel with her pale skin and nearly white blond hair.

"Clasp your hands behind your back, sweet girl." His voice was husky even to his own ears.

She not only reached back to grab one wrist with the other, but she pulled her shoulders back, lowered her face, and spread her feet wider. A stance she was trained to assume.

"Did you submit to your husband twenty-four seven, Faith?" Surely all bets were off and she would answer his questions.

"Yes, Sir. When he was home."

"And you miss that." It wasn't a question. He stroked her soft skin up and down her biceps.

"Yes, Sir," she whispered.

"You've been so alone."

"Yes..." Her voice trailed off.

"Does anyone in your family know about your lifestyle choices?"

"No, Sir."

"I'm proud of you for confiding in me. I won't take it for granted."

"Thank you, Sir."

"You won't stop looking until you can find someone who can dominate you the way you crave again, will you, sweet girl?"

She hesitated.

He slid one finger to lift her chin, forcing her to meet his gaze.

"I'm not looking for anything permanent, Sir. I won't do it again."

He cocked his head to one side. "Why's that?"

"I don't have the strength to do it again. I've given my heart to two men. Both of them left me. I won't live through that again. I can't take the risk."

Still holding her chin, Rowen considered her words. His chest tightened at the pain he saw in her eyes. She was both hard and soft at the same time. In her mind, she thought she could not give her heart away again. But her heart craved the love and connection.

Rowen had no idea if he could make her see how wrong she was to close herself off from love at the age of twenty-eight. However, at the same time, he wasn't remotely sure he could be that man even if he wanted to be.

She had thrown a lot of information at him in a short amount of time. Intellectually he understood why she felt the way she did about her parents, but part of him couldn't accept that there was no way to work things out with them. He wouldn't want anyone to be estranged from their parents. Surely her relationship could be repaired.

A tear ran down her face, and she shifted her gaze downward even though he still held her chin. She did not release her hands to wipe away the tear.

With a lump in his throat, Rowen slid his hand from her chin to her cheek and swiped the tear with his thumb. "No one is pressuring you here, sweet girl. Let it go for tonight. Submit to me."

"Yes, Sir." Her shoulders relaxed subtly. When she submitted, she was in her safe space. A place where she could escape the pressures of her life and turn them over to someone else. She craved this more than her next breath. All of that was obvious to Rowen.

And he could do this for her. He simply prayed he didn't make things worse by dominating her.

"Please, Sir. I need this," she stated as if she'd read his mind.

"Okay, sweet girl. I've got you." Releasing her, he grabbed the two small pillows from the sofa and rose to set them on one end of the coffee table. "I want you on the table, hands and knees, knees on the pillows, wide."

She turned around to do as he instructed while he headed to the office door to lock it. He wasn't sure why he felt the need to ensure their privacy, but he did know he wanted Faith to be as relaxed as possible. She wasn't out as submissive to many people besides him, so her privacy was important.

He grabbed the bag of toys on his way back toward her, glad she had brought it with her. His mind was working double-time to come up with a plan.

When he returned to her side, he set his fingers on her lower back, pushing the lace hem of her lingerie several inches higher. He had one more question he wanted the answer to before he made her body hum. "Why did you transfer your membership from Breeze to Zodiac, Faith?"

"To start fresh. People look at me with so much sorrow there. They knew Victor. I needed to go somewhere I could start over. Where I could ease back into the scene as a Domme. Where no one would feel the need to say how sorry they are anymore." Her voice trailed off.

He understood her so much better now than he had an hour ago. And every word tugged at his heart strings. He wanted to take away some of her pain. And he could do that.

He stepped behind her and set his hands on her bare hips, admiring the creamy skin as he spread his fingers to mold her soft flesh. The thin lace of her thong made his mouth water. He would taste her tonight. No matter what, the scene would not end until he wrapped his lips around her clit.

His cock ached to be let loose, but he needed to control his physical reaction to her incredibly sexy body. Or maybe his reaction had more to do with how sweetly she submitted to him.

He closed his eyes and inhaled slowly. Was it possible she could be his? Her submission was so thorough and so perfect. Her baggage was so monumental. He wasn't sure. He hoped it wasn't insurmountable. Time would tell. In the meantime, he needed to hold his emotions close and guard his heart.

He shook all thoughts of the future from his head and focused on Faith's incredible body, sliding his hands up her sides. He pressed his knees against the curved end of his oval coffee table and cupped her breasts gently where they hung free.

Her lower back dipped as she arched her chest and moaned. Already he had her in the zone, right where he wanted her. Right where she was her authentic self.

"That's a good girl. Just feel. Let me explore." He set his fingers and thumbs on her nipples and gave a sharp tug.

She arched further, moaning again.

"So responsive. I love watching you come undone. I even love listening to you do it on the phone." He smiled at the memory of her masturbating for him in her bed and later on the cock he'd had her use in her kitchen. He couldn't wait to make her do that in front of him while he watched.

In addition, he had six other unopened boxes in that mystery bag he'd had delivered. So many more plans...

Shoving the barely existent material of her shear top over her breasts, he left it gathered under her chin. Her tits hanging free, he cupped them again, feeling their weight, stroking her nipples until they were hard pebbles, enjoying the way she swayed and whimpered in response.

When her noises grew louder, he released her breasts and eased his hands down her body again until he cupped her soft cheeks, spreading them apart. He tapped the entrance to her tight hole, the thin strip of lace doing nothing to hide the puckered flesh. "One of those packages has a plug in it, sweet girl. Have you worn a plug before?"

"Yes, Sir." She instinctively pulled her cheeks in.

"Relax your bottom, Faith. Let me explore."

She drew in a breath and let it out slowly while she released the tight grip of her butt cheeks.

"Good girl." He tugged at the sensitive flesh next to her rear hole, opening her to his gaze, proud of her for this level of submission. "Do you own a plug?"

"Not anymore, Sir."

"Okay. So it's been a while."

"Yes, Sir."

How much experience did she have with ass play? He didn't want to continue to ask her questions about her past for fear he was bringing up painful memories. She was with him now. For however long that lasted, he would cherish her and take care of her needs. "It makes you wet thinking about me inserting something into your bottom, doesn't it?"

"Yes, Sir." Breathy. Whispered.

"I like that." He released her cheeks and slid a finger under the lace at the small of her back, giving it a tug.

She thrust her bottom toward him slightly as the thin strip of elastic teased both her tight hole and undoubtedly her pussy.

Finally, he removed his hands and reached into the bag at his side, rummaging around for the box he wanted. He had them memorized. He knew exactly which one held the toy he would use on her tonight.

As he slowly ripped the paper from the small box, she flinched. He loved watching her body tense in anticipation. Making as much noise as possible, he opened the box to draw out the contents, and then he stepped to one side of her body.

She undoubtedly expected a plug after their discussion, but that wasn't what he had in mind. He wanted to adorn those sweet tits with dainty clamps that would hang down and sway with her movements.

Reaching for her closest nipple, he pinched it between two fingers and gave a slight tug.

Faith rocked forward.

"Stay still. Have you worn clamps before?"

"Yes, Sir."

"So you know how the added weight pulling on your nipples can make you insane with desire."

"Yes, Sir." She whimpered.

He crouched down at her side and pinched her swollen nipple with the small rubber clamp. Rounding to her other side, he did the same. She held herself steady this time, knowing what was coming.

With the two small chains hanging toward the surface of the table, she looked sexier than ever. Rowen gave them both a flick to make them sway. "Are they too tight?"

"No, Sir."

"Lower to your elbows, sweet girl. Your arms are shaking. They won't hold you up while I play."

She gracefully did as he instructed, setting her forehead on her folded arms while he rounded to stand behind her again.

"That's my girl. So open and needy. So obedient." He stroked her thighs, dancing his fingers over the soft white flesh, inching closer to her pussy. A glance at her chest revealed she was holding her breasts off the surface of the table. "Lower your nipples, Faith. Let them drag over the cool wood."

She released some of the tension in her spine to follow his directive. The smooth, cool surface of the coffee table would tease her nipples further, frustrating her while helping his cause.

Her legs were trembling now as badly as her arms had been, so he reached for the two pillows under her knees and slid them toward her chest, spreading her wider. "Lower your bottom. Relax your body."

There was nothing sexier than a woman submitting so thoroughly to him like this. It made his cock harder than a rock while it humbled him to receive such a gift.

He set one hand on her lower back to steady her while he eased his other hand between her legs and tapped her pussy through the thin barrier of the small swatch of silk. He had no idea why women bothered wearing thongs. It didn't seem they provided any protection at all. But they were sure sexy.

Rowen dipped a finger under the edge of silk and lace and stroked it through her folds. "So wet for me…" He gave another tug to the fabric, dragging it across her clit this time.

She moaned.

He slid his hand farther up her back to hold her down between her shoulder blades, assuming the pressure would increase her arousal. And he was right.

She squirmed, lifting her chin a few inches before setting it back down.

He stroked two fingers through her folds and then pressed them deep into her. Slowly.

She sucked in a breath.

He eased those fingers back out and drew them forward to circle her clit and then flick over the swollen tip.

"Rowen..." His name on her lips drove him crazy. Not *Sir. Rowen.* She had slipped out of her role, but he didn't think she realized it.

He had to have her. He had gone days taking himself in hand. More than once a day in fact. He needed more. He needed to look in her eyes and take her completely. But first, he needed to taste her.

He grabbed her hips and pulled her backward until her ass pressed against his cock. Without giving it another thought, he spread one hand over her belly and smoothed it up to her chest. He lifted her up onto her knees, guiding her with his hand until her back was flattened against his chest.

She was breathing heavily, her head lolling against his shoulder, her top falling over his hand and the tiny clamps on her nipples. "Rowen..." she repeated. Her eyes were closed, her lips moving only enough to whisper his name. It was as if she were in a trance. Hypnotized. So aroused.

He set his mouth on her ear. "Sweet girl. I need to taste you." He nibbled her ear while he slid his other hand up her body to cup her face. He angled her head toward his and flicked his tongue over her lips. They had not kissed. Kissing was so intimate. It meant something to Rowen.

But suddenly he needed to own her lips and then her pussy. Taste them both. Devour her.

She licked her lips in that way she always did that made his dick take notice.

He closed the distance, taking advantage of her parted mouth to capture her tongue between his lips and suckle it.

She reached around to cup his face with her free hand, twisting her body slightly to make it easier to deepen the kiss.

Her touch. It unmanned him. He needed more.

He angled his head to one side and slipped his tongue into her mouth, tangling, dancing, tasting, wanting.

More.

She moaned into his mouth. He pressed his cock into her lower back.

A tiny flicker of reality flashed through his mind. He was dancing in unchartered territory. He did not kiss women like this. He did not let his cock lead him into temptation. He was breaking all the rules to have this woman. And he had no intention of stopping.

Gripping her chin, he parted his lips from hers. "Look at me."

She blinked, her eyes glassy, her lips swollen and wet. Her tongue darting out to stroke along the bottom one.

"I want you on your back. I need to taste you."

She nodded.

He held her chin steady. "I need to fuck you, Faith."

Her face flushed. She nodded again.

"Words, Faith."

"Please, Sir. Please. God. Please. I need you inside me."

Blessed angels.

CHAPTER 17

Now, Rowen was stepping into *dangerous* territory. If he had sex with her, it would be even more difficult to let her go. But he needed her so badly it was impossible to ignore anymore.

The best thing to do would be to slow this down. Take things in a different direction. Give them both relief without sliding his cock into her pussy just yet. He was rushing things.

He released her chin to guide her onto her back.

She flattened her hands at her sides on the table.

He shoved the sheer top up her body again and cupped her breasts, making the jewels hanging from her nipples shake. When she moaned and arched her chest upward, he reached with both hands and unclipped them simultaneously.

A sharp gasp escaped her lips as she froze for several seconds, but Rowen dropped the clamps to her sides and immediately pinched her nipples to ease the sting. Slowly, he lessened the pressure as she resumed breathing and let her back relax against the table. "That's it, sweet girl. Better?"

"Yes, Sir."

Stuffing one pillow under her hips to lift her butt into the air, he lowered to his knees between her legs and reached for the thong to slide it over her hips and down her legs. He tossed it aside and wrapped his hands around her thighs, pressing them high and then wide.

He stared down at her pussy, open and pink and swollen for him. Wet.

She arched her hips upward, using her shoulder blades for leverage.

"Ass on the pillow, sweet girl." Pressing his elbow against her thigh, he set his forearm over her hips.

"Sir..." She grabbed the sides of the table with her hands.

He lowered his face, inhaling her essence. So sweet. So wet.

Before devouring her, he flicked his tongue over her clit and then dragged it through her folds. She bucked. Or tried to. He held her steady.

With his free hand, he pulled her folds open and then stabbed into her with his tongue.

She called out his name. *"Rowen."*

Music. Such sweet music. He had no idea how he was going to deal with her lack of submission later, but he couldn't imagine a day when he wouldn't want to hear his name falling from her lips laced with so much desire.

He closed the distance, opening his mouth over her clit and sucking. The taste of her sweetness on his tongue undid him. All he could think was how badly he wanted more.

He sucked harder, flicking over her clit with the tip of his tongue while she attempted to writhe.

Her hands released the table to thread into his hair. She held his head against her pussy, and he didn't have the heart to stop her. Damn, she felt good.

Rowen kept sucking, noticing every second how her tension increased until her hips managed to lift slightly beneath his grip.

She stiffened. And then she came. On his lips. Sweet, sweet heaven.

He suckled her right through the pulses of her orgasm until her muscles loosened and she relaxed her hips.

For about two seconds she sighed. And then like a bullet she shot to sitting, batting him out of the way until she straddled the table, her sexy baby doll lacy top falling over her breasts.

As if she suddenly recovered enough brain cells to realize the insanity of her actions, she lifted her gaze and licked her lips. "Please, Sir. May I return the favor?" With her head tipped back and her eyes wide, he couldn't help but smile. Her face was flushed a gorgeous shade of pink.

He unbuttoned the top two buttons on his shirt and then tugged it over his head in one swoop, popping the button on his jeans and kicking off his shoes next. Two seconds later, his jeans were over his hips and then on the floor. He was naked. For the first time with Faith.

Those lips. She licked them again, her gaze on his cock as he palmed the base and stroked upward. He stepped closer, cupped the back of her head, and teased those swollen lips with the tip.

She flicked out her tongue to taste him and hummed.

"Faith..." He didn't know how to finish that thought. His head swam with the need to have her lips around him, her pussy around him, anything at all. After days of needing her, he was finally going to take her.

She leaned forward, parting her lips.

He wrapped his hand in her hair and pulled back, getting her attention. "Who's in charge here?"

"You are, Sir." She lifted her gaze, her face blank.

"Then how about you stop moving and let me control this, yeah?"

"Yes, Sir." Another swipe of her tongue. Destroying him.

He held her head steady and guided his cock to her parted lips. The moment he felt the warmth of her mouth around his length, he shuddered. Damn. He was in so much trouble.

As much as he enjoyed dominating her, and as much as he

enjoyed receiving a blowjob, he didn't want her to have the impression he was a shit when it came to taking him in her mouth. So, he released her head and set his hands on her shoulders. "Take what you need, sweet girl."

She drew him into her mouth so deep, so fast, so hard, he rose onto his toes.

Fuck me.

If he wasn't mistaken, she smiled against his cock as she drew off, hollowing her mouth to increase the pressure.

Yeah, he was going to come. Too fast. "Faith…"

She lifted her hands and grabbed his hips.

He should have stopped her, but he couldn't do it. His brain wasn't firing orders to his mouth or his limbs. All demands were aimed at his dick as it swelled further. He gritted his teeth, figuring he'd done everything he could to warn her.

With her fingers digging into his thighs, he held his breath, tipped his head back, and came, pulsing into the back of her throat.

Faith swallowed every drop, not letting him slide out of her mouth until he was depleted. When she set her chin on his stomach, he melted. "Sweet girl…" He smoothed his hands from her shoulders into her hair. "That was amazing."

"Thank you, Sir."

"However, that was not how I envisioned coming." He smiled but narrowed his eyes and gripped her chin. "Later."

Her face flushed. "Looking forward to it, Sir."

"I have to be downstairs soon. I'm the dungeon monitor for several shifts tonight." He still held her chin. "I want you to wait in my office."

"Okay, Sir." Her lips curved into a slight smile.

Good. She liked the idea. She might not like exactly what he had in mind, however. He released her chin. "Stand."

She obediently drew herself to her full height.

He reached for the hem of her top and pulled it over her head, leaving her naked. "I want you on your knees facing the loveseat."

She nodded and hurried to do his bidding.

While he watched her settle into the most basic of all submissive positions, he dressed. His cock stiffened again. He would relieve the need to be inside her later. For now, he would give her something to think about while he worked the floor in the club. Perhaps he could get a few people to fill in for him later or trade slots. If not, she could wait.

He reached into the black bag and pulled out the largest box. It didn't weigh much, but he knew it would make her shudder. Reaching around her, he set it on the couch. "Next box, sweet girl."

She released her hands from behind her to tear the wrapping and open the package. When the paper was tossed aside and the box opened, she pulled out a thick length of rope. She held it reverently before offering it to him. "It's so soft, Sir."

He didn't mess around when it came to Shibari. Injuring a submissive with rough threads was never his intention. "I'm going to restrain you and leave you here while I go downstairs. I want you to hold the position I leave you in while I'm gone."

"Yes, Sir." She swallowed as she stared up at him.

"Don't worry. I'll check on you often. Stand for me, sweet girl."

She elegantly rose, still facing the loveseat. He flattened his chest to her back and set his palm on her belly, lowering his lips to her ear. "I'm good with rope bondage, Faith. You'll never be unsafe."

"Okay, Sir."

"Set your arms at your sides." As he spoke, he slid his hand down to her pussy and cupped the warm flesh. "Legs wider."

She spread her feet apart as he unraveled the rope. With practiced skill, he started at one wrist and wound the soft white rope up her arms, weaving back and forth between them so that

BECCA JAMESON

her shoulders were forced back and her elbows and wrists came closer together at her back.

As he worked, he threaded one end of the rope through the center of the entire weave in a way that would allow her to easily tug the end and release her arms at any moment. When he had her secure, he continued by capturing her breasts in a figure eight, the gorgeous globes swelling between the gaps.

"You look so beautiful, sweet girl," he whispered. "How does it feel?"

"Sexy, Sir. Like a work of art."

He kissed her shoulder and nibbled a path along her neck. "I love restraining you like this. My cock is already completely at attention again. I wish I had time to fuck you against the couch before I go downstairs."

She shivered. "Me too, Sir."

"Later. The anticipation will make it worth it." He stepped back, releasing her to grab the bag and set it on the coffee table. As he rummaged through it in search of another item, he spoke to her back. "I guess I'll have to open the next box for you, since you're tied up."

He was glad to see she had included all eight items in the bag when she came because he was about to put the lube to use for the second time. It also reminded him that she had come to his office prepared to return his gifts and walk away. That stung, but he was to blame. His silence that afternoon had hurt her.

As soon as he had the next small package open, he closed the distance, to press into her back again. With one hand he covered her eyes and tipped her head back, and then he ran the tip of his next toy over her lips. "Open your mouth, sweet girl."

She parted her lips without hesitation. So sexy. Trusting.

Rowen slid the clear glass plug between her lips slowly until the widest part was inside her mouth while he held the outer ball. He spun the plug around inside her, swirling it over her tongue.

She moaned.

172

Jesus.

"You know where this is going, right?"

She nodded, closing her lips around the thinnest part of the plug and sucking. Any man would come in his pants watching her. Hell, most women would too. She was that spectacular. And she was all his. Completely at his bidding.

His head grew two sizes as he considered that few people inside the club knew this side of her. None of them had seen her in action as a submissive, and most of the members and guests believed her to be a Domme.

This was a different side of Faith, one he hoped he could continue to nurture as she resumed her more authentic role. He gritted his teeth as he tried not to dwell on the thought. Just because she was in his office submitting to him once again didn't mean they had worked out their differences. Far from it.

But for tonight—one day at a time—he would ignore their possible disagreements and enjoy her submission. Watching her suckle the plug was enough to make his heartrate increase.

Finally, he released her eyes, still holding her head tipped back. She blinked up at him as he popped the plug from her mouth. "Will you wear this for me?" He lowered it to trail it down her body, stopping when he tapped her clit and then continuing to drag it through her folds.

"Yes, Sir." The words were breathy. She lifted onto her toes.

He released her to step back again, pressing on her shoulder blades. "Bend over. Set your forehead on the couch."

He held her shoulders, easing her forward. So eager. So willing. So obedient.

So perfect.

Tapping her feet wider with his shoe, he watched the smooth skin of her bottom spread open for him. There weren't many things on earth sexier than a woman in bondage bent at the waist obediently taking his plug. But Faith was sensational.

After he grabbed the lube and let a generous amount dribble

down the tip of the plug, he pulled her cheeks apart with one hand and settled the tip at her tight opening with the other.

She tensed. Expected. No matter how much experience she may have had previously with plugs, it had been a long time, and she had never received a plug from him. She couldn't know what to expect. "Relax your bottom, sweet girl. Let it slide inside."

She took a few deep breaths and visibly did as she was told.

The moment he saw the tension disappear slightly at her entrance, he pressed the heavier end of the glass against her hole, slowly letting it slip into her. It only took a few seconds, and then it was seated. He twisted it around several times to increase the sensations she would be feeling. "Good girl. I'm proud of you. You okay?"

"Yes, Sir." Her knees were shaking a bit.

"Can you take more?"

"More what, Sir?" she murmured.

He stroked the skin of her bottom around the plug and then reached between her legs to tease her pussy. "More of anything I want to dole out."

"Yes, Sir."

After parting her lips to open her pussy to the cooler air of the room, he went back to the bag. "Too bad you're missing out on all the fun of opening these. It's a shame."

She shuddered but said nothing as he opened the next box and then lifted the larger of the two items out of the soft interior. Grabbing her hip with one hand, he slid the tip of the silicone egg through the wetness between her lower lips.

Her legs buckled.

He held her, propping her up with a knee at the base of her ass. "My girl is overwhelmed."

She moaned.

He slid the egg inside her without warning, an incredibly easy task considering how wet she was. When the only visible part was the loop that extended from her pussy, he stroked her clit a few times and then removed his hand. "Lower to your knees, Faith."

He helped by guiding her hips until her forehead rested on the edge of the loveseat, her tits hanging in front of her, and her knees spread on the carpet. "Hang on, sweet girl." He grabbed the two pillows from earlier and tucked them under her knees. "Comfortable?"

"Yes, Sir." He could hardly hear her words. Was she in subspace? It was possible. At the very least, she was concentrating on all the sensations bombarding her.

He picked up the end of the rope that wove through the crisscross down her back and set it in her hand. "I want you to remain in this position while I'm gone, but if for any reason you can't, pull this rope. It will release your hands. Understood?"

"Yes, Sir."

"Good girl." He picked up the second item from the last box and pushed a few buttons, smiling as he watched her spine stiffen. The vibrations inside her pussy would keep her on edge for the next hour. "I'll be back after my first shift." He leaned over and kissed her shoulder. Walking away was one of the hardest things he'd ever done.

CHAPTER 18

Faith's mind was filled with a mix of emotions and thoughts that had multiplied exponentially over the last hour. She had come to Rowen's office prepared to end things. Not wanting to walk away, but knowing it was a possibility.

But he'd softened, listened to her deepest secrets, and backed down. At least for the time being. She had no idea if he could fully embrace her unusual situation, but she was grateful he had taken control and turned their precarious relationship in the direction she craved.

Submitting to him came naturally. Every moment since he'd ended their difficult discussion and taken control was precious and embedded in her mind. The bombardment of sensations all over her body served as a constant reminder that he was the consummate Dom.

He hadn't been kidding about his ability with ropes. Her arms were securely fastened at her back, but not stretched so far that her shoulders would hurt. Only someone with a great deal of skill could leave a safety release. No Dom had ever done so with her.

The slight stretch in her ass served as a constant reminder it was filled. The weight of the glass plug was enough to keep her on edge, but combined with the surprisingly large egg inside her channel, the effects of both devices kept her alert and conscious of every erogenous zone.

Even her nipples still tingled from the clamps she'd worn not too long ago. Her breasts swayed with every movement, the globes swollen between the crisscross of ropes.

Victor had used ropes on her, but he'd done so because he knew she liked the restraint. He had not been as proficient nor artistic. She wished she could see the results, and considered asking Rowen to take a picture before he released her. That would be a giant step in a direction she had never strayed before. Evidence of her submission in the form of photos made her almost as nervous as the idea of dining with her family.

Had he been serious when he suggested coming to her parents' house for dinner Sunday? If so, she wasn't sure she could go through with it. He seemed to live in a dream world where he couldn't conceptualize a family as dysfunctional as hers.

The truth was much worse than she could describe. Her mother would slaughter him with her words and her glares. Or she could possibly ignore him entirely in the hopes her rudeness would cause him to disappear.

No matter what happened, it would not be pretty, and even at the expense of losing Rowen's respect and trust, she wasn't sure she could do as she'd promised. Taking him home to meet her family would cost her. A piece of her dignity would be lost.

He would never see her through the same eyes again. Was it worth the price? Or would it be better to accept the fact he wouldn't want to have anything to do with her if she refused to go through with it?

The reality was, there was only a snowball's chance in hell he would still want to continue their arrangement after he met her family anyway, so why put herself through the humiliation? If family was as important to him as he'd implied, he would be sorely disappointed when he met hers.

She shook the worrisome thoughts from her head and turned her attention back to the stretch of her rear hole and the slight vibration inside her pussy. When the speed and intensity suddenly picked up, she gasped.

Holy shit. He had a remote, and he was changing the settings from downstairs.

Faith rocked forward, her breasts brushing against the cushion of the couch and increasing her sensitivity. She squeezed the rope in her hand, knowing one pull would release her from this pleasurable prison.

She had no intention of ending the scene, but knowing it was possible gave her a great sense of relief. This total submission was made more so by the fact that he'd given her the control to continue. In a way, it increased her role, heightening his level of dominance. Her compliance was in her hands.

Time ticked by, the egg inside her going through waves of increased vibrations and then almost completely stopping. Her frustration mounted every time he changed the settings.

She had never wanted to be fucked so badly in her life. Did he know that? Did he do it on purpose?

Even after the orgasm he'd given her with his mouth, she was not sated. She had craved his cock inside her from the moment she'd come down from her high.

She had craved his cock in her mouth worse, however, thus erasing the possibility he would fuck her at that moment. She wasn't sorry, though. Sucking him had been as heady as having his mouth on her clit.

How much time had passed? She willed him to return.

Finally, the door opened softly behind her, making her moan with anticipation.

As his footfalls grew closer, she inhaled slowly, silently pleading with him to fuck her fast and hard and now.

His hands were warm when they hit her hips and pulled her onto her feet, kicking the pillows out of the way. "So proud of you, sweet girl," he whispered. "I know that wasn't easy. Your submission makes my cock so hard I can't stand it."

Thank God. Her forehead remained on the couch, her butt now higher than her shoulders.

He reached between her legs, grabbed the loop at the entrance to her pussy, and pulled the egg out so fast she gasped. "Sir..."

"Shhh. I know. No words."

She pursed her lips, hoping she could contain herself, knowing it would serve her well.

The sound of his zipper lowering followed by the unmistakable rip of a condom wrapper made her whimper and squirm.

One of his hands was on her hip again seconds later, holding her steady. His cock was at her entrance. He swiped it through her folds slowly from top to bottom, and then he stunned her by slamming all the way to the hilt.

Their combined groans filled the silence.

Yes. Oh, hell yes.

She hadn't needed words or discussion or preparation. She had needed to be filled. And he'd given her that.

She wasn't just full from his cock. The combination of him inside her pussy while the plug still filled her tight rear doubled the sensations.

He didn't pull back out. Instead, he slid his hands up her belly until they cupped her breasts. He toyed with her nipples, twisting and pinching them until she opened her mouth, instinctively intending to beg him to stop teasing her and fuck her.

She stopped herself, and he rewarded her—intentionally or otherwise—by drawing himself back several inches and then thrusting forward again.

Yes.

The base of his cock hit the glass ball of her plug, pressing against the toy maddeningly.

His grip remained on her breasts, tightening over them,

encompassing them completely in his palms so that they no longer swayed. He repeated the same sensational motion two more times, thrusting into her seemingly deeper with each pass.

She arched her chest into his palms, fisting her hands at her back. So good. So very good.

It had been so long since she'd been with a man that it nearly overwhelmed her. When Rowen released her breasts to grab her hips, he had more leverage to fuck her harder and faster.

Her clit ached to be stroked, but she wouldn't dare utter a single word. Rowen knew exactly what he was doing. If she tried to top him from the bottom, there was no telling how he might punish her.

Half of her considered doing so just to find out. She imagined his punishments would be sweet torture any submissive would be happy to endure. The two quick spanks to her bottom Saturday night had given her a taste of his brand of discipline, leaving her pussy pulsing with need and her clit throbbing for hours.

The slight sting to her butt cheeks reminded her of his control well into the night. Even long after the effects of his swats would surely have dissipated entirely, she could still feel the imagined sting. And she loved it.

As Rowen picked up the pace, his breathing came heavier to her ears. She lifted her forehead, setting her chin on the cushion to arch her neck. Her lips fell apart, no sound coming from her mouth.

She knew by his tightened grip on her hips and the soft rhythmic moans coming from his mouth he was close. And then heaven shined down on her. He released one hip, reached around to her front, and pinched her clit hard.

She came instantly, a scream escaping her lips as his own moan of completion competed with her audible release.

Several thrusts later, he stilled, deep inside her, still stroking her clit. When he eased his hand from her sensitive nub, a shiver raced down her spine.

He reached between her hands for the lost end of the rope and gave a sharp tug. As her arms were released, they fell apart at her sides uselessly. His cock slid from her pussy as he leaned forward to flatten a hand on her chest and pull her upright.

With one hand holding her tight, he grabbed a tissue from the end table and removed the condom.

Her legs shook, but he had her secure with his other arm quickly tucked under her breasts. "You are so damn hot," he whispered in her ear. "I will never forget this gift." He kissed her neck and then spun them both around, lowered himself onto the loveseat, and pulled her down onto his lap.

He cradled her in his arms while she nestled her head against his shoulder.

His hands worked to rub her arms up and down. "Talk to me, Faith. Do your arms hurt?"

"No, Sir. They're fine." The circulation was coming back. Nothing hurt. "You are truly skilled with a rope."

He kissed the top of her head. "There's nothing sexier than a woman intricately bound and naked."

She burrowed deeper against him, grasping his shirt with her fingers, more worried than ever about how deeply she was falling for him. She held her breath as tears welled up in her eyes, fighting to hold them back, not wanting him to see her weakness.

But she lost that battle when one tear slid down her face, forcing her to swipe it away.

"Hey." Rowen grabbed her shoulders and held her a few inches away from his chest. "What's wrong?"

She shook her head, staring at his chest. "Nothing, Sir. Everything is too right."

"People don't usually cry when everything is right."

"Sure they do." She forced a smile, lifting her gaze while she wiped her cheeks again.

His brows rose. "Seems corny." He must have felt her shudder because he tugged a blanket from the arm of the loveseat and wrapped it around her, tucking her against him again. He grabbed a bottle of water from the end table next. "You need to drink, sweet girl."

She took a sip and leaned her weight into his chest once more. "Thank you, Sir."

"I have to get back downstairs soon. Lincoln is covering for me. Will you stay? Maybe take a nap here on the couch? I'll drive you home later."

"I'd like that, Sir."

"Good." He gave her a squeeze and then spoke again. "Would you like me to remove the plug, or would you rather take care of it yourself? There's a bathroom across the hall if you'd like to clean up a bit."

"That would be nice, Sir." She would much rather remove the plug herself than have him do it. Maybe if they were together for weeks or months she would loosen up, but after less than a week and only a few hours together, she felt a twinge of modesty about that level of intimacy.

Rowen rose to his feet, taking her with him and setting her on her feet. He tucked the blanket around her and led her toward the office door. After glancing into the hallway, he pushed the door all the way open and declared the coast clear. "I'll wait right here for you."

She was grateful for that too. It would be mortifying if she came out of the bathroom to find someone unexpected in the hall while she was naked under a blanket.

She hurried into the small bathroom, unwrapped the blanket, and folded it to set it on the corner of the vanity. Working quickly, she removed the plug, used the toilet, and cleaned herself up. She wrapped the washed glass phallus in a paper towel and rushed to open the door.

No one but Rowen was outside. He smiled at her as she returned, taking the wrapped plug from her hand. "You're stunning when you blush."

She rolled her eyes and made her way back to his loveseat, suddenly drained and in great need of that nap.

Rowen didn't rush off and leave her. No. Of course not. He was nothing if not thorough in his aftercare. He helped her settle curled on her side, tucked the blanket around her, and kissed her forehead. "Rest, sweet girl. I'll be back."

As he left, he turned off the overhead lights, leaving her in near darkness. Her eyes slowly adjusted to a room bathed in streams of light coming from outside, but it was soothing. Relaxing. In moments she fell asleep.

CHAPTER 19

Faith had no idea how much time had passed before Rowen set his hand on her shoulder and gently shook her awake. "Sweet girl, I'm so sorry. It's late. Let me take you home."

She blinked her eyes open, trying to shake the sleep away. "What time is it?" she murmured.

"Midnight."

"Don't you have to work still?"

"I'll come back and finish up after I drop you off." He brushed a lock of hair from her face and cupped her cheek. "Let's get you home. You'll sleep better in your own bed."

She wanted to ask him to stay. She wanted to *beg* him to stay. The idea of sleeping next to his warm body sounded so appealing all of the sudden that she wasn't sure who she was or what woman had inhabited her body.

She hadn't felt this strongly about anyone since Victor, and while it scared her to let herself feel again, she needed to admit Victor would have wanted this for her. He never would have wanted her to pine over him forever.

She pushed herself to sitting, watching as Rowen rummaged

around, putting a few items back in the bag of toys and then adding her flimsy white top and thong. There were still two unopened toys in that bag, and she'd give anything to find out what they were.

But that wasn't in the cards. Rowen had intentionally set up this game to keep her guessing. Genius of him. The possibilities were endless. She couldn't recall what the sizes of the last two boxes even were. Since she hadn't been the one to open the previous few, she couldn't eliminate them from the running.

When he stepped in front of her holding her jacket, she lifted her gaze. "Can you stand, sweet girl? Are you awake?"

She didn't want to leave. She didn't want this evening to end. "I don't mind staying, Sir. I can wait for you to finish working." If he had to return to work, their time would be cut short. She would rather sleep in his office than be clear across town in her apartment while he was back at Zodiac. Anything to avoid breaking the spell.

Rowen lifted a brow. "This isn't multiple choice, Faith. I'm taking you home."

She swallowed, unable to move. It had been so long since she'd submitted to someone. She was rusty. She should know better than to challenge a Dom when he made a decision. She *did* know better.

She held his gaze for a long moment, reading correctly that he wasn't a pushover. He was truly as firm as he'd promised. He was also losing his patience. "I'm sorry, Sir." She pushed to standing, letting the blanket fall, took her coat from his hand, and slid her arms into it. Apparently he expected her to go naked under the jacket.

Not that it made a bit of difference. The outfit she'd arrived in would have raised more eyebrows if anyone would have seen it than if she'd been completely naked.

He bent down to button her in and handed her the silver heels she'd worn to the club next. After perching on the sofa to get her shoes back on, she stood, marginally more awake than a few minutes ago.

"Ready?"

"Yes, Sir."

He led her to the door, opened it, and then squared her shoulders with his and lifted her chin with two fingers. "I'm going down before you. I'll get the car and pull up to the door. I'll send someone to escort you downstairs in a minute."

"I'm sure I'll be fine, Sir. Thanks."

A female voice in the hallway made Faith glance around Rowen to find Sasha approaching.

"Oh, hey," Sasha said, a smile lighting up her face. "Are you guys leaving?"

Faith's face heated. She hadn't spoken to Sasha since last weekend, and she definitely hadn't publically acknowledged her relationship with Sasha's brother.

Rowen spoke. "Yes. Would you walk Faith to the door in a few minutes? I'll pull the car up."

"Sure. Go on. We'll follow."

Faith groaned inside. This was so unnecessary. "I said I would be fine," she whispered. "I'm a big girl. I can walk down the stairs and step outside without incident."

Rowen faced her more fully, his brow furrowed, his back to Sasha. He lowered his lips to her ear and whispered, "Sweet girl, how about you stop arguing with me and let's get out of here, huh?"

She nodded, lowering her gaze as she realized she had stepped out of her role and displeased him.

He gave her shoulder a quick squeeze, kissed her neck, and left her standing there. Shit.

Sasha was smiling, her head cocked to one side, when Faith lifted her gaze. "So you and my brother, huh?"

If Faith could flush more, she would. "Maybe?"

Sasha giggled. "Are you asking me? Because if you are, I'd say go for it. He's a gem. And I sense you are too. You have my blessing."

Faith wasn't sure how much she should divulge to Rowen's sister, so when her mouth fell open, she found herself tongue-tied. "Thank you. It's...complicated."

Sasha smiled again. "It always is." She nodded over her shoulder. "Come on. I'll walk you to the car."

"Your brother is—"

"Overprotective?" Sasha joked, glancing over her shoulder. "Yes. Very. He forbade me from even joining Zodiac and I'm a grown woman. I'm not sure my situation improved any now that I got what I wanted." She giggled. "After all, Lincoln might be even more overprotective. But at least I reap far more benefits under his care." She winked.

Faith couldn't keep from grinning at Sasha's back. If by some miracle Faith and Rowen managed to work out their differences and forge a relationship, Faith knew she would have a fantastic new friend in Sasha. It was a longshot, though, so Faith kept the thought to herself.

"Why exactly does my brother think you need an escort to the front door?" Sasha asked when they were in the stairwell.

"I have no idea." She shuddered.

Sasha twisted around to face Faith. "A few people asked where you were tonight."

"Really?" Faith hadn't spent much time thinking about how her absence might be perceived. Apparently, she was missed. "What did you tell them?"

"That I had no idea. I heard Brooke was here earlier too. She left before you got here, though."

Faith winced. "Did she do a scene with anyone?"

"I don't think so. Lincoln said she watched from the sidelines for a while."

"I feel bad that I had to cancel on her. I was supposed to meet her before the club opened."

"I'm sure she'll understand." Sasha turned to smile. They had reached the second floor, the floor where Zodiac would be in full swing, but Sasha stepped between Faith and the doorway to the club and swung a hand toward the next set of stairs, indicating Faith should keep going while at the same time blocking her from view.

Yeah. Sasha was a good person. Faith felt a tightening in her chest as she continued down the stairs. If only there wasn't so much to work out between her and Rowen, so many unresolved issues, then she would feel like she could get to know this new friend better. His sister. She swallowed past a sudden wall of emotions. If Faith somehow managed to make things work with Rowen, Sasha would be like a sister to her. It stung that her biological sister, Hope, was so different from Faith that they were more like strangers.

Faith barely had a moment to thank Sasha for her help before she was swept into Rowen's sports car and they pulled away from the curb. The lingering pressure on her chest made her stare out the window, hoping to control her emotional overload and not let Rowen see it.

The last thing she wanted to do was tell him why her mood had shifted in the five minutes she'd been with his sister.

Rowen was quiet too. Neither of them said a word while they drove to her apartment.

She wasn't surprised when he parked and rounded the hood of his car to let her out. Nor was she shocked that he intended to walk her to her door. If the man was concerned about her taking two flights of stairs to his car in his own club, he would never drop her off at the front entrance of her building and drive away. He'd already proven that Saturday night.

When she pulled her keys from her jacket pocket, he took them silently from her and then held her hand as they rode the elevator to her floor. He guided her to her apartment with a hand at the small of her back and unlocked her door. A second later, he led her inside, set the black bag on the floor, and shut the door.

Without a word still, he faced her and unbuttoned her jacket.

As he slid it off her body and set it over the back of her couch, she shuddered. Somehow the silence made her self-conscious. She wanted to cross her arms to cover herself, but she forced herself to grip one wrist with her other hand at her back instead.

Was he pissed?

Rowen pointed toward the hallway. "Do what you need in the bathroom. I'll be right behind you." Finally, words. But what did they mean? She couldn't read him.

For the first time since she'd started submitting to him, she felt nervous. She made her way to her bedroom and straight to her closet on wobbly legs. After removing her heels, she angled for the bathroom to remove her makeup and brush her teeth.

The entire time, she wondered what Rowen was thinking? Maybe he was just tired. Or maybe he was the sort of man who didn't need to constantly be talking. Or maybe he was done with her...

She was absurdly nervous when she stepped out of the bathroom to find him standing in her bedroom. He'd pulled the comforter down on her bed. "Sir?"

"Come here, sweet girl."

Ah, so *sweet girl*... If he was still using that endearment, the world surely wasn't too far out of whack.

She approached him, clasping her hands into fists at her sides, head bowed, shoulders pulled back as far as she could manage.

He was fully clothed, as usual. She was fully naked, as usual.

He met her gaze. "I can be pretty demanding, Faith." He set his hands on her shoulders and ran them down to her biceps.

"I see that."

"It's in my nature. It's who I am. It's the reason why I've never had a permanent submissive that lasted more than a short time."

"Because you're overprotective?"

"Did my sister say that?"

She shrugged, her skin heating from her chest to her cheeks. "She didn't have to. I already gathered that."

"And yet you argued with me. Twice." He lifted a brow.

She swallowed. She should have known he wouldn't go for that. It was possible in her subconscious mind she'd topped him on purpose to test him. He'd passed. "I'm sorry, Sir. I didn't think. I was trying not to inconvenience you or anyone else."

"When I make a decision, I expect you to follow it without argument."

"Yes, Sir."

"I shouldn't have to explain myself."

"You're right, Sir." Damn, but he was right. And he was unbelievably in control at all times. Even Victor hadn't been this dominant with her.

"I think you tested me on purpose."

She flushed. "Perhaps, Sir." And he called her out on it too.

He lifted her chin with a finger, forcing her to meet his gaze more fully. "Do I have your attention?"

"Yes, Sir."

He lifted a brow. "Why do you think I went out of my way to sneak you out of the building with an escort?"

She winced.

"Yeah. I was hoping to spare you having to run into anyone from the club and face questions about where you'd been. The members only know you as a Domme. I thought you might appreciate keeping your submission to me a secret for now."

Shit. She hadn't thought about it from that perspective. "I'm sorry, Sir."

His fingers slid to hers and he lifted her hands to his lips, kissing her knuckles. "We're still feeling each other out, but I've made it pretty clear I'm incredibly dominant."

"Yes, Sir."

"And if I've read you correctly, you thrive under the control."

"Yes, Sir." He was right. She had fucked up.

"Then I need you to keep that in mind next time you feel like arguing with me. The reason I brought you home was because I need to work later than I expected. I need to close the club tonight."

She nodded. "I understand, Sir."

"And I didn't make arrangements to have someone escort you to my car because I thought you couldn't walk down stairs without falling. I did it to shield you from being bombarded by questions from the members."

She lowered her face farther.

He dropped her fingers and cupped her breasts, his thumbs brushing over her nipples. His voice was deeper when he continued. "You were naked under that coat."

"Yes, Sir."

"When I give you an order, it's for a reason."

"Yes, Sir."

"I know we hadn't intended to see each other tonight, but I'm glad you came to my office. I'm glad we had the chance to clear the air between us. And I want us to finish this week as originally planned. I want you to submit to me for the rest of the week. I've been hard on you. Are you still interested?"

He was also testing her. "Yes, Sir." Her pussy had been clenched in frustration for the last half hour. Suddenly wetness coated her skin. The tone of his voice did that to her no matter what his words were.

"I'd like to take you out Saturday night. A date. Dinner. Is that okay?" Just like that, he was done explaining himself.

She leaned closer to him. Nothing had ever sounded better. "Yes, Sir."

"We can go to the club afterward. But first something normal."

She lifted her face. "When you say normal...?"

He narrowed his gaze and hauled her even closer until their faces were inches apart. "When I say normal, I mean we'll appear to be a regular couple to everyone else we encounter, but you'll still be submitting to me."

At that, the moisture between her legs increased until she felt a line of it on her thigh. "Yes, Sir." Her voice was hoarse.

Rowen slid a hand down her belly and then farther to cup her pussy. When his fingers pushed her lips apart and dipped inside, he smiled. "You like the idea."

"I do, Sir." She swayed closer to him.

His hand disappeared as fast as it had arrived. "I have to punish you now. You won't be permitted to come."

She gulped. "Yes, Sir." Did she expect him to forget? If she were honest with herself, she would have been disappointed if he let her off the hook for being argumentative.

"We haven't discussed other forms of punishment yet, so I'm going to spank you. Five swats. Hard. When I spank you for punishment, you'll know the difference. You won't argue with me Saturday night."

"Yes, Sir." Her mouth was suddenly dry.

He sat on the edge of her bed and angled her to his side, leaning her over his lap. He didn't clasp her hands at her back like he had last time. This time he permitted her to brace her upper body on the mattress, elbows on the bed.

He smoothed his hand over her butt cheeks. "Safeword?"

"Red, Sir."

When he lifted his hand, she stiffened, holding her breath. He'd spanked her two times Saturday night, but she wasn't familiar enough with him yet to know what to expect, so she tensed.

The first swat took her breath away. It stung. There would be a pink mark where he'd spanked her. Instead of striking her butt again immediately as she expected, he smoothed his palm over the burning skin, rubbing it.

Finally, the second swat landed, followed by him commenting,

"Your bottom is so gorgeous with my palm print on it. Maybe I'll enjoy having you disobey me more often."

She held her breath, thinking she too would enjoy being spanked by him more often. She wouldn't suggest such a thing out loud, but it felt so good to have someone take control of her like this. It had been so long. She'd nearly forgotten how it felt to turn over the reins to a Dom and let him manage her every move.

She hadn't thought anything of it when she'd argued with him about getting herself to his car without help earlier. Old habits. She was rusty. She hadn't submitted so thoroughly to anyone for so long that she'd slipped from the role. But Rowen meant it when he said he was demanding. He'd also meant it when he said he liked to have complete control at all times.

She craved his kind of dominance. It brought her back to life. The feel of his palm on her ass was something she longed for so badly that emotions climbed up her throat, choking her.

Thank God she wasn't facing him.

A tear slid from her eye. She shouldn't permit herself to get used to this. It wouldn't last. If nothing else, he would probably stomp from her parents' home Sunday night and never look back. And that stung more than anything she'd endured in the last eighteen months.

Alone. So very alone.

She needed to find a way to break the engagement. No way was she taking him to meet her parents. There was little to no chance she could keep up this charade with Rowen if she sabotaged it by bringing him home.

No fucking way.

His next strike yanked her from her thoughts. Higher. Harder. Perfect.

It felt so good to feel.

She'd never been a brat. But maybe she'd consider it if it got her to feel like this.

Another strike. That was four, wasn't it? It landed on the other cheek. Her entire butt was on fire now.

And then the fifth. Right in the center, close to her thighs. The burn was intense on top of already stinging skin.

She lowered her face to the pillow and moaned. Her pussy ached for attention even though he'd given her two amazing orgasms earlier.

He wasn't kidding. When he spanked for punishment, he did so in a way that shouldn't have made her horny. But it backfired on him. It backfired on both of them.

She'd never been the sort of submissive who got off on being punished. At least not before. Had she changed? Or was she so empty inside that any amount of dominance for any reason would get her off?

"Sweet girl..." His voice trailed away. "Your bottom is so damn sexy. And my cock is so damn hard."

She couldn't respond. It wouldn't be prudent. So she bit her lip.

"You enjoyed that, I believe."

Still she didn't move.

He rubbed her skin for several more moments and then slid his hand between her legs to stroke through her folds. "Oh, yeah. My sweet girl indeed enjoyed that. Fuck me."

He dragged his fingers through her wetness again and then glided them back to her burning skin. "Warm," he murmured. "Tomorrow morning I want a picture of this bottom on my phone as my morning text."

Her breath hitched.

"Nothing else. Just your bottom. Take it in the full-length mirror so I can make sure you didn't bruise. I told you that will never be my intention."

"I bruise easily, Sir. I don't mind a few marks." Never before had those words left her lips. No one had ever struck her hard enough to leave a mark beyond the pink glow from a spanking.

But suddenly Faith felt a new desire wash through her body. She wanted Rowen to leave a mark. She wanted to see his palm print on her butt. In fact, she wanted to run into the bathroom and see what he was looking at.

If she could make out his fingers, it would send a thrill down her spine.

What the hell was happening to her?

"We'll revisit this topic another day. For now, I want proof that my palm print is no longer noticeable in the morning. If you can't or won't provide that proof, I'll find other ways to discipline you."

She whimpered.

"Don't worry about the picture. No one will see it but me, and no one would ever know whose bottom it was if you take the picture carefully enough."

"Yes, Sir."

The thought of photographing her own ass still didn't sit well with her. Funny how earlier in the evening she had pondered the desire to have him take pictures of her roped arms. She hated that she would never see the beauty of his work.

Maybe one day she would let him take pictures of her. Except that day would never come. It required a level of trust that took weeks, months, or even years to build. She didn't have that kind of time with him.

Chances were Saturday night would be their one and only date. Sunday, she would either piss him off by refusing to bring him to her parents' home or she would drive him away by bringing him. Either way, Rowen Easton was not going to be hers by the end of the weekend.

She'd be selfish to bring him with her. It would be easier to cut him off beforehand and wallow in her pity party without the drama. Because she knew with certainty it would be a deal breaker for him if she refused to take him to her parents'.

Rowen lifted his hand from her butt and pulled her around until she was sitting on his lap and he had her face cupped in his palms. He frowned, wiping away the remnants of another round of uninvited tears. "What were these from, sweet girl? I spend a lot of time making you cry."

She forced a smiled, cocking her face into one of his palms. "I got emotional. It's been a long time since I felt this. I forgot how good it can be," she admitted.

He smiled. "I hope that's a good thing. Because I love dominating you, Faith. It's fulfilling. It centers me. I feel grounded when I'm with you. My best me."

Her heart pounded. *For how long? A few more days?*

He kissed her lips, gently at first, and then with more passion. On a groan, he broke the kiss and lifted her off his lap. He stood and pointed at the bed. "Climb in. You need sleep. I'll lock the door on my way out."

She slid between the sheets, wishing she had the guts to ask him to stay. She didn't want the evening to end. She wanted him to take off his clothes, climb into bed with her, and hold her all night.

But she said nothing. After all, he was already displeased from her arguing with him earlier. If she made such a request, he would think she was topping from the bottom.

He tucked the sheets around her and leaned over to kiss her temple. "Sleep well, sweet girl." And then he left her, slipping from her room and then her apartment.

For a long time she stared at the place she'd last seen him, willing the clock back five minutes so she could beg him to stay. Fuck topping. She wanted him in her bed.

Finally, she closed her eyes and concentrated on breathing. Her butt stung against the coolness of the sheets. She considered turning over to alleviate the burn, but decided she liked it. It reminder her she had a new Dom. A stern Dom who wouldn't permit argument. And in her heart, she knew Victor would be happy for her.

Her pussy pulsed with the need to come, but she kept her

hands folded on her belly. There was no way she could touch herself without instantly coming. And Rowen had forbidden her to do so.

Deep cleansing breaths.

She thought she would have trouble falling asleep with her mind racing, but instead, a sense of peace she hadn't felt in a long time settled over her. She let go of her concerns and drifted away.

CHAPTER 20

Rowen leaned back in his chair in his home office and stared at the picture on his phone for the hundredth time since Faith had sent it that morning. Her pink bottom. Perfection. Not bruised. Not so red she couldn't sit. But pink enough to serve as a reminder that his palm had swatted her five times last night.

The cell phone still in his hand buzzed, indicating he had an email.

He smiled when he saw the screen flash across the top. It was from Faith. The fact that she sent another correspondence made him irrationally excited. He really needed to get ahold of himself.

Even though she had opened up to him last night and spilled her soul, there was no way to ensure things would work out between them. It concerned him greatly that she was so adamant about keeping her distance from her family.

He also worried that her money would get in the way eventually too. He couldn't imagine a world in which he forged a full-time D/s relationship with a woman who was so loaded she could buy her own club. Not just shoes or purses or paintings. She was undoubtedly far wealthier than that. No matter how irrational it was, he didn't think he could ever get past his need to care for Faith or any other woman who submitted to him.

Even if he could get past those two road blocks, there was no guarantee Faith could be the kind of submissive he desperately craved. He'd crashed and burned in this area multiple times, the last being with Rayne. Finding a woman who wanted to submit to him twenty-four seven was a monumental task. Some people went their entire lives and never found that perfect match.

Rayne hadn't been willing to do it. Neither had any other woman before her. Although Faith said she was interested in that sort of arrangement, there was no proof she could live those words. For one thing, she hadn't really had a full-time arrangement with her husband since he'd been deployed a good portion of their marriage. For another thing, she found ways to top Rowen when he least expected it.

Rowen turned toward his computer to open his email, preferring to read her latest words on the larger screen. As it powered up, he closed his eyes and pictured her arguing with him last night about having an escort to the front door. He added the memory of her trying to convince him to let her stay at the club while he closed.

His cock stiffened irrationally. Why would he get aroused at the thought of her defying him? He stared into space across his office, seeing nothing while he pondered the possibility that she enjoyed being punished and perhaps even thrived on it.

Could he fulfill that need for her? It wasn't that she was a brat. She didn't intentionally whine or set out to defy him. It happened by accident. He wasn't sure she had realized she'd defied him at the time. But she had undeniably gotten aroused when he spanked her.

And so had he.

Whether consciously or subconsciously, she had tried to top him twice last night. Did she have a bratty side? Was she unable to fully submit? Or had she been testing him? He prayed it was the last.

Rowen shifted his gaze to the email from Faith.

Sir,

There were only a few unanswered questions left after last night. I don't want there to be any lingering holes in what you know about me, so let me answer them now.

Do I get aroused when I dominate others? No. Dominating for me is like a Band-Aid. It gives me pleasure. I enjoy helping other people fill a need. I've never gotten off from it. Other than the rush of knowing someone would sleep better that night because of something I gave them.

Do I get aroused when I submit to others? Depends. When I'm submitting for the purpose of learning the ins and outs of a new apparatus, no. When I'm with a Dom I'm not physically attracted to, no. When I'm with someone I want to submit to, yes.

When I'm with you, so much yes.

When I'm not with you, I'm always submitting to you even from a distance, so I'm in a constant state of arousal.

I'm aroused now, Sir.

Rowen couldn't take his eyes off the screen. His cock was so hard he had to pop the button on his jeans and lower the zipper. His hands shook so badly he had trouble moving the mouse around to scroll up and down the screen.

I'm aroused now, Sir.

He could hear the sweet lilt of her voice as if she'd spoken the words out loud.

He wanted to push away from the desk and drive to her apartment. He wanted to fuck her so hard she saw stars. He wanted to fill her pussy and never let her go.

Instead, he circled his cock with his hand and stroked up and down with a firm grip. Now was not the time to drag things out. He needed relief.

When his vision grew so blurry that he no longer saw her words, he let his eyes slide closed and savored the feel of his dick wrapped in his fingers. It didn't take long. He was on the edge in moments. After reaching to yank a few tissues out of the box on his desk, he covered the tip of his cock and let himself come.

He moaned, his voice reverberating in the office. Every pulse jerked his hands forward. Finally, the last bursts of semen left him panting and shaky. He tossed the tissues in the trash and leaned against the edge of the desk to catch his breath.

Faith Robbins was taking over his world. He both loved and feared what that might mean.

Rowen was slightly disappointed that he had plans with the other guys from work that night. He was even more aggravated that it was his turn to host. But they had a standing poker night one Thursday a month, and eyebrows would raise if he canceled at the last minute for no apparent reason.

Lincoln and Carter were aware of his clandestine arrangement with Faith. The rest of the staff was not. Three other guys worked part-time at Zodiac. Dayton, Tyler, and Aaron. All five would be arriving at seven.

Since the club was open Wednesdays, Fridays, and Saturdays, Thursdays were the perfect night to socialize outside of work.

At six forty-five Rowen checked his email for the last time. Nothing new from Faith. He'd responded to her message simply.

I like knowing your pussy is wet with desire even when I'm not with you. I wish I could watch you fingering yourself. Remember not to come without permission.

Fifteen minutes later, Lincoln arrived, the rest of the guys trickling in soon after. Rowen found he was glad for the distraction as they opened the poker surface on top of his table and then settled down with beer, pizza, and chips.

Dayton was the first to break the ice. "What's up with you and Faith?" he asked as he shuffled the cards, the smirk on his face telling. "She's hot. I've seen her work. Are you letting her top you upstairs where no one can see?"

Rowen flushed slightly as he nearly choked on his beer. Is that what the other employees thought?

Carter laughed. "Rowen? Bottom?"

Rowen needed to put this fire out before it got started. "What are you talking about?"

Aaron chuckled. "Dude, you've been caught twice sneaking her out of the club. Don't deny it."

Rowen took a deep breath and counted to ten, wondering how to handle the damage control. He and Faith hadn't discussed this possibility. Would she be pissed that people knew about them? He wasn't sure. He assumed she simply didn't want to out herself as a submissive yet in a world where she'd been a practicing Domme for several weeks.

But could it be more than that? "You guys need more to do on the floor if you have time to gossip about something you've totally invented in your heads," he retorted with a bit too much vehemence. He could feel the tension in his face.

"Jeez, Rowen, lighten up," Tyler said. "It's not like everyone in the club knows. Aaron just happened to be working near the door Saturday night when you left with Faith. And I was there Wednesday night. It's not gossip. It's an observation. Between friends."

Rowen rubbed the back of his neck. "I'm sorry. I didn't mean to snap. You all know how fiercely some people protect their privacy."

Lincoln's distinctly low voice filled the room next. "Rowen, we're friends. No one at this table would say a word to anyone about Faith. We've all been in the lifestyle long enough to know better."

Rowen blew out a breath. "Right. Of course. Sorry. This is sensitive territory."

The air sucked out of the room, and he lifted his gaze to find every man staring at him. Aaron's, Tyler's, and Dayton's eyes were wide. Finally, he realized what he had inadvertently suggested. Fine. Let them think whatever they wanted. It wasn't his place to give them any more information than what they'd surmised from what they'd seen.

A smile spread across Dayton's face. "I get it."

Tyler chuckled. "Yep."

Aaron set his elbows on the table, leaning closer. "You know none of us would say a word. To anyone. Ever."

Rowen wondered what they thought they "got" from his total lack of information. But for now, he decided it would be prudent to keep his lips closed and let them invent whatever story made them happy. Either way would stun anyone. If Rowen was submitting to Faith, his closest friends would stop breathing in shock. Then again, none of them could probably imagine Faith submitting to him either. It was a toss-up. Let them wonder.

Rowen did have another concern however. "Are people talking? The other members, I mean?"

Lincoln cleared his throat. "I can field that one from Sasha's perspective. A few people asked her where Faith was Wednesday night, but she blew them off. It's not like Faith habitually came in every night we were open. It was easy."

Carter spoke next. "I did have a member ask if she could book a time with Faith for Saturday night."

"Who?" Rowen asked, his back straightening.

"Brooke."

Rowen frowned, pondering that possibility. "I'll talk to Faith."

Carter lowered his gaze to pick up the hand of cards he'd been dealt. "Faith has been working with Brooke. I think she's skittish.

She hasn't performed publicly. I haven't seen her sub for any men since she joined either. Only Faith, and only in private."

Lincoln picked up his cards too. "Now we're switching from judging Faith to judging Brooke? Who cares if she submits to men or women?"

Rowen eyed Carter who seemed nervous as he rolled his eyes. "You know I'm not judging anyone. Don't be ridiculous. I just think there's something about her."

"Brooke?" Aaron clarified. "Or Faith?"

"Brooke." He shrugged. "What can I say? She's cute. I've been watching her." Yep, his face was red.

Lincoln cocked his head to one side. "How about you ask her to submit to you then? Have you tried that?"

"Not a chance. She's as closed off as a woman can be when I speak to her."

"But you're interested," Rowen pointed out.

"Maybe." Carter straightened his back and glared at everyone. "How the hell did I become the center of this conversation? We were talking about Faith, not Brooke."

Aaron tapped the table and set his gaze on Rowen. "You know none of us care who's topping whom while the two of you are sequestered in your office, but how long are you going to try and conceal this thing? People will start talking if you keep sneaking up and down the stairs like you have something to hide."

"He's right," Lincoln added.

Rowen glanced around at all their faces. They deserved at least some answers. Too bad he didn't have them.

Carter cleared his throat. "Is this about money?"

Rowen flinched.

Carter groaned. "Dude, please don't tell me you're lurking around in the shadows with a woman because you're hung up on her wealth."

He took a deep breath. "Maybe." He sat up straighter. "It's complicated."

Carter leaned forward, getting in his face. "Look, I know you have issues with money. I get it. You've had some stupid experiences, and you get all the crazies coming to you to do their taxes, but you can't judge every single person based on a few."

Now *this* was an intervention.

Lincoln apparently thought he should weigh in too, and damn if he didn't hit the nail on the head. "It's not just that she has money. You know Rowen. He likes to take care of his women."

All the guys groaned before Carter spoke again. "Rowen, jeez. The two are not mutually exclusive. You can take care of a woman without getting hung up on her ability to buy designer purses and shoes. Who cares? Her wealth shouldn't have anything to do with her ability to submit to you...or vice versa," he joked.

Rowen grabbed a handful of popcorn and launched it across the table toward his friend. Carter wasn't far from the truth. Rowen did like to take care of his women, and at the moment that included protecting her privacy and not divulging who was topping whom to the entire room. "Are we going to play cards or what?"

His friends had managed to plant some ideas in his head, though. He needed to examine his obsession with being a caregiver in all ways. Faith's money shouldn't be a deal breaker from the standpoint of him caring for her, and she'd called him on that herself.

The next hour passed in a far more normal fashion with everyone talking over each other, exchanging barbs, eating, drinking, and dealing cards.

And then Rowen's phone buzzed in his pocket. They were between hands. Tyler was about to deal when Rowen leaned on one hip to reach into the front of his jeans and extract his cell.

He nearly dropped it.

Faith: Permission to come, Sir.

He shoved from the table and stood. Without looking at anyone, he spoke. "I've gotta take this call. I'll sit this round out. Be right back." And then he bolted down the hallway to his bedroom, shut the door, locked it, and tapped the screen to call Faith.

"Sir…" Her voice was breathy.

"Faith…" He sounded just as breathy, and he had to adjust his cock at the sound of her voice.

"I've been thinking about you all day, Sir."

"I like to hear that, sweet girl." He held his breath a moment to center himself and get in control. "Did you work today?"

"Yes, but from home. I had several calls to make, but I never left the house, Sir."

"So, you've been naked all day."

"Yes…" That one word, hissed more than spoken. "It was… distracting, Sir."

He smiled. "Good. Then I guess you deserve some relief."

"Thank you, Sir."

"I want you to get that egg from the bag, sweet girl. Push it up into your pussy."

She panted as he listened to her move around the apartment and then rustle in the bag. And then she moaned.

Rowen grabbed the front of his jeans to squeeze his dick. He could help Faith get off, but he didn't intend to masturbate in his bedroom while five of his coworkers sat in his kitchen. "Is it inside you, Faith?"

"Yes," she whispered.

"Good girl. Grab the remote."

He pictured her bending over the bag again to find the small black key fob.

"Got it, Sir."

"Push the top button three times." He waited, smiling when she gasped. He remembered that was the highest setting. He hadn't used it on her last night.

"Sit down somewhere, sweet girl."

"O-Okay, Sir."

He waited a few seconds. "Where are you?"

"On the couch, Sir."

"Good. Now I don't want you to touch your clit with your fingers. I want you to use the loop of the vibrator. It should be hanging out of your pussy, yeah?"

She panted again. "Rowen..."

Damn. His name on her lips always got to him. She broke form to use it, but he found it impossible to reprimand her. "Use both hands if you want. Put the phone on speaker. Set it somewhere where I can hear you, and flick the loop over your clit until you come."

A soft moan filled his ear as she switched to speaker and then must have done as instructed. "That's a good girl. I'll just listen. You give yourself the relief you need."

He closed his eyes as he pictured her on her back, the phone probably sitting on her chest, both hands between her spread legs. Would she be lifting her ass off the cushion as she teased herself?

It didn't take long before her breathing grew heavier and her moans louder. After all, she'd been on the edge without touching herself before she called. "Come for me, Faith."

A sharp squeal met his ear. Music. So gorgeous. And then she slowly came back to herself, her breathing returning to normal as he listened. "That was so amazing, Sir. I can't believe you're able to get me off like that."

"My pleasure, sweet girl. I'm proud of you for obeying me and calling to ask permission. I have to go now. I have the guys from work over. It's poker night." He tried to sound as lighthearted as possible, adjusting his cock and bracing himself to return to the kitchen.

"What? Oh my God. Rowen? Are you serious?" Her voice was slightly elevated and shaky.

"Relax. No one has any idea who I called. I excused myself and

207

went to my bedroom." That probably wasn't true. He hadn't told anyone who was on the phone. But no one currently sitting in his kitchen was oblivious enough not to suspect who had texted.

She sighed. "You're insane...Sir."

"Get ready for bed, Faith. Text me when you're going to sleep."

"Okay. Thank you, Sir." The sultry tone was back.

Damn, how he loved the sultry tone.

CHAPTER 21

Faith was so nervous on Saturday that she was frazzled from the moment she got up. It was just a date. There was no reason for her overreaction.

Except she knew it was more than a date. It was likely the beginning of the end. The first and only date she would ever have with Rowen Easton. And no matter what, she wanted it to be good. No—great.

So she spent the day preparing—hair, nails, facial, new outfit. By the time she stood in front of the mirror at six o'clock, she had to smile at the futility of her efforts. Rowen didn't care about things like hair and nails. He wasn't likely to even notice. But they made her feel good.

When his knock sounded at her door, she took one last look in the mirror and inhaled long and slow, releasing the cleansing breath just as languidly.

She wore a white dress. Tight. Short. Plenty of cleavage. But tasteful. It was something she'd carefully selected that could be worn in public at whatever place he'd chosen for dinner and then later at the club without raising an eyebrow at either venue.

The bodice of the dress was fitted, and she wasn't wearing a bra or thong. Her only other article of clothing was her favorite silver strappy heels, and she concentrated on remaining balanced on them as she made her way to the door.

Rowen took her breath away when she opened the door. He wore black slacks and a classy black dress shirt with a black tie. The yin and yang between them didn't escape her notice.

His hair was its usual tousled mess from running a hand through it. His mouth was lifted on one side in a half smile. His green eyes twinkled. But the best part was the single red rose he held in his hand.

After making no effort to hide his obvious appraisal of her from head to toe, he stepped forward and stroked one rose petal across her shoulder, up her neck, and over the curve of her chin. When he tapped her lips with it, she shivered.

She drew in a deep breath through her nose, inhaling the sweet scent of the rose.

Not a single word had been spoken yet as he backed her up several steps and shut the door behind him with his foot. His gaze remained locked on hers, his expression serious.

Her entire body was alert, the arousal she'd experienced all week shooting to a new height. Her nipples tingled against the fabric of her dress. She clenched her thighs together and pursed her lips behind the rose.

Finally, Rowen lowered the rose, letting it drift down to her cleavage, his gaze following the path. "Faith, you take my breath away every time I see you. But this...this dress..." He set his free hand on her forearm and eased it down to her hand, lifting her fingers to his lips. The gentle kiss on her knuckles nearly undid her.

"Thank you, Sir."

"Where is the bag of gifts, sweet girl?"

"On the kitchen table," she murmured. She had wondered when he might reveal the last few items. She'd been nosy enough that she knew both items were small. The largest of the boxes had been opened already.

Still holding her hand, Rowen threaded their fingers together and lured her across the room. He set the rose on the table next to the bag and reached inside. After rummaging through the contents, he pulled out the last two small boxes. "I find it interesting that you keep everything I've given you all together in this bag."

She didn't respond. She did so for self-preservation, knowing that at any given moment this bubble might burst and she would return his purchases to him.

Rowen opened one of the boxes first and removed a soft, thick, black blindfold. He held it up, grinning. "For later." And then he tucked it in the front pocket of his pants.

She shuddered.

He opened the last box next, dropping the black paper on the table. He was moving the small box around so much that she couldn't get a clear enough view to know what it contained. A white box with mostly pink lettering. Finally, he opened it and pulled out a tube of something. Lube?

He'd already included lube. She'd used it the day she opened the cock which she had suctioned to the chair he now stood next to. The memory of her fucking herself to completion right where he stood while he listened over the phone overwhelmed her.

Rowen still didn't let her see the tube. It wasn't that he hid it. He simply didn't hold it steadily in front of her. "Turn around, sweet girl. Legs spread. Hands on the table. Lean over slightly."

She did as instructed without hesitation, but her body betrayed her, shaking with nerves.

He set one hand on her thigh and eased it underneath her dress, pushing the material up as he went until her butt was exposed and her dress was bunched around her waist. She shuddered. How was his every move so sensual?

"Legs wider, Faith," he commanded.

She parted them obscenely farther and then listened as he popped the lid on the tube, still not understanding why he would need to apply any sort of lubricant to her pussy.

When his fingers reached between her legs, she whimpered. She was already so wet it was embarrassing. She'd been wet before he arrived, and now she was soaked from the overwhelming arousal brought on by everything that was Rowen. His clothes. His hair. His smile. His voice. Damn, his voice. So sexy. Every carefully chosen word made her clit throb.

The coolness of whatever lube he had on the tips of his fingers hit her clit first.

She lifted up on her toes at the contact, sucking in a breath.

He set his free hand on her lower back, his fingers spreading across her butt. "Stay still, Faith." As he continued to torment her with the slightest touch of his fingers over her clit and then her lower lips, she held her breath. And then his hand disappeared and he pulled her dress back down over her ass.

She didn't dare move without permission.

"Let's go, sweet girl. I'm starving." His voice was huskier now, filled with his own need.

She righted herself and turned around, drawing her legs together. Thank God the material of her skirt was stretchy enough to accommodate the spread of her thighs. She opened her mouth to question his motives with the lube as he slipped it into his pocket. But he set a gentle kiss on her lips, cutting her off.

Before she knew it, she was in the hallway, her small white evening purse resting on one shoulder by the thin strap. Rowen took her keys from her hand, locked her door, and pocketed them.

With a hand at the small of her back, he led her toward the elevator. If she wasn't mistaken, his expression wasn't schooled enough to hide a slight smirk.

It wasn't until they stepped out of the elevator on the ground floor that she hesitated, set a hand on the wall, and gasped. "Sir..."

He was smiling now, his eyes twinkling as he rounded to

stand face to face with her. He cupped her cheeks and set a second gentle kiss on her lips. "For the next three hours the world will see nothing more than a man and a woman out on a date. No one will know you're my submissive." His voice was low, barely above a whisper. There was no one else in the lobby, but they would have needed to lean in close to hear him anyway.

Faith had trouble concentrating on anything he said over the tingling sensation that had her clit and lower lips pulsing with desire. Whatever he'd spread on her had been an aphrodisiac. Not a lubricant.

He kept speaking as one hand threaded in her hair at the back of her head and tipped her face up to meet his. He held her firmly. He was good. If anyone walked by, they would see nothing but a sensual exchange between lovers, but the truth was his grip was tighter than it appeared. Demanding. Controlling.

His voice was even lower this time. "But you'll know better, sweet girl. You'll know I'm in charge of your every move. I'll decide when and what you eat and drink and even how you sit and where."

She licked her lips. "Yes, Sir." The tingling increased, making her squirm.

"You'll obey my every command, won't you?"

"Yes, Sir."

He held her gaze a few more moments, smiling, and then he took her hand and led her from the building.

Every step exacerbated the sensitivity of her clit. Even separating her legs slightly didn't help. It was going to be a long dinner.

It was going to be the best three hours of her life.

And it needed to be to sustain her throughout the rest of her days on earth because deep in her heart she knew this precarious arrangement was just that. It held no guarantees for a tomorrow. She needed to grab onto it and enjoy every second.

Tomorrow would come all too soon, and there was no way Rowen would still be hers.

~

Rowen was in his element. A dream. Perfection. He'd imagined a woman like this for most of his life, someone who looked like an angel and submitted to him so thoroughly that she gave every ounce of her trust over to his control.

He wasn't stupid. He knew they had obstacles between them that seemed insurmountable, but for tonight he wanted to put them aside and enjoy the perfection that was this easy balance of power he had with Faith.

The world was playing a cruel trick on him. It was obvious as the nose on his face. He wasn't in denial. He knew there was a giant elephant blocking their ability to fully connect, but he had hope. Surely the rift between her and her parents could be repaired. He needed to believe things could be fixed. No one should spend years of their life avoiding family, especially when they lived in the same city.

He shook the melancholy from his mind. It had no place at dinner. Tonight Faith was all his.

As he helped her into his car and then reached across to buckle her seat belt, he stared down at her dress. She looked like a million bucks. The material hugged her body to perfection. It probably also cost a fortune. A reminder that she would always have money that could buy her anything her heart desired, and he would never be able to provide her the kinds of things she was used to.

But did it matter? Maybe his friends were right. He shouldn't care if she had money and could buy expensive things. She wasn't the type to rub it in his face. He had other qualities she was attracted to. Most importantly he could give her the dominance she craved. And, if her family was truly as fucked up as she insisted, he could also give her a loving home, a soft place to fall. His family was small. It consisted of one blood relative and several close friends, but it was strong. It was enough.

He planted a soft kiss on her forehead. No one was making life decisions tonight. They were going to dinner. He'd chosen the location. It was one of his favorites. It wasn't a five-star restaurant, but in his opinion it was a culinary experience all the same.

"Sir?"

He realized he had lingered too long, inhaling her scent, staring down at her fucking amazing cleavage under the stretchy white material. Letting his thoughts carry him in a direction he had no intention of going tonight.

He forced a smile, ducked back out of the car, and shut the door.

Several deep breaths accompanied his trip around the hood of the car, and then they were off. As soon as they were headed in the right direction, he set his right hand on her knee and spread his fingers. "I like knowing you're bare under the tight material of this dress. You look amazing."

"Thank you, Sir." She squirmed.

"Sit still, Faith."

"Yes, Sir," she whispered.

"How was your day?"

She swallowed. "Long, Sir."

He chuckled in agreement. It had been the longest day he could recall in years, waiting for the moment he could pick her up. He had gone for a run, hit the gym, taken care of some Zodiac business, and ensured he had his appointments lined up for the coming week. Throughout the entire day he'd thought of Faith repeatedly, his cock hard and demanding.

He'd taken himself in hand first thing that morning in the shower after her wake-up text and then again a few hours ago when he'd showered again before getting ready. The two orgasms had done nothing to control his dick, however. At the moment he felt like a randy teenager on his first date who'd never had sex before.

"What did you do to occupy yourself?" he asked conversationally, hoping to lessen the tension. It wasn't the kind of stress he would normally feel on a first date. It wasn't even uncomfortable. He was as calm in her presence as if they'd been together for months or years. The tension was sexual. And it was overwhelming. If he managed to keep her for years, would it still feel like this?

She hesitated. Why? "I, uh...boring girl things, Sir."

He glanced at her, squeezing her thigh. "Girl things?"

"You know, nails, pampering, shopping, stuff like that."

"All day?" he teased.

"Well..."

"I get it, Faith. Not sure why it makes you flush, but whatever you did all day, it paid off. Every inch of you is delectable." He meant that. Her gorgeous hair was down, but styled. Her manicure was fresh. He bet her toes matched. Her makeup was professional.

She'd probably spent more money getting ready for tonight than he made in a week. He wouldn't allow himself to dwell on that, however. Instead, he concentrated on the effort she'd made to impress him. What mattered was that she cared enough to do so.

"Thank you, Sir." She squirmed again.

"Faith, sit still," he commanded. "I know your sweet pussy is distracting the hell out of you, but I want you to concentrate on not letting anyone know you're distracted."

"Yes, Sir," she whispered before biting her bottom lip as if transferring the need to wiggle from her torso to the slight pain she caused would divert her attention.

He glanced out the side window to hide his smile.

As he drove, he casually teased the soft skin of her inner thigh with his pinky, precariously close to her pussy.

She amazed him with her ability to remain still and relatively composed.

When he pulled into the parking lot of his favorite Italian restaurant, he eased into a spot and turned off the engine. He then lifted one hip to extract the stimulant from his pocket. "Pull up your skirt and spread your legs open, sweet girl."

She trembled as she followed his directions, her fingers white against her thighs.

Rowen intentionally made a production out of opening the ointment and squeezing some onto two fingers. He let her see what he was doing as he reached between her legs to reapply the aphrodisiac.

The effects would last about a half hour on most skin. Based on the way Faith had responded during the drive, he surmised it had not yet worn off, but he wanted to have her attention while they started dinner too.

Her breath hitched as he tapped her clit and then smoothed the rest down to her lower lips. When he pushed both fingers up inside her, she lifted her hips on a moan.

"So needy. Did I say to lift your bottom?"

"No, Sir." She set her ass back down slowly.

"Good girl." He wiped the excess ointment and her own juices on her inner thighs and put the tube back in his pocket. "Ready?"

CHAPTER 22

Faith didn't know how she made it from the car to the table. It was a blur of sensation. The additional application of whatever that evil substance was increased her arousal tenfold.

She hadn't been the one to right her clothing as they exited the car. Rowen had tugged her skirt over her butt and straightened her dress to his satisfaction. She was pretty sure he was fighting the urge to laugh the entire time.

Now they were seated across from each other, and the waiter was pouring their wine. He nodded and set the bottle on the table when Rowen told him they needed a few minutes.

The restaurant had a romantic atmosphere. Dim lighting. Small intimate tables. Black tablecloths. Candles on every table. Soft easy music playing in the background.

It seemed Rowen had made a reservation and requested this particular table in a back corner. If she kept her gaze on him, she could almost pretend they were alone.

He tapped her shin with one foot. "Spread your legs, Faith."

She swallowed as she uncrossed her legs and let him plant one foot between hers, trapping one ankle, thereby forcing her thighs to be spread as far apart as his knee. A flush rushed over her face.

He smiled and took her hands in his on the table. "You are the singularly sexiest woman alive."

The flush deepened as he held her fingers and squeezed gently. "Is there anything you don't like to eat?"

She shook her head, pleased that he asked her opinion after telling her he would be choosing everything for her as they left the house. He'd also checked to make sure she liked red wine before ordering. She had yet to take a sip. He hadn't given her permission, and it seemed prudent to wait for him to do so. "I'm not a picky eater."

"Good." He released her right hand. "Try the wine."

She loved the way he controlled everything in a subtle enough fashion that no one else would notice even if they were sitting next to them.

She lifted her glass and took a sip. It was dry with a hint of blackberry. "Mmm. It's good."

He gripped her leg between his and slid it a few inches out, widening her thighs more.

While she was struggling with the fact that her bare pussy was exposed so blatantly under the table, the waiter reappeared.

Rowen ordered, but she didn't listen to a word he said. Instead, she concentrated on easing her other knee over to touch his.

"Faith," he admonished as the waiter walked away.

She swallowed and spread her legs apart again. "Sorry, Sir. Instinct."

He stroked the back of her hand with his thumb. "Look at me, sweet girl."

She lifted her gaze.

"That's my girl. Have you ever submitted to anyone in public?"

"No, Sir. Not like this. Not outside of the club. Not so... thoroughly. Playfully on occasion, maybe."

"Scale of one to ten, how aroused are you?" He leaned forward, holding her hand tighter.

"Eleven...Sir."

His smile grew. "Then I'm doing my job. Let it go. Give me control."

She held his gaze, finding it hard to breathe. "Yes, Sir." For the first time since he'd arrived at her apartment, she let her shoulders relax and blew out a breath. She could do this. Trust him. She needed to stop wondering what anyone was thinking and trust him to make the right decisions for her. He had never failed her yet.

"That's a girl. Let go of the reins. I've got you. Your only job is to obey me. For the entire evening let all that control you usually exert go."

She nodded, swallowing for the millionth time.

He lifted his wine and took another sip, nodding toward her as he did so.

The nonverbal permission was welcomed. She needed the fortification of a few glasses of wine. And it was a delicious Malbec, the perfect blend. Expensive.

She took a few sips, savoring the flavors on her tongue as she thought about her parents' wine cellar. They probably had a thousand bottles, every one of which cost more than this bottle. But Faith wasn't a wine snob. She appreciated a good vintage, but she would never be able to tell the difference between a fifty-dollar bottle and a five-hundred-dollar bottle.

In reality she doubted her father could either, but he liked to talk the talk.

As if Rowen read her mind, he asked her about her family. "Tell me about your sister."

"Hope?" She flinched as she set her glass down.

"Do you have more than one?"

"No, Sir. I do not. One is enough. Someone should have cut my parents off at zero," she muttered.

He stiffened.

She hastened to get back on track. "Hope is bubbly and fun. She has always fit in better than me. Played the game. I can't stand the thought of meeting whoever this man is she's reportedly smitten with."

"Why?" He cocked his head to one side.

Faith shrugged. How much should she tell him? Was he trying to gather information for tomorrow night? Because she was still committed to ensuring tomorrow night never happened.

She did not, however, want to ruin this perfect evening by bringing up their never-going-to-happen dinner with her family. "It will make me sad to find out she's involved with someone she doesn't even like."

He jerked in his seat. "Why do you think she doesn't like her boyfriend? You've never met him."

"Because that's how things work in my world. My mother probably picked him out. Or he's the son of some important politician my father knows. I doubt Hope even met him before my mother had the wedding invitations ordered. Trust me. She tried the same stunt with me many times."

"Come on." He rolled his eyes. "Surely you're exaggerating."

When he said things like that, she thought maybe she should go ahead with dinner tomorrow just to show him the truth. It was a catch-22. Lose-lose. Which was worse? Having him break things off with her because she refused to take him? Or allowing him to learn the harsh reality that was her life before turning away and running as fast as he could?

She licked her lips just before he reached forward and brushed his thumb across the bottom one. "Makes my cock hard when you do that."

She met his gaze. Did that mean he wanted her to stop, or keep doing it? She didn't ask.

He released her lip slowly. "Go on. You were explaining the ancient practice of arranged marriages."

She narrowed her gaze. "Rowen, if you want me to open up, you can't mock me the entire time. It doesn't make me feel safe and willing to share." She stiffened, not sure how he would take her abrupt change of demeanor from pliant submissive to feisty bitch.

He slid his hand up her arm and tugged her forward with a grip on her shoulder until their faces were inches apart. "You're right. I apologize. I shouldn't be so judgmental. I've never walked in your shoes. I haven't met your parents. Perhaps they're ogres." He smoothed his hand back down her arm and took her fingers in his again. "I promise to stop interrupting you. Please, continue."

She glanced at her wine.

"Go ahead, sweet girl. You have permission to drink that wine at whatever speed you'd like, but I'll decide when to refill your glass."

"Thank you, Sir." She lifted the glass and took another sip, finding it interesting how he managed to manipulate even that small thing.

"Your sister," he prompted.

"It will hurt me if I don't think she's happy. I'm worried I'll find her acting fake and subservient to both him and our parents, going along with a relationship to a man she isn't interested in. I'd hate to see her spend her life in a loveless marriage of convenience just to appease my mother."

He nodded slowly, seemingly taking in her words. Finally, he spoke. One word. "Subservient?" One corner of his mouth lifted in a smirk.

She laughed, realizing how funny that sounded. "There's a difference, you know. I'm submissive by nature and by choice. And only to men who make my entire body flush with need under their command. It makes my heart race to submit to you. And it doesn't extend to my professional life or have any correlation with my actual domineering personality—the one I exude all day when I'm in charge of ensuring hundreds of people enjoy a charity event."

He didn't move.

She leaned closer. "It's heady to submit to you. Not the same thing at all as being kowtowed into doing someone else's bidding completely against my will. It's not like my sister has a safeword."

"I understand. Thank you for your honesty."

"You're welcome, Sir." She relaxed a bit more at his praise.

The food arrived, forcing Rowen to release her hand. The waiter set three platters down in the center of the table, family style, before placing a clean plate in front of each of them.

After Rowen assured him they had everything they needed, the waiter left.

"Sir, this is enough food for half the restaurant."

He smiled. "Don't worry. Just eat what you want. If there's much left, we'll take the leftovers to the club. The guys will go crazy over it in the breakroom."

Good. She hated the thought of throwing over half of this spread away. She had never felt right about wasting food.

Rowen kept her leg hostage between his throughout the meal, but other than that he didn't make her uncomfortable in any way. He served her, dishing food onto her plate, but only after checking with her first and giving her the amount she indicated.

His method of dominance made her come alive. She found she liked it. A lot. He didn't force her to eat more or less than she wanted, but he did control when she would be served and point at her silverware to indicate she had permission to begin. Subtle commands. He was completely in charge, and yet no one around them knew. Faith knew, however. And it was hot.

He let her wine glass remain empty for a while before filling it, thus controlling how much she drank without making an issue out of when she chose to do so or at what speed. Genius.

When she was full, she set her fork across the plate and took a long drink of water. "That was delicious, Sir."

"I'm glad you liked it. I come here often. Both the food and the service are supreme." He sat back, sipping his wine while staring at her over the lip of the glass. "We should discuss what we're planning to do at the club tonight."

"Yes." Their dynamic was important. She'd thought about it several times during the week.

"Carter said Brooke came in Wednesday night and asked for an appointment with you for tonight."

"Oh, good. I felt bad cancelling on her. I'm glad she came in anyway. She's never come when the club was open."

"Is that something you'd like to do? Domme for her tonight?"

"If it's okay with you, Sir, I'd like to work with her. She's...I don't know...skittish. I've never seen her submit to a man, but I don't get the feeling she's interested in women, sexually, I mean. I'm afraid she's been burned in the past and doesn't trust easily."

He nodded. "I've heard a few details. The guys were talking about her the other night while we were playing poker."

Faith furrowed her brow, running her finger along the edge of her glass as she considered his words. "Is that appropriate, Sir?"

He leaned forward, setting his elbows on the table. "You mean discussing someone from the club?"

"Yes." It made her nervous. Lines could be crossed. *Did they discuss me too?* There were club rules to protect people's anonymity. Being a member of a fetish club was something people took very seriously. If their privacy was in jeopardy...

"Faith, look at me."

She lifted her gaze.

"I'm part owner of Zodiac. You have to know I would never engage in or condone any discussion that was unethical."

She nodded.

"My poker group is composed of employees only. Lincoln and Carter and I, in addition to three other employees who have worked there for years. Tyler, Aaron, and Dayton. Occasionally when it's necessary, we do discuss members, but only when we feel like something needs to be addressed."

"Okay, Sir."

"Members are never present when we discuss them, and we do not gossip."

She nodded again, half hating herself for doubting him and half concerned still about what had been said about her. "Did you...discuss me, Sir?"

He hesitated for a moment and then answered. "Yes, but only because my employees were curious about us. They've seen us leave together. They're wondering if I'm topping you or vice versa." He grinned.

"Did you tell them?" She sounded breathless even to her own ears.

"Nope. And I can only imagine how hard they've been scratching their heads in confusion."

Her heart resumed its regular rhythm. He hadn't told them. Not even his own employees. He'd let them believe he might be a switch just to protect her. Holy shit.

He cocked his head to one side. "I'm only speaking of Aaron, Tyler, and Dayton, of course. I'm sure Sasha does not keep secrets from Lincoln. I can also assure you Lincoln would never break that confidence. As for Carter, we've been friends for fourteen years. He knows me well. He hasn't asked, but he's not stupid."

She nodded. Of course.

Rowen jerked her back to the more important subject. "As for Brooke, I'm going to permit you to do a scene with her tonight, but I want you to understand my reasons."

"Okay, Sir." Her heart pounded.

He stared at her for a long time, tapping his fingers on the table. So long she fought the urge to squirm. Finally, he cleared his throat. "For one thing, I'm concerned about Brooke. She seems to thrive best under your domination. I hope you can break through and help her. Maybe you can get her to talk to you."

Faith nodded. That had been her intention the last time she dominated Brooke, but the redhead had clammed up and said nothing. She wanted to try again. This would be their first public scene.

"Another reason I'm going to consent is because I think it

would be good for you to switch tonight to see how it makes you feel. You've been in a new role for the first time in a long time, submitting to me for the past week. You need to make some decisions for yourself. You can't hide forever. I think dominating Brooke will help you get inside your head and figure yourself out. Do you want to go back to topping? Do you want to switch? Or are you in a place where you want to give up dominating to submit to someone instead?"

She winced at his word choice that did not specifically indicate he meant to be the one who dominated her if she chose that path. What he didn't realize was that she would not submit to someone else. If he left her, she would be right where she started, floundering in a world where she didn't quite fit in.

He continued. "There's one more reason I'm going to permit you to top Brooke and that's because I like the way you asked my permission. I like the fact that you're taking this thing between us seriously. I like that you recognize you're mine tonight and don't automatically get to decide what you will and won't be doing in the club."

"Thank you, Sir." She sat up straighter, feeling pleased with herself at the way she'd diplomatically handled things.

He grabbed her hand again, pulling it to his face to stroke her knuckles against his cheek. "Do not take advantage of this concession, Faith. You have permission to dominate one person tonight. Brooke. No one else. Don't ask."

"Yes, Sir."

"I'll let *you* decide whether or not you want to come out to other members tonight. I'll totally understand if you'd prefer to keep our arrangement secret for now. It's new. It's admittedly precarious. I'll be watching you top Brooke, of course. But I won't say a word. You think about how you want me to dominate you before and after you do this scene. Secretly or publicly. I won't hold it against you either way."

She had mixed emotions about his statement. On the one

hand, she was glad he was giving her options. He could have demanded she bottom for him without discussion. On the other hand, it spoke volumes about how far he saw their relationship going that he would keep it behind closed doors. Nowhere.

He tugged her hand as he leaned forward, silently asking her to do the same. When their faces came together, he kissed her lips gently. "You're still mine tonight. All night. You'll use the apparatus of my choosing for Brooke and follow my instructions with regard to timing and boundaries. Understood?"

"Yes, Sir." She was breathless. As usual. In addition, her belly clenched, the need to be fucked right on the edge. She had no idea how she was going to dominate another person knowing Rowen was watching so intently. Was it possible for her to dominate someone while under the control of another?

She prayed it looked like the way he dominated her during dinner. Giving her options in a controlled environment.

CHAPTER 23

Rowen leaned against the wall in the darkest corner of Zodiac and watched as Faith prepared for her scene.

Brooke stood to one side, shuffling her feet as she distributed her weight back and forth between legs. She rubbed her arms several times.

Faith stepped over to her and whispered something in her ear.

Brooke nodded and then lowered her gaze and grasp her hands behind her back. She also planted her feet shoulder-width apart and stopped fidgeting.

Faith was good. She was amazing actually.

Rowen had watched her perform like this several times, but this was the first time he was doing so overtly with Faith fully aware of his presence and the fact that he'd given her strict instructions about her scene.

It was still her scene. He wouldn't interfere in Brooke's experience just to keep Faith in her place. That wouldn't be fair to Brooke.

Rowen had given Faith a choice of several apparatus to use tonight. He hadn't been surprised when she chose the new spider web. He'd had daydreams of attaching Faith to the same piece of equipment one day. It didn't shock him that she was lured to the web also.

He had given her permission to use whatever toys Brooke desired as long as blood wasn't drawn, but he had not agreed to Brooke being naked.

It wasn't that he thought it mattered one way or the other with regard to Faith. He wasn't worried about her arousal or how she felt when she topped a nude submissive. She had already told him she didn't get aroused dominating others. He trusted her.

No. He had other motives. One was that he didn't recall ever having seen Brooke naked inside the club, so he felt confident the redhead wouldn't likely request such a thing.

But the main reason why Rowen had set that boundary and several others was because he wanted to impose his will on Faith in subtle, unmistakable ways. He had also insisted she remain completely clothed, wear her heels, and keep the scene under an hour. He'd added the part about her heels simply because he liked to watch her shapely legs while she moved.

Faith had readily agreed to his demands, keeping her head bowed and her submission to him at the forefront while he spoke to her in his office earlier. When she'd questioned Brooke's aftercare, Rowen had assured her he would arrange for Carter to step in and take over after the scene. It was obvious Carter had an interest in Brooke, and Rowen knew without a doubt his friend would see to her care.

Before they'd headed downstairs, he'd given her one last challenge. A choice. Either she could leave quietly with him after the scene and go to his apartment, or he would arrange to dominate her in a private room of the club. People might notice she went into the room with him, but they would not know what happened after the door closed or who topped whom. Let them wonder.

Faith had chosen the private room.

He still had trouble thinking straight as he thought about how he would handle her as soon as he got her alone.

Shaking his plans for later to the back of his mind, he watched as Faith led Brooke to the spider web and then had her face the chain links. Interesting choice. It was one thing to lower a submissive onto his or her back against the chains. He'd yet to see anyone lying on the links face first.

But he trusted Faith to know what she was doing. No way would Rowen interrupt her scene. It was against Zodiac policy to ever interrupt a scene, besides, never once since Rowen had known Faith had she done anything to place any doubt in his mind as to her abilities as a Domme.

This scene was well planned and prepared for. Faith had even met privately with Brooke in Rowen's office before they descended to start the scene. Faith would have made certain Brooke was ready for this public display.

As Brooke lifted her hands up in a V above her head, Faith used soft Velcro cuffs to attach her to the chain links.

Rowen let his gaze wander down to Brooke's body. She was shorter than Faith, maybe five two, and so small as to seem fragile, though he doubted that was the case. Her skin was as pale as Faith's with a sprinkle of freckles. Her curly red hair was braided down her back tonight, and Faith tucked it over her shoulder as she switched to attach her other wrist.

Brooke wore jeans and a loose-fitting, long-sleeved, black shirt. It caught Rowen's attention. Members of the club wore all sorts of clothing on any given night, so no one surprised him ever. But Brooke... She was hiding.

Rowen realized he wasn't alone a moment before Carter spoke from his side. "You might think it's none of my business, but what exactly is going on here?"

Rowen glanced at Carter and then back at the women, unsure how much he wanted to divulge. Yes. Carter definitely had a stake in this situation. Even if Brooke didn't know it yet.

Under any other normal situation, Rowen wouldn't reveal a member's secrets even to his closest friends and coworkers if they asked him not to. And he'd watched the tension ebb from Faith's shoulders at dinner when he'd told her he hadn't revealed the nature of their relationship to his employees.

But Carter's arms were crossed and he was planted next to Rowen, sucking the oxygen out of the room. He deserved more than silence. He cared more about Brooke than he was probably fully aware of yet.

"Faith is helping Brooke."

"Helping her?"

Rowen leaned closer to ensure their conversation could not be overheard while he kept his gaze on his woman and the woman Carter was preoccupied with. "You said yourself she has issues. She only submits to women. She prefers Faith. Cutting her off with no explanation would be cruel. I thought it was best if Faith worked with her tonight in an attempt to make a breakthrough."

"*You* thought it was best..." Carter deadpanned.

"Yes."

"Because cutting Brooke off would be cruel..." he continued.

"Yes."

"So this is the last time Faith is going to dominate Brooke?"

"Quite possibly."

"Quite possibly," he repeated. "That's clear as mud."

"Isn't it, though?" Rowen asked without looking at Carter's face.

Carter's stance relaxed slightly. "Maybe. Though this cryptic game we're playing is making me think too hard."

Rowen took a breath. "I apologize."

"I get it. Don't apologize. I'm a smart guy. Contrary to the confusion you planted in everyone else's mind Thursday night, I know you better. No fucking way is that woman dominating you in private. You're not protecting your *own* reputation. You're protecting *hers*. And it makes perfect sense. I totally understand why she would want to hold her secrets close until she's positive of her stance and willing to out herself to others."

Rowen said nothing. It wasn't necessary.

"Do you have a plan for aftercare here? Who's going to work with Brooke an hour from now when Faith walks away?"

Rowen did glance at his friend at those questions. "You busy tonight?"

Faith moved around Brooke, taking things slow. Half of her felt like she slid right back into her element, her role as Domme, without a hitch. After all, she'd done this so many times it came naturally.

But it wasn't natural. It was a learned behavior. And after a week of doing what was truly natural she was well aware of the way she mechanically maneuvered around a scene like this. No one would ever know it wasn't her true calling. She was that good. But in her heart, she knew. She simply couldn't allow it to affect her performance.

As usual, dozens of people were watching. She tuned them out, also as usual. However, she was super aware of Rowen. She knew exactly where he was standing, and in addition, she wasn't surprised to find Carter next to him, arms crossed, face scrunched in concern. The blond man had an interest in Brooke, which was convenient because he was the perfect person to take over Brooke's aftercare when Faith finished this scene.

Faith had no proof that Brooke was even interested in men, but she hoped to pull off the performance of a lifetime right here and get the woman to talk to her, both before and after the scene.

Already Faith had accomplished one goal—she knew with certainty that she didn't thrive as a Domme. She could do it. That was never in doubt, but it didn't bring her to her knees and make her feel whole like submitting did.

No matter what happened between her and Rowen in the next few days, Faith would have to admit her true submission to herself. Unfortunately, that fierce revelation was wrought with problems.

If the shit hit the fan—as it surely would—between her and Rowen, she would be left without a club and without a Dom. The hardest part to swallow about that would be that she couldn't envision putting herself out there for another Dom.

It was bad enough coming to terms with how good Rowen made her feel and how much she was willing to sacrifice for him. She had sworn off men to guard her heart, and she'd meant it. But Rowen had snuck up on her and burrowed under her skin before she could stop the advance.

Submitting to him later tonight would cost her dearly. She knew it, but she couldn't stop it. Her heart was in jeopardy of betraying her completely when soon afterward her world would crumble, leaving her without a Dom and with a new chink in her armor that would cause her to bury herself even deeper from future possible hurt.

She never should have let things go this far. She'd known all week she was falling harder for Rowen with each passing day. She'd even found peace with losing Victor and allowed herself to open up again. However, she'd known with equal certainty that Rowen would never survive her parents.

The two warring issues lived in separate compartments in her mind. She'd allowed herself to feel, to submit thoroughly, to love again. Meanwhile, the sane half of her head knew it couldn't last, and she would inevitably get hurt.

The loss already weighed heavily on her shoulders.

She closed her eyes, drew in a deep breath, and forced herself to concentrate on Brooke. Faith's ponytail fell over her shoulder, reminding her she was only playing the role of Domme for the next thirty minutes. Rowen had put her hair in that band, and he was ultimately in charge of her.

She stepped around the spider web holding a paddle, a flogger, and a whip in her hands. "Look at me, Brooke."

The skittish redhead lifted her gaze. "Ma'am."

"You said you didn't want me to hold back tonight."

"Yes, Ma'am."

"I'm going to let you choose which item you'd like me to strike you with, but there's a catch."

Brooke's eyes widened. "A catch?"

"Yes. I'm going to expect you to open up to me. Talk to me. Answer my questions while I top you."

Brooke swallowed, her pale cheeks pinkening. "Why...Ma'am?"

"Because you're using me to escape and hide from yourself. If you don't let some of that out, you're never going to make any headway."

Brooke held Faith's gaze for so long Faith worried she might turn down the offer. Finally, she nodded. "The whip please, Ma'am."

Faith wasn't surprised. The sting from the whip was usually more piercing and quick than any other implement. If the goal of a submissive was pain, he or she would get the most bang for their buck with the whip.

Faith didn't have the luxury of striking Brooke's bare skin. For one thing, Rowen had forbidden it. For another thing, Brooke had never indicated she craved the exposure. So, Faith would make do with knowing whatever pink lines landed on Brooke's skin would be seen later only by Brooke. Faith was professional enough to know how hard to strike to avoid blood. And she would be extra cautious tonight without being able to see the results.

Stepping out of Brooke's line of sight, Faith took a position behind Brooke, set a hand on her shoulder, and spoke into her ear. "Are you sure you're ready for this?"

"Yes, Ma'am. I want to push myself tonight."

Faith had spoken to Brooke for a while before they stepped

into the main room. It was a big deal for Brooke to open up in public like this. A huge step.

"Safeword?"

"Red, Ma'am."

Deep breath. "I'm going to start now. Easy at first and then harder."

"Yes, Ma'am."

Faith slid into the zone she'd trained herself to assume and stepped back to strike Brooke's small rounded butt, watching the redhead clench her cheeks together with every swoosh of the whip.

She set up a pattern, landing her strikes down the backs of Brooke's thighs and then back up until she reached her shoulders. Every so often she increased the force, watching every flinch to gauge Brooke's reactions.

When Brooke stopped fighting against herself and relaxed into the scene, moaning softly, Faith paused to rub her hand along the welts and leaned in toward Brooke's ear. "Do you get aroused when I whip you, Brooke?" She knew the answer to that question, but she wanted to hear Brooke say it aloud.

"No, Ma'am."

"That's a girl." She continued to soothe Brooke's back with her palm. "There's no right or wrong answer, you know."

"Okay, Ma'am." Her voice was soft.

"Did someone in your past hurt you, Brooke?" Faith was treading into difficult territory, knowing she was taking a gamble.

"Yes, Ma'am," she whispered.

"A past lover?" Faith held her breath. The answer to that question held the key to unraveling Brooke.

CHAPTER 24

Faith was mentally exhausted when she was finally finished with Brooke. She had pulled so much information out of the smaller woman that there had been a seismic shift in the universe that left the air around them thick.

Between every round of strikes with the whip, Faith had spoken quietly to Brooke, helping her release her past. The woman had a long way to go, but hopefully what they had accomplished had been a start that would help launch Brooke into a healing path.

After they finished the scene, Faith helped Brooke over to a sofa and sat next to her, holding her hand as she drank a bottle of water. It took a while for Brooke to come out of her daze and meet Faith's gaze with seeing eyes. "Thank you."

Faith smiled. "You're welcome. My pleasure."

"I said a lot of things."

"I know." Faith squeezed her hand. "That's good. You need to get that stuff off your chest. You need to release it."

Brooke nodded, tipping her head down toward her lap. "It would be different if I let a man top me, wouldn't it?"

"Yes." Finally, a breakthrough. The segue Faith needed. "Can I make a recommendation?"

Brooke flinched, not having expected Faith to push the issue further so fast.

Faith continued. "I'd like to ask one of the owners to work with you. He's a very gentle Dom. And he knows what he's doing. He's safe. I think you would benefit from letting him help you."

"You're not going to top me again, are you?" Brooke asked.

Faith shook her head. "No, sweetie, I'm not. For many reasons."

Brooke nodded. "Which owner?"

"Carter Ellis. He and Rowen have been watching you closely. They're keeping an eye on us even now. Will you let me step away so he can talk to you?"

She hesitated for a long time and then tipped her head to one side. "The blond?"

"Yes."

"He's so...big."

Faith smiled. "You aren't lying. But he's a gentle giant." Faith didn't need Rowen to tell her that. She'd seen him in action many times herself. "Trust me?"

"Okay."

Faith lifted her gaze toward the men hovering just out of hearing distance and nodded. Two seconds later, Rowen had his hands on Faith's shoulders, guiding her away from Brooke while Carter took her spot on the sofa.

Damn but she hoped she had made the right decision.

Rowen said nothing until they were out of the main room and he had guided her upstairs into his office. He shut the door and faced her again, his hands cupping her cheeks. "I know we discussed using a private room here tonight, but I'd rather take you to my place if you don't mind."

She smiled. "I'd like that, Sir." The extra time it would take to get to his apartment would help her recover from her experience with Brooke. Besides, with every passing moment she felt more certain tonight would be their last night together, so she wanted to make the most of it. She preferred submitting to him someplace where she didn't have to worry about anyone seeing her, where she could let down her inhibitions in private, where she could have amazing sex on a bed with a sexy man who worshipped her.

Yeah, she wanted to go home with Rowen.

"Wait here." He left her by the door and headed across the room to shut down his computer and grab a few things off his desk. "You okay walking out of the club with me? We can leave separately again if you'd prefer."

"No, Sir. It's fine." She grinned. "I'm pretty sure most people who have seen us think you secretly submit to me in private."

He narrowed his gaze at her, clasping one of her ass cheeks with his hand and hauling her to his front. "You think you're funny?" His voice was serious, but his expression gave him away. He couldn't hide the mirth dancing in his eyes.

"Yes, Sir."

"Sassy girl." He backed her up until she was flattened against the door, lifted both her hands over her head, and clasped her wrists with one of his hands. His free hand was on her breast in less than a second.

She gasped, sobering.

He pinched her nipple through the fabric of her dress.

Her pussy flooded as she rose onto her toes.

Two seconds later he released her breast and yanked her dress up over her hips. "Spread your legs."

She did so without hesitation, adrenaline pumping through her body. A minute ago she had felt the need to rest and regroup. Now she was on full alert. Deep ragged breaths.

He grabbed her leg and hitched it up high on his thigh. "How wet are you, Faith?"

She swallowed, blinking. Befuddled. "Very wet, Sir," she whispered, hating how her body betrayed her without warning.

He cupped her ass with his enormous hand and swiped his fingers through her folds.

She moaned loudly, instantly needing release.

His hand came up between them, two fingers wet with her come. He wiped it on her mouth. "Taste yourself."

She licked her lips.

His fingers slid into her mouth next. "Suck."

She did as he instructed, surprised to find her flavor sweeter than expected.

When he pulled his fingers out of her mouth, he lowered his hand back to her pussy and thrust those fingers up inside her.

"Rowen..." A louder moan she could not stop.

He thrust again, harder, practically lifting her off the floor. His thumb landed on her clit and pressed while he fucked her pussy, adding a third finger.

Her eyes rolled back into her head as she leaned against the door. Her breasts felt full and tight behind the confines of her dress. And Rowen relentlessly fucked her with his fingers until she couldn't think.

"Do you need to come, Faith?"

"Yes, Sir," she panted.

"Ask for permission."

"Please... Sir... Please let me come." It was a wonder she was able to speak the words.

His thumb against her clit disappeared and one finger slid into her tight rear hole so that every thrust included both holes now. It took seconds for her to fall apart, exploding around his palm.

She gasped for every breath as his hand disappeared. Too soon. Before the pulsing stopped. Before she was fully satisfied. He released her hands and her leg and tugged her skirt over her butt.

Her vision was still blurry and her brain confused when he

grabbed her chin and looked her in the eye. "Who's in charge of your body?"

"You are, Sir." There was no doubt.

"If I wanted to march you down to the club right now, cuff you to that spider web, and make you scream for release, would you do it?"

"Yes, Sir," she responded on a deflated breath. She would. She wasn't kidding. She would do anything he asked. He had that much control over her.

"That's what I thought." He released her chin, grabbed their constant companion—the black bag of surprises—and took her hand. "Now you have something else to recover from while you're in the car. And I suggest you take the time to think about what it means to submit to me, because when we get to the apartment, I'm going to remind you a few more times."

As Rowen let them into his apartment, he wondered if he'd pushed her too far.

When she pulled out her sassy card, he couldn't resist the urge to ensure she understood who was in charge. Even though she'd just finished topping Brooke, she was still *his* submissive, and she'd clearly needed the reminder.

And damn but she proved to him in less than two seconds that she knew good and well she was his in every way.

He watched as she looked around. "Go ahead, explore."

She wandered in farther and he headed for the kitchen table to deposit the bag. He opened the fridge to grab two bottles of water next and then leaned against the counter to watch her as he tugged off his tie and unbuttoned the top two buttons on his shirt.

She had managed to recover enough from her scene with Brooke and him unbalancing her in his office to move around on steady feet, her shoulders pulled back, her hands clasped behind her. When she reached his side, she lifted her gaze. "I love your place, Sir. It's warm."

"Seriously? I thought you would hate it. Your apartment is so open and bright. Cheery, I suppose. I thought the darkness of mine would make you cringe."

She shook her head and took the water bottle he offered her. "I didn't choose the décor. My mother did. My sister helped. They thought I needed a new apartment and a fresh start after Victor died, so they set me up with no input from me at all."

Huh. Go figure. He took another drink of water.

"I'm not sure I was even ready to move yet. Emotionally. My mother swooped in fast, hoping to get me to forget Victor and fall back in line." She rolled her eyes and then her face hardened.

He frowned at her. It really bothered him that she had such a bad relationship with her family. So much sarcasm in her voice as if she truly hated the mother who gave birth to her. It made him sad. Hell, it pissed him off. Was he judging her wrong or was her mother truly the bitch Faith made her out to be?

Tonight was not about that, though. Tonight was about the two of them. Tomorrow they could deal with family issues.

When she turned around as if to walk away, he wrapped an arm around her waist and pulled her back against his chest. He set his lips on her ear. "I'm glad you like my place. Now, as much as I have enjoyed watching you move in this sexy white dress all evening, it's time to take it off." He set his water on the counter and reached for the hem to pull the dress over her head, leaving her totally naked except for the strappy silver heels. He liked the look, so he left them.

She lowered her face, her ponytail falling to one side as he returned his arm to rest under her tits and pulled her lower back into his erection.

"No more words," he whispered against her ear again. "Unless I ask you a direct question, your job for the rest of the night is total obedience."

She said nothing, but her body shivered in his grip, and her nipples stiffened as he watched.

He smiled. "Good girl."

Releasing her, he took her hand, led her to a kitchen chair, pulled it away from the table, and guided her to sit. "Spread your knees, sweet girl. Reach your arms behind the chair."

She straightened her spine and did as he asked, although her thighs were still not wide enough for him to get between them.

He waited, not moving, seeing if she would realize what he wanted and comply on her own. Finally, she slowly spread her knees wider. "That's better."

She shuddered.

He pulled the blindfold from his pocket and held it in front of her. "Our last unused toy." He slid it over her head and tightened it to ensure she couldn't see anything. "Bend your arms so you can hold on to your wrists with both hands."

She followed his instructions.

After rummaging around in the bag, he found the rope and turned around to let one end of it dangle over her shoulder, grazing her nipples. She wiggled just enough to avoid the touch as if it burned when really it simply teased.

He stepped behind her as he prepared the rope, folding it several times to create the perfect loop that would secure her arms behind the chair but not injure her skin or pull too tight. The moment he touched her skin, he was in his zone, creating art. He took his time intricately wrapping the rope around her arms, securing her to the chair with a beautiful swirly pattern.

When he rounded to face her and kneel in front of her, he set his hands on her knees. "Is it too tight?"

"No, Sir."

He pressed the inside of her knees. "Since you seem to find it necessary to keep your legs too close together, I'm going to bind them open."

She licked her lips and then bit the lower one.

242

He plucked it from her mouth, causing her breath to hitch, and then he smoothed his hand down one leg until he gripped her ankle. Angling himself to the side of the chair, he used one of the lengths of rope hanging from her biceps to attach her ankle to the rear leg of the chair.

Her breathing picked up. Not surprising. Her knee was now pressing against the side of the seat. There was no way to close it. After securing her other leg in the same fashion, he stepped back. "So gorgeous," he murmured. "Do you mind if I take a few pictures? From behind. I won't show your nipples or your pussy. Not even your face."

"If that's what you'd like, Sir."

"Good girl." He pulled his phone from his pocket and rounded to take several shots from a variety of angles. Every time the flash went off she flinched. "These are perfect, sweet girl. You're going to like them." He set the phone down and kneeled in front of her again.

He settled between her knees, smoothing his hands up and down her inner thighs. "So wet for me."

She whimpered.

"The blindfold heightens your arousal, doesn't it?"

"Yes, Sir."

He pulled her swollen lower lips apart, but didn't touch her pussy directly. Instead, he watched her face as she squirmed and tipped her head back. Her mouth opened to draw in much-needed oxygen. Watching her made his dick so hard it pressed against his dress pants.

Rowen leaned forward enough to blow gently against her pussy.

She arched her belly on a moan.

He lifted his gaze to her amazing tits and flicked his tongue over each one. "Are you comfortable, Faith?"

"Yes, Sir."

"Whose pussy is this?" He tapped right above her clit with one

243

finger.

"Yours, Sir."

"Good girl." He rose again to grab some things from the bag on the table, returning with everything he intended to use to torment her. He toyed with her nipples first, cupping her breasts and thumbing them until they were stiff peaks.

When he thought she might come from the nipple play alone, he released them, but only long enough to pinch one of them and settle the little clamp on the offended bud. Seconds later, he had the other secured to match its mate.

He gave the delicate chains a pull to make them sway.

Every tiny reaction from her, every whimper, every arch, every flinch made his cock harder. She was the perfect submissive. More than he could have dreamed of.

But was she his? Would she be his tomorrow? Something in the air gave him the distinct impression their perfect bubble would burst tomorrow night and this game they were playing would be over as fast as it started.

She had said very little about the fact that he'd insisted they go to her parents' for dinner. He wasn't sure she'd even informed them she was coming or bringing a guest. He hadn't pushed her, but he got a vibe that she either had no intention of going through with her promise or planned to skip town in order to avoid it. Preposterous, but he couldn't avoid the dense air that surrounded every conversation involving her family.

With both hands on her thighs again, he parted her lower lips and leaned forward to flick his tongue over her clit.

She let out a sharp noise and tried to lift her butt.

"So needy."

She whimpered again. Music. The flush on her cheeks was sexy too. The way she licked her lips repeatedly and then let them fall apart to breathe through her mouth. Also hot as hell.

He reached for the vibrator next, turning it on low so the sound made her squirm with renewed effort. Her head fell forward, her ponytail swaying with the movement. "Oh, God. Sir. Oh my God."

"Did I give you permission to speak?"

She sucked in a breath, shaking her head. "No, Sir. I'm sorry, Sir. Sorry." She was mumbling, almost incoherently, while he listened to her with a smile. "So aroused. I think I'm going to explode. Please, Sir." She gasped for oxygen as if there weren't enough of it in the room.

"That's kind of the idea, isn't it, sweet girl?"

"Yes, Sir." She stiffened, inhaling long and slow, perhaps telling herself how to regain control.

"Nevertheless, you still don't have permission to speak. Every time you do, I'm keeping a tally."

She pursed her lips.

"I think you enjoy being punished."

She didn't move, but she did bite her lip again.

He stroked his free hand up and down her thigh. "Or perhaps you're testing me to see what I'll do to discipline you. Pushing your boundaries. Understandable. In many respects we're new to each other. You can't be sure I'll live up to your expectations."

Her lips parted as if she were going to argue, but she stopped herself.

"I get you, Faith. I know you need a firm Dom. I know you need someone to set tight boundaries and enforce strict rules. It soothes you to submit fully like that. And I'm letting you know that I'm up to that task. I've searched my entire life for someone like you." He leaned forward. "Let go. Let me lead. Don't fight it." *You're home.*

Those last words were on the tip of his tongue, but he thought they would scare her to death, and he truly believed she wasn't on the same page as him. She was submitting completely—her body anyway. But her mind wasn't fully his. She was still holding back.

Sure, she'd told him everything about her life. She'd been an open book. But he sensed she was still holding back emotionally.

If she went through with their plan to dine with the Davenports tomorrow night, he hoped to be able to understand the entire dynamic. Either she was an ungrateful brat who refused to be kind to her parents, or her parents were evil beings who didn't deserve Faith in their lives. The former seemed unreasonable. The latter made his heart hurt.

The conundrum was that he felt pulled in two directions. He couldn't stomach the thought that Faith was a different person in her parents' home—one he would not like. He also couldn't stomach finding out her parents were as horrifying as she insisted.

She lowered her head, but her chest was rising and falling rapidly.

God, she was gorgeous.

He lifted the egg toward her ear to remind her it was in his hand.

She sucked in a sharp breath but didn't otherwise move.

He set it against the chain hanging from one nipple, making her arch. When he switched it to the other chain, she leaned to one side. "I bet that feels weird," he commented. "Brings attention to those clamps, doesn't it?"

She didn't answer. He didn't need her to.

When he set the tip of the egg directly on the tip of one nipple, she shrank away from the shocking contact. Without warning, he pressed the egg directly against her clit and turned up the speed.

Her ass lifted off the chair as far as she could move while a groan left her mouth.

He set his free hand on her thigh to hold her down and pressed deeper.

"Oh... God. Oh, no. Sir..." Her leg trembled under his palm, and within seconds she came.

A scream filled the room. He waited until she started squirming in earnest to remove the egg from her clit, but only to push it up into her pussy.

Her head rolled back.

He reached in with two fingers to angle the vibrations against her G-spot.

"No. No no no no no."

"Faith..." he warned. "Unless you mean to use your safeword—which is not *no*—close your lips."

She clamped her mouth shut, her entire body stiff and wiggling.

He still held her thigh, but he angled his hand so he could stroke her clit with his thumb.

Faith moaned, a deep unintelligible sound that signaled she was close again.

"Come for me, sweet girl. Come on my hand."

At his command, she came, the inside of her pussy clutching at his fingers while her clit throbbed against his thumb. A gush of wetness hit his palm. "Ohmygod," she murmured. It was the most beautiful thing he'd ever seen, her so completely at his mercy and undone.

He would bet money that was her first G-spot orgasm.

When she winced, he turned off the vibrations and removed his thumb, but he left the egg inside her. While she was still gasping for air, her body shaking with the aftereffects of two hard orgasms, he reached up and removed both clamps at once.

"*Fuck*," she screamed. "That hurts."

He chuckled. "Sweet girl, you're incorrigible. No matter what I do to punish you, you add to the infractions."

She licked her lips. "Sorry, Sir."

"Normally I would rub out the sting after removing the clamps, but you didn't earn that privilege. Now you've made it worse."

She pursed her lips.

"You're going to be a handful when it comes to discipline, aren't you? Normally, if you were anyone else, I would use a whip on your bottom. But your skin is too sensitive for the welts. I won't do that to you."

He stroked a finger down her cheek. "You're intentionally pushing the limits to see what I'll do, aren't you, Faith?"

She hesitated. "Yes, Sir."

He leaned in closer, gripping her chin but setting his lips on her ear. "You're testing me. You want to know deep down if I'm a firm enough Dom to handle you."

"Yes, Sir." Her voice was stronger.

"Good girl. I'm proud of you for telling the truth. I'm creative, sweet girl. I will always give you what you need. But I will also warn you that you won't like it. So if you think it's a good idea to antagonize me in order to get a gentle spanking or a rush of orgasms, you would be wrong." He let go of her chin and rose to his feet.

He knew she was nervous, wondering what he would do next. Goose bumps rose on her skin. He also knew this night was crucial. Whatever was going on in that twisted head of hers included testing his worthiness. Though he had no idea what he needed to do to prove to her he was a firm Dom who could handle her.

He had no choice but to take a chance, choose a punishment, and see how she reacted. Silently, he left her in the kitchen. He'd done more shopping that week than what she'd been privy to in the bag he'd sent to her house.

He headed for his bedroom closet, unlocked the deep drawer at the bottom of his built-in shelves, and prayed he chose correctly. If he wasn't mistaken, she would endure anything. If he was wrong, he could lose her.

His own hands were shaking as badly as hers when he made his selection, and a minute later he was in front of her again.

"Open your mouth." He tugged on her chin, waiting for her to comply.

She parted her lips.

"Wider."

She held her breath as she tipped her head back and spread her jaw open farther.

He tucked the O ring behind her teeth and pulled the leather straps around to the back of her head to hold the ring in place. It wasn't overly large, but it wasn't the smallest one on the market either. He wanted her to feel the stress of not being able to speak. He wanted her to be uncomfortable and unable to swallow properly. He wanted to do something to discipline her so she would know he took his job seriously without marking her skin.

When he had the straps tightened, he tipped her head forward toward her lap and made sure her blindfold was still in place.

She moaned, fighting the ring.

He reached behind her and set a golf ball in her hand. "Hold on to the ball, Faith."

She gripped it.

"Good girl. You're being punished for speaking out of turn. The ring stays in your mouth for fifteen minutes. Since you can't use your safeword, the ball is your safety net. If you drop it, I'll remove the ring and the scene is over."

She moaned unintelligibly behind the ring. He kneeled in front of her and ran a finger around her lips, teasing them. "Keep your head down. I want you to drool between your legs."

A shudder spread down her torso.

"That's my girl." He stroked her hair. "I have dozens of ways to discipline you. You don't need to test me to find out what all of them are." He thumbed her nipples, making her writhe. They stiffened to sharp points. He pinched them both hard and held them away from her body as he spoke again. "I have the perfect little crop for these. Next time you tempt me, I might be inclined to bind your tits and give your nipples a sharp swat. Just one will make you wish you had never disobeyed me. I know because I've had it done before."

He leaned in closer, tugging harder to remind her what part of her body he was discussing. "Have you ever had your nipples cropped, sweet girl?"

"Un-uh." She shook her head.

"Do you like the idea?"

"Un-uh."

"Then maybe you'll trust me to guide you and teach you how I like my submissives to behave without testing me, yeah?"

She nodded, a line of drool running down her chin.

He released her nipples and stroked a finger through her folds. She moaned again as he flicked across her clit. "For someone who just had two orgasms, you sure are horny." After teasing her for another minute, he removed his hand entirely. "You won't be permitted to come again tonight. Though you will climb on top of me and ride me when your punishment is over."

She sucked in a sharp breath, probably wondering how the hell that would be possible.

"I know you can do it." He left her again. She had five more minutes. He wanted her to spend them without knowing where he was or what he was doing or how much time had passed.

When her time was up, he returned with her bottle of water. He unlatched the O ring from the back of her head first, and then he rubbed her jaw. "You okay, sweet girl?"

"Yes, Sir." Her voice was far meeker. Obedient. He liked it. Maybe she was done testing him for now.

He rounded to her back to untie her ankles and her arms. When they were free, he rubbed the circulation back into her biceps and shook them out.

"Thank you, Sir."

He pulled her legs to the front next and rubbed her thighs and then her shins. "Keep your hands at your sides. Leave the blindfold. You don't have permission to look at me while you fuck me."

When he was certain she was okay to stand, he took her hand.

"Follow me, sweet girl." He led her down the hallway to his bedroom.

He'd anticipated bringing her back here tonight, so he had changed the sheets, made the bed, and straightened up.

He led her to the bed and then kneeled in front of her to unbuckle the strappy heels she wore, lifting first one foot and then the other out of their confines.

Leaving her where she stood, he pulled the comforter down to the foot of the bed and then returned to lift her by the waist and set her on the cool surface of his black sheets.

He didn't delay in removing his clothes and rolling on a condom. His cock had been hard enough to break things for hours. After climbing up next to her and lying on his back, he reached for her waist. "Climb over me, Faith. No words. Just fuck me. I'll let you control how fast and deep you want to go, but you don't have permission to come. Understood?"

"Yes, Sir," she whispered as she felt around for him and straddled his body, her pussy then hovering over his cock.

"Lucky for you, I'm going to come in about two minutes, so you won't have to restrain yourself for too long." He lined his cock up with her entrance and guided her over him with his other hand on her hip. And then he released her and lifted his hand over his head to cradle his neck and watch the most gorgeous submissive woman he'd ever met fuck him as part of her own punishment.

She set her hands on his chest and lifted off several inches, slamming back down with enough force to make him gasp. "Faith..." he warned. "If you come, I'll tie you spread eagle to this bed and torture you with orgasm denial until the sun comes up."

She bit her lip and then released it and nodded. Her face was tight as she continued to fuck him. She arched her back spectacularly, her breasts lifting high on her chest as she rose and fell over his dick.

He gritted his teeth to keep from coming, wanting this

moment to last longer, but it was no use. He was totally gone for her. No way could he hold back with her riding him so gloriously.

On a groan, he came. Hard. It lasted longer than normal, too. Nearly a minute went by before the last of his come pulsed into the condom. When he could convince his arms to follow directions, he grabbed her waist, lifted her off him, and settled her at his side.

She was shivering, her breaths fast with need.

Instead of heading to the bathroom to clean up, he grabbed a tissue from the end table and wrapped the condom in it to toss it on the floor. And then he turned off the lamp next to the bed, pulled the sheet and comforter up from the foot of the bed, and drew her back into his chest, spooning her securely.

It wasn't until he had her cocooned that he removed the blindfold. The room was dark. It would take her a while to adjust. He kissed her temple. "You may speak freely now. I'm so proud of you."

"Thank you, Sir." She gripped his arms with her small hands. "Thank you." There was a hitch in her voice, and he lifted one hand to stroke her cheeks.

Tears. Of regret? Or relief? "Tell me about the tears, Faith. Happy or sad or angry?"

"Happy, Sir." Her voice was so soft he barely heard her.

"Because?"

"Because I never thought I'd feel like this again."

"Like what, sweet girl?"

"Like I'm home." She dipped her head and kissed his arm at her breasts.

Thank. God.

He brushed her hair out of her face. Most of it had come loose from the ponytail as she'd ridden him. He needed to kiss her, so he pulled her onto her back and leaned over her, taking her lips. Instantly, the kiss was hot and needy.

He took. She gave. He slid his tongue into her open mouth and tasted every inch of her sweetness.

They kissed until he couldn't breathe properly which meant she couldn't either, and then he pulled back, still nibbling on the corner of her mouth. "You're an amazing submissive, Faith. This evening was perfection."

"It really was." Her voice was hoarse.

"You gonna test me like that when I give you an order next time?" he teased.

"Probably sometimes, Sir."

"Good. I'll enjoy coming up with creative ways to let you know I care."

"Looking forward to it, Sir." She relaxed in his arms.

He wanted to ask her one more question before he let her sleep. "Was that your first internal orgasm?"

"Yes." The one word was breathy.

Something inside him unraveled at the admission. He owned a piece of her no one else could claim. It endeared her to him even more. He kissed her temple reverently.

"Your bed is very comfortable." She snuggled in closer. "Your entire apartment is more inviting than mine."

"I'm glad you like it." He drew circles on her arm with one finger. She liked his place. She wasn't just saying that. There was no need. She genuinely liked it.

Her body finally relaxed, and her breathing evened out as she faded.

He'd worn her out. The stress of submitting to him all week from a distance and then dominating another woman earlier in the evening would have been enough to exhaust a normal human being. But Faith had shown grit and determination, allowing him the pleasure of demonstrating what a future with him would look like.

He tried to relax next to her, still holding her tight against his side, but all he could do was worry about what tomorrow would bring. He was determined to show her they were perfect together.

She had said so little about dinner with her parents that he was pretty sure she was equally determined to show him how deep she could dig in her heels.

What if she refused to take him to dinner? Was it a deal breaker?

He shuddered. He didn't know the answer.

He thought about the lecture Carter and Lincoln had given him about her wealth. They were right. She was not pretentious in any way. She'd never shown any indication she gave a shit about money. It was probable that her parents had a lot of it, and chances were she had a sizable inheritance, but suddenly he didn't care. He wasn't sure why he ever cared.

He took several cleansing breaths, fighting to push his next thoughts out of his mind.

The situation with her parents was a much bigger deal. It was a boulder between them that wouldn't budge. He needed to bite his tongue and withhold further judgment until he met her family. But damn, he was stressed about it.

As he closed his eyes and took several deep cleansing breaths, he knew why he was so worried.

Because he had fallen for Faith hard. He wanted her. Permanently.

He wanted to be her Dom. All day every day.

And that unnerved him because it would hurt like hell if this family situation of hers came between them. He considered waking her and forcing the issue. Now. Making her see reason.

A bargaining chip might work. He knew she craved being his submissive as much as he wanted to be her Dom. Maybe he could promise to give her everything she needed and wanted in exchange for encouraging her to work out the rift with her family.

He wouldn't wake her. That was crazy. She was dead tired from submitting to him. She needed to sleep. But tomorrow. Tomorrow he would plead his case.

CHAPTER 25

Faith woke slowly, wondering why she was so warm for a moment before she realized an enormous arm was draped across her chest, weighing her down. An equally large leg was stretched over her thighs.

Jeez, was he afraid she might escape?

She sobered on that very real thought.

Her bladder was screaming at her, though, so she needed to extricate herself and find his bathroom. She pushed on his arm and wiggled out from under his leg, but he rolled closer and murmured in her ear, "Where are you going, sweet girl?"

"Bathroom."

He kissed her temple and released her. "It's straight across from where you're lying. I know it's dark in here. Can you see well enough?"

She blinked several times as she slid to the floor, trying to get her bearings, and then she spotted the opening to the bathroom and headed that direction. "I think I've got it. If I run into a wall, I'm blaming you, however." At the doorway, she grabbed the frame and turned to toss one last word over her shoulder. "Sir."

She smiled as she entered the bathroom, shut the door, and flipped on the light.

Lord. Even his bathroom was dark. The man loved the color black. Though she did prefer the calming effects of darker colors over stark white, if she lived here, she would toss some bright colors around to give the place character.

After using the toilet and washing her hands, she splashed water on her face and stared at herself in the mirror. What the hell was she thinking? She would never live here.

She closed her eyes and sucked in a breath at how painful the thought was. She had permitted herself to live a double life for an entire week—half of her pretending she belonged to Rowen as his permanent submissive while the other half tried to tamp down the reality that he would never be able to accept the entire package that made up Faith Robbins.

She'd seen him cringe last night at dinner while she spoke about her family. He didn't believe her. He couldn't accept that some families were too dysfunctional to carry on.

She wasn't right for him. She had pretended for a week because it felt so fucking good. But he needed someone more wholesome and normal. Not a rich, crazy girl who was nearly estranged from her family and refused to let her heart love again.

She held the edge of the counter as she forced herself to face that last and most important thought.

She was falling in love with him.

It scared the fuck out of her.

She needed to get out of his house. Like now. Fast.

She needed to run.

She needed to protect her heart from future possible pain.

When she finally had the strength to open the door and face him, prepared to tell him she was going to call a cab and go back to her apartment, she nearly jumped out of her skin.

His entire naked frame was lounging in the doorway, meaning

he'd been facing the closed door, probably touching it with his nose, waiting for her to come out.

"Jesus, Rowen." She tossed her hand over her heart. "You scared me to death."

He lifted a brow, reminding her she hadn't turned off the light. His eyes were narrowed, squinting into the brightness, but his expression was hard. "Why do I bet you don't need me to scare you because you're so damn scared on your own that no one can even top that level of fear?"

She swallowed and stepped back. "Why do you say that?"

He took a step forward, crowding her. "Because you've been in here for half an hour, which means you spent the majority of that time staring at yourself in the mirror and coming up with excuses to get out of my apartment as fast as possible."

Her shoulders fell. Could she hide nothing from this man?

"Come back to bed, Faith." He reached out a hand and waited patiently for her to take it.

She finally did, realizing she was just as naked as him as he pulled her into his embrace. Suddenly, he bent slightly at the knees, tucked his hands under her ass, and hitched her up in the air so she was forced to wrap her legs around him to keep from falling over backward. *"Rowen,"* she chided.

He ignored her, spinning around, flipping off the light, and taking her back to bed. He dropped her unceremoniously on the mattress and then climbed over her. As he landed on his back, he pulled her into his side. "I have no idea what's going through that head of yours, but it scares the fuck out of me. So, I suggest you start talking, or I'll resort to extreme measures to get you to share."

"I don't know what you mean," she lied.

"Sweet girl, do you have any idea how I might go about disciplining a submissive who lies to me?"

"No, Sir," she muttered, her cheek pressed against his rock-hard chest.

He stroked his hand gently up and down her arm. "I'll demonstrate later. For now, I need you to talk. Openly. You gave me a huge piece of yourself the other night. I want the rest. Now."

"It's the middle of the night."

"Yep."

"Let's talk about it in the morning."

"Let's talk about it now."

"I'm tired."

"You weren't tired enough to put forth some cockamamie argument and present a good case for leaving my bed in the middle of the night, so you aren't too tired to tell me what you're running from."

"I'm not running," she defended, stopping short at the last word when it occurred to her she was lying again.

He pulled away from her several inches, his upper body stretching toward the other side of the bed. The next thing she knew, the lamp was on, and he was back at her side, leaning against the headboard, staring down at her. "Are you testing me?"

"No, Sir." She swallowed as she pushed to sitting, facing him, tucking the sheet around her chest.

"Okay, listen, we haven't had an opportunity to discuss a single particular about what a permanent relationship between us might look like, but let me paint it for you because I know in the long run that's what you need."

She didn't dare move, scared out of her mind about what he might say because she knew it would be enticing, and now wasn't a good time for him to point out how fucking perfect he was for her. He could easily get her to cave.

He continued. "We know each other well enough from a week of correspondence and three encounters to realize we match really, really well. You're super clear on the fact that I haven't had many long-term relationships because I'm a demanding Dom who likes to control things and provide for and protect my woman.

"You know perfectly well I'm exactly the sort of Dom you

crave. I'd even hedge a bet that it kind of stresses you out to realize how good we are together."

She stiffened. He was right. It scared her to death. She fit with him even better than she had with Victor, and that made her feel guilty. Intellectually, she knew it was unwarranted, but she couldn't keep the idea from invading her mind.

As if he read her thoughts, he brought Victor into the conversation. He reached for her hand and tugged her closer. "I know you had a full-time relationship with your husband. And I know you loved him deeply. But he wasn't home many times, which left you having to switch in and out of sub mode.

"When he was away for months at a time, you would have needed to step up to the plate and take care of far more than you wanted to. I'm not suggesting there was another way or that you would do anything different if you could do it over. I'm simply pointing out that I know it had to be hard for you."

She nodded. He was right. She sometimes had whiplash from submitting for several months and then being alone and in charge of everything for the next few months. It had been stressful even though she had never said a word.

Rowen's voice softened. "Sweet girl, I get it. Now let me tell you something about what I would expect from you. What I *do* expect from you."

She met his gaze and held her breath.

"In the long run, I'm looking for twenty-four seven. I never thought it would be possible to find it with anyone."

She opened her mouth to offer a lame protest in order to get him to shut up before she became putty, but he stopped her with a finger to her lips.

"Let me finish." He stroked her bottom lip as he removed his finger. "If you choose to submit to me, giving it one hundred percent, it won't mean I never let you relax and have down time to yourself or just to *be* when we're together."

She furrowed her brow, having no idea what he meant.

259

"What I'm saying is that you will have times when I don't want you to use 'Sir' with me, when I don't want you to have to think about every move, wondering how I'll react. No one can be expected to truly give every waking moment to a 'yes, Sir' submission without getting totally exhausted.

"There will be times when I give you permission to speak freely and relax without fear of retribution. What makes me the Dom is that I will choose those times and/or consent to your request for that kind of relief." He dipped his head farther. "There will be times when I insist upon it. Now is one of those times."

She didn't move a muscle as she took in his words. He wanted her to open up to him. And he wanted her to do so without submitting. In fact, he demanded it.

It felt right. It felt warm and good. She would be a fool to turn him down. She would miss out on an opportunity she hadn't fully admitted to herself was important enough to fight for until that moment.

The truth was she wanted him. She wanted to fight for him.

Taking the cowardly way out and running wasn't going to work because he'd gotten so far under her skin that she knew she would never be the same.

She took a deep breath. "It scares me to allow myself to love again."

He pulled her closer. "I know, sweet girl."

A tear slid down her face and she brushed it away. "I'm afraid of what will happen if I lose another man."

"I know." He tucked a lock of her hair behind her ear. He didn't say more, as if sensing correctly there was no way he could promise her he wouldn't leave her, especially to death. She appreciated his silent acceptance.

She continued. "You have a serious hang-up with my parents."

"Yes, I do." At least he didn't deny it. That would have rankled too.

"I never intended to take you home with me later tonight."

"I figured that." He smiled.

"One of two things would happen. Either they treat you like shit and you decide you can't take the heat and run as fast and as far as you can, or..." she hesitated, unsure how to continue.

"Or what, sweet girl?"

She had backed herself right into this corner. What she should have done was stopped at reason number one. Now she had no choice. She lowered her voice and her face. "Or my mother will say something to turn you against me or even offer to pay you to stay away from me and I end up far more humiliated than I was before we went to dinner. In my mind, I lose either way. I don't see another outcome."

He stiffened before he dropped her hand, and then he reached for her and pulled her sideways onto his lap. With one hand at her back and one hand under her chin, he met her gaze. "First of all, have I not made it perfectly clear how I feel about money?"

"Yes." He had. Repeatedly. He didn't like it. That was the next topic of conversation she needed to bring up in full disclosure.

"I rather abhor it. It makes people act like fools."

She almost laughed. He had no idea how correct he was.

"I make plenty of money. Enough to keep me comfortable. Enough to keep a significant other also fed and clothed and housed. Hell, I could raise a few kids too. I'm not poor. I do not need or want more. It wouldn't matter if your parents offered me six trillion dollars, I would walk away. So know that right now."

"Okay." She believed him.

"In addition, I've realized I judged you unfairly when it comes to money. I knew from the moment I saw you that you had plenty, and it got under my skin. I judged you before I even met you. It was wrong. You're not that kind of person. I've known that from the start. I apologize if you worried about that with me. It wasn't fair.

"Now as for our other problem, bring it on. I don't have to impress your parents. I have to impress you. If they want to try to sabotage what we have, they're welcome to try, but I will not be so easily persuaded, and I'm quite sure you won't be either."

She stared at him. He had no idea what he was asking for.

"Rowen, they are absolutely the shittiest people you will ever meet. My mother will get right in your face and belittle you. My father will stand by and let her—equally shitty." Suddenly, she realized something and shook her head. "And yet, the only way I can prove that to you is to show you. So please, be my guest. Dinner tonight at my parents' house. It'll be a hoot. We can bring balloons."

"Balloons?" He stared at her quizzically.

"Sure. Why not? Then we'll have something to pop in the car on the way home after the shitstorm. Maybe they can serve as a stress reliever."

He chuckled. "You're on. I'll get balloons."

CHAPTER 26

Faith was a mess. There was no hiding her tension as she stood next to Rowen at her parents' front door.

Rowen had already knocked. If he hadn't done it, she might have changed her mind and turned around, chickening out. This was going to be a total disaster, and it made her literally sick to her stomach to realize how much power her parents had over her. They even had the power to destroy everything good in her life, either directly or indirectly.

Sure, Rowen was full of hot air and big words, insisting it couldn't be that bad and he could handle it, but he had no clue what he was about to walk into.

The elderly woman who opened the door wasn't someone Faith had ever met, but she didn't hesitate to let the two of them inside. She mumbled a few words in greeting without making eye contact.

"Faith? Is that you?" Her mother's high-pitched, grating voice made her cringe before the woman stepped into view. Jane made her appearance by regally stepping out of the library several yards away to the left of the ridiculous grand entrance.

Faith had given her mother only four hours' notice that she

was coming and bringing a date, leaving all this information on voicemail at the exact moment in the day when she could reasonably be assured her mother would be taking her afternoon nap.

A lady should always rest in the afternoon so that she'll look her best in the evening.

Rowen set a hand on Faith's lower back as Jane strode in their direction. Jane wore a navy skirt, a white blouse, and nude heels. The blouse looked like it had been taken from the dry-cleaning bag five minutes ago.

Jane pasted on a ridiculous smile as she reached Faith and leaned in to air kiss first one cheek and then the other, as if she were French. The woman had been to France several times, but she was certainly not French.

Her hair was arranged perfectly on top of her head as usual. If Faith wasn't mistaken, she'd had it bleached earlier that day. It was amazing how she never looked like she needed her roots done. It was a wonder it hadn't all fallen out from overtreatment.

"Is that Faith?" her father asked, emerging from the library behind his wife. He was a large man. Almost as tall as Rowen and almost as big.

Faith smiled inside. It gave her pleasure to realize the father she had grown up thinking was a giant was actually not as big as her current boyfriend. She grabbed Rowen's forearm and squeezed it. "Mother. Dad. This is Rowen Easton."

Her father glanced at Rowen, brow furrowed, saying nothing. Instead, he pointed over his shoulder toward the library, asking, "Does anyone want a drink?" Not surprising. After all, it wouldn't be proper to fail to offer houseguests a beverage as soon as they stepped inside.

Ignoring Faith's introduction altogether, Jane spun around to follow her husband, William. "I certainly would. White wine spritzer if you will, dear." Even her voice grated on Faith's nerves.

Faith realized she hadn't moved to follow her parents when

Rowen pressed against her lower back. He leaned his lips close to her ear. "They seem nice," he joked.

She twisted her neck to glance at him. "They didn't even introduce themselves, Rowen."

He smirked. "True."

Rowen looked hot enough to eat. He wore perfectly fitting khaki dress pants, a navy button-down, and even a matching navy tie. When he'd picked her up, she'd lost her breath.

"Sweet girl?" he encouraged, sliding his hand from her back to her fingers and giving a tug.

Finally, she followed.

He pulled her close to his side and whispered in her ear, "Have I mentioned how fucking hot you are in that dress?"

He had. A few times. But she flushed again anyway. Mostly because she wasn't wearing anything underneath and it made her feel sexy.

Of the four people she'd set eyes on so far, she was the least formal. She'd intentionally worn a white fitted dress that had more than a small amount of Lycra in it and hugged her curves seductively. It left her shoulders bare, a thin strip of the fabric reaching from her chest to tie at the back of her neck. It wasn't obscene. After all, the front had a built-in bra and lifted her breasts just right. But she knew her mother would hate it and Rowen would drool over it. Win-win.

Working her way toward the library on her silver strappy heals, she squeezed Rowen's hand. "Let the hurricane begin."

He shook his head.

He was about to get the shock of a lifetime.

As soon as they rounded the door to the enormous library where her parents frequently entertained their guests before moving to the dining room, Faith spotted Hope sitting like a statue on one of the mahogany room's leather loveseats.

The man standing next to her was older and he looked like he needed to take a shit. His face was drawn up in a serious expression that wrinkled his forehead and made her believe it was his usual look.

Hope stood, smiling fakely. "Faith," she drawled as if she were from a southern plantation. "I haven't seen you in forever." She made her way around the coffee table and a few leather armchairs, taking her time, her back so straight it looked like she'd been practicing with books on her head.

Faith thought—not for the first time—that she was surely switched at birth.

Hope was dressed similar to their mother—who probably picked out her clothes. Both her boyfriend and Faith's father wore suits. Jackets and all.

"Hello, Hope," Faith finally said. "This is my boyfriend, Rowen." She turned her gaze up toward him and smiled. After all, he was the highlight of the room.

Hope didn't look at Rowen or acknowledge him. Instead, she turned around and nodded toward the man she'd been seated by. "The handsome man I'm dating is Montgomery Ainsley." She batted her eyes in his direction, tipping her head to one side.

Montgomery at least had the decency to nod in their general direction, but he looked bored out of his mind or like he needed to be somewhere else.

"Nice to meet you all," Rowen stated, causing Faith's skin to warm. He was far more polite than any of the rich fools in her family.

Faith lifted onto her tiptoes and whispered in Rowen's ear, "Gonna grab us both a beer."

He nodded, sauntering farther into the room to take a seat on one of the long leather couches even though not a soul had addressed him and he hadn't been invited to sit.

Faith thought it was perfect. Fuck them. She was proud to have a man with her who had the gumption to work the scene while everyone else seemed intent to act exactly like the very rich snobby fucks he despised.

"A beer? Faith. Have you no couth?" her mother chided as Faith returned to Rowen's side, handed him a bottle, and lowered onto the sofa next to him.

He took a long draw. She couldn't blame him. In fact, she did the same, ignoring her mother's taunt.

Finally, William and Jane stepped into the circle of seats. Her father sat in one of the armchairs with a high ball. Her mother stooped herself on the corner of the loveseat Hope had returned to, her wine spritzer in hand.

Montgomery remained rooted to his spot, standing while everyone else sat.

It was almost comical. If it hadn't been so sad and absurd, Faith would have buckled over laughing.

"How was your event the other night, Faith?" her mother asked. "Did you get a lot of good contributors?"

"Yes. It was lovely. You were there."

"There's no need to be snippy. I'm simply making small talk."

Whatever.

"That dress is dreadful on you, Faith. Did you get it at a thrift shop?"

Rowen stiffened. He shifted his beer to his far hand and lifted the other to settle on the back of her neck, lightly gripping her.

Faith ignored her mother's taunt.

The woman kept speaking. "Haven't you taken about enough time playing around with your little fundraiser project?"

Rowen's fingers tightened on her neck. She wasn't sure he was breathing. She glanced at him to find his eyes wide and unblinking.

Oh, yeah. He asked for this. Faith took another drink at the same time Rowen did. A long one. There wasn't enough alcohol in the house.

To top things off, her mother continued. "I'm sure it was a fun diversion for a while, but you should really think about marrying a suitable man soon and settling down."

Rowen is sitting right next to me. My date. My boyfriend. My life.

It was like he wore an invisibility cloak.

Jane sighed. "Really, Faith. I understand how you'd want to sow your oats. Find a few buff boys to have a fling with, but you're twenty-eight years old. It's time for someone serious with a college degree and a prestigious job. Someone with connections."

Rowen calmly leaned forward and set his bottle on the coffee table, ignoring the coasters.

Faith set her bottle on the hardwood floor and rose to her feet as Rowen stood next to her. "Well, this was fun." She took Rowen's hand with the intention of pulling him from the room.

Turned out she didn't have to. He threaded his fingers with hers and took control. At the entrance to the hallway, while both her mother and her sister were talking over each other, Rowen looked over his shoulder. "Thanks for the enlightenment."

Faith nearly choked as she hurried her steps to get out of there as fast as possible.

Rowen held his hands over his ears and cringed at the incredibly loud noise that filled the inside of his car with each balloon explosion as Faith used the hoop of her earing to pop every single balloon one by one until the inside of the car was covered with flying bits of colorful rubber. Several pieces were even stuck in her hair.

He removed his hands, glancing around to make sure not one remaining balloon was left behind to sneak up on him and deafen him for good. "You done?" he teased, grabbing her wrist after she put her earing back in and hauling her toward him. She was forced to lean awkwardly across the console to meet his lips.

"Yeah," she breathed. "But it would have been better if we'd gotten another dozen. I've never felt such freedom before. Like punching a wall or something."

He flexed his hand. "I tried that a few months ago. I don't recommend it. The balloon trick was a much better way to relieve stress." He glanced out the window of the car at the front of her parents' house and shuddered.

"You believe me now?"

"Yes. I'll never doubt you again." He released her to start the engine. He didn't want to sit in her parents' roundabout for another moment.

Her parents were every bit as insane as she'd explained, perhaps more so. He was shocked by how fast he'd been schooled.

It was also true that Rowen never in a million years could have taken her word for it and allowed himself to imagine parents existed who had so much more love for money than their own children.

Listening to Jane Davenport berate her daughter for making another horrible choice when it came to men had shocked him speechless.

It was incredible to think anyone could speak that way so blatantly in front of a guest as if he were nothing more than dog shit on the bottoms of her shoes. The woman knew nothing about Rowen. She clearly assumed he was some sort of flunky. Sure, he was built and a little rough from years in the army, but he was also an accountant with a reputable business. Not that it should matter who Faith dated.

Now he was educated. He'd seen it for himself. Neither of her parents had looked him in the eye or shook his hand.

Her sister had fidgeted across the room while whoever the apparently appropriate man she had next to her pretended he was too engrossed in the expensive paintings on the walls of the library to notice there was a squabble going on. Neither Hope nor her suitor said a word in support of Faith.

Twenty minutes had been about eighteen minutes too long as far as Rowen was concerned. He would never again put Faith in a position where anyone anywhere for any reason treated her poorly. He actually felt like an ass for permitting it to go on as long as he had.

The reality was he'd been too stunned to move, and part of him wondered how far her mother would really go. She'd proven she would go any length necessary to lure the black sheep back into the flock.

Faith turned to him as he sped away from the asylum. "What did you say to my dad as I stomped ahead of you to the car?"

"I told him if he or his wife ever wanted a relationship with you, they were welcome to contact us, but only if they did so knowing I would not tolerate you being mistreated ever again for even one second. Their choice."

Faith was smiling when he glanced at her.

"If it makes you feel any better, I think your father heard me and knew I meant it. He nodded as I walked away."

"Really? My father rarely gets a word in edgewise. I'm not even sure he's had an opinion of his own for thirty-five years."

Rowen laughed and reached across the console to grab her hand as he pulled up to a red light. "Frankly, now that I've seen your parents in person, I'm surprised you would agree to any communication at all."

Faith squeezed his fingers. "Like I told you before, I do it for my dad. After all, he is a congressman. It would create a scandal if I never showed my face. Even though he's a crappy, uninvolved parent, he's good at his job. I don't want to jeopardize that."

"You're a bigger person than I could probably be. I'll give you that." He lifted her fingers to his lips and kissed them. "Come home with me."

She didn't hesitate. "Okay."

"I mean, I want you to pick up some things and plan to stay."

"Overnight, you mean?"

"Longer." He squeezed her hand. "I'm not suggesting you move in. But I'd like to explore this thing between us further, and the best way to do that is to have you in my home."

"After the way you dominated me without seeing me this past week, I can assure you my proximity isn't a factor," she joked.

"I want more," he stated firmly, glancing at her.

"Okay." She leaned closer and set her head on his shoulder. "But I hope you mean it because I've already fallen so hard for you that I don't think I can retreat now. If there was any doubt, you chased it away in the last half hour. I thought you'd want to bail after that shitshow, but you stuck up for me in a way no one ever has." She lifted her face. "I'm in love with you."

He grinned, his heart soaring. "After one week?" he teased.

She flushed, apparently not catching his intonation. "You don't have to say it back. I didn't mean to—"

He cut her off with another kiss to her knuckles. "I was kidding, sweet girl. I think I fell in love with you before I knew your name."

Her smile grew slowly wider. "Yeah?"

The light turned green and he pushed on the gas. "Don't even think it will make me soft or lenient toward you. I'm so totally going to spank your bottom when we get home."

"Why...Sir?" She straightened her spine, sitting up taller.

"Because it's the fastest way to lull you into a subspace that makes you so wet and horny you can't say no to me." He shot her another smile and then focused on the road.

She leaned back in her seat, pensive. It wasn't until he pulled the car into a spot in the parking garage under his apartment building that she spoke again. "Sir?"

"Yes, sweet girl?" He faced her fully.

"All it takes to get me horny is to speak to me in that commanding tone. My pussy is already wet and swollen. You never have to spank me to accomplish that. The suggestion alone does the trick."

"Ah," he said. Instead of responding to her right away, he climbed from the car, rounded the back, and helped her out of her side. But then he turned her to face him and flattened her to the door with his much larger body, nudging her legs apart to situate his knee between them. "Are you saying that for informational purposes, or did you hope to manipulate me into not swatting your bottom as soon as we walk in the door?" He lifted one brow.

She winced. "It was more of an observation, Sir. I didn't mean to imply anything by it. I simply noticed how aroused I get when you dominate me. It only takes a voice command to bring me to my knees."

"Ah, well, that's good to know. Then you won't mind spending some time on your knees servicing me tonight, will you?"

She shook her head. "No, Sir. I would be delighted."

He lowered his face to take her lips, deepening the kiss as soon as they touched. His hands burrowed in her thick blond hair, and neither of them came up for air until someone giggled behind him.

He grinned at Faith as he broke the kiss and turned around to find two teenage girls rushing away. "We probably just ruined them for life with our heat."

"Yeah. Lucky them." Her voice was dreamy as she returned her attention to him. "I dare you to ruin me for life, Sir."

"I totally intend to do so, starting right now." He took her hand and rushed her toward the elevator, not wanting to waste another second in public.

His heart was full.

Two hours later Faith was lounging in Rowen's bed, her head against his chest, drawing circles on his pecs with one finger.

He was leaning against a pile of pillows at the headboard, his fingers trailing up and down her spine. "You're quiet," he pointed out. "I wish I could attribute it to me wearing you out, first by occupying your mouth and then by making you squirm against my lips, but I'm betting you're inside your head."

"Yeah."

"Talk to me."

"Just thinking about all the baggage we have and where we go from here."

He slid his hand into her hair and pulled her head back to meet his. His eyes were questioning.

She shrugged. "Money. Family. You know. The usual luggage." She pushed off him to sit up and meet his gaze. She needed to say some things. If they were going to make a go of this relationship, she needed to be sure he was over his hang-ups.

"Faith."

She licked her lips. "Just let me get this off my chest."

"Of course."

She took a breath and jumped right in. "I can't fix your money issues, Rowen. I'm wealthy. It's just dollars in a bank account. I like to think I'm not a bitch about it. I don't live recklessly or throw money around like it's candy. I use it for good. I donate to charities, and I made a decision years ago to put my abilities to use serving those charities.

"In fact," she sat up straighter, "I'd go so far as to say that to spite my parents, I live rather frugally, all things considered. I hate the way they have flaunted their wealth all my life. That's why I removed myself from them in the first place, met normal men, dated regular guys, and got burned now twice by the men I loved."

"Whoever the guy was who didn't have the spine to stand up to your parents in college, he missed out. He wasn't worthy of you. And you know in your heart that Victor didn't leave you. Not on purpose."

A tear fell. "You're right. I need to stop viewing it as him leaving me and instead acknowledge it was just something bad that happened. It was out of his control and mine."

He nodded. "I'm sure he loved you more than anything in the world. I'm certain you were his last thought. And, Faith, it's okay that you still think about him sometimes. It's natural. You loved him. There is no reason to feel guilty about that. Your feelings don't disappear just because he's gone. A part of you will always love him."

She choked up for a moment and then whispered, "Stop being nice."

"Sweet girl, I may be firm and set boundaries that make you feel loved and cared for, but I will always be a nice guy."

"I like that plan."

"The one with the boundaries?" He lifted a brow.

"Yes. You're right. Submitting to you calms me. It's an enormous relief. I crave the entire package."

He cupped her face with both hands. "And I want to so completely dominate you that you don't have to think. It fulfills me too. There's something in my soul that makes me crave the total domination. Maybe it's a product of years of caring for my mother and my sister. Or maybe it's just in my genetic make-up. It doesn't matter. Either way, it's what I need."

She held his gaze for so long her eyes burned. Was it possible this could work out between them? "You've had your own doubts about us this week too, Rowen. You've hidden them from me, but you've also spoken in the present tense with me several times as if this arrangement truly was for nothing more than the week."

He leaned closer. "You're right. I won't deny it. I've worried about the money. I've obsessed over your estrangement from your family. But more importantly, I didn't believe in my heart that someone could be such a perfect match for me. I didn't trust it was possible I might meet someone who could submit to me so thoroughly.

"I've been burned before. I've also tried to convince a few women to try. It never works out that way. Rayne, for example. I cared about her. I wanted it to work. She isn't that committed to the lifestyle. We clashed. I tried to be what she needed. She tried to be what I needed. It was never going to work.

"Honestly I've been unrealistically reticent about the existence of such a unicorn for several months. Perhaps years. So, I didn't trust this to work out. I didn't trust you to be as committed as all signs indicated. I didn't believe it was possible. And I sure as hell would never pressure a woman to submit to me at a level she wasn't comfortable with."

Feeling bold, Faith twisted her body around and swung a leg over him so that she straddled his lap and cupped his face. "I can understand why you would be skeptical. It makes sense. I would be too if I were you. And I would worry about the damn money, and I would feel sad about the estrangement. You have a right to all those emotions. They're totally legit.

"But you need to know that I *am* that unicorn. It's true I need to trust that you won't leave me, and I need to accept that sometimes people unintentionally die. It's true I have to take that chance to love again and let someone burrow into my heart so deep I never want to be let free.

"But you have to trust me too, Rowen. You have to trust I won't make you uncomfortable with my money. You need to get over some of your hang-ups about it and relax, knowing that no matter what you do to provide for me—and these fictitious kids you seem to be imagining—we will never want for anything. Think of it at a safety net if you want.

"In addition, you needed to see my parents for yourself, take in all that is their insanity, and accept that any real relationship with them is probably not in the cards. Granted, as long as I live in Miami and continue working for nonprofits, we will see them from time to time, and if we're in public, I'll want to be amicable for my father's sake." She shrugged. "And not just him but my job as well. It wouldn't look good for a city employee to publicly scorn her well-known family."

He stroked her back. "I get that."

"I know it made your skin crawl to find out I'm not close to my family, but Rowen, family isn't just blood. It's what you make it. I'd much rather have a family of close friends and a man I love than spend my life being fake to impress people."

His face softened.

She continued before he could stop her. "And finally, you have to believe in us. Sure, we'll be feeling each other out for a while until we settle into a routine that works for both of us, but don't turn your back on me out of some unfounded fear that no one can ever love you the way you deserve."

He blinked, his eyes wide. "Faith..."

She shook her head. "No. I mean it, Rowen. You know what you want. Don't turn it down when it's offered to you because you don't believe it can exist or you somehow don't deserve it." She grabbed his shoulders and gave him a shake.

Shocking her, he gripped her waist and flipped her onto her back, coming over her, his body between her legs. "Okay, enough chatting. I need to be inside you. I need to fuck you hard. And I need you to come screaming my name."

"I'd like that, Sir." She recognized the time for talking was over. It was time to submit again.

She waited impatiently while he grabbed a condom from the bedside table and rolled it on, and then she cried out when he plunged into her without another word.

So full her eyes rolled back and she dug her nails into his shoulders.

So perfect.

So right.

EPILOGUE

Four months later...

Rowen stood casually in the doorway to Faith's apartment, leaning against the frame, arms crossed, fighting the urge to smirk. "You're sure about this?"

"Yes. Positive." She spun around to face the movers and winced. "Be careful with that one." Rowen thought she might actually try to help the man remove the painting from the wall to ensure it wouldn't get damaged. Finally, she faced him, hands on her hips. "Why wouldn't I be? We've discussed this several times. Are *you* having second thoughts?"

He laughed. "Sweet girl, I was certain I wanted you to move in with me within days of meeting you. I'm not the one with issues. You're stressed." He reached out a hand. "Come here."

She came to him.

Luckily the movers ignored them. Rowen stepped out of the doorway so they could take another load down to the truck. He tugged Faith into his embrace and frowned down at her. "We don't have to do this if you're not ready. There's no rush."

She rolled her eyes. "You've asked me to move in with you a dozen times in the last month."

He smiled and kissed her nose. "That's because I love you, and I hate it when you're not in my bed every night."

"I'm almost always in your bed. We're wasting rent money."

That was a joke. She had enough money to buy the building. But by now Rowen knew another side of Faith. She was not wasteful. She hemmed and hawed over nearly every purchase she made. She donated anything she didn't use without flinching. She hated leaving food on her plate. She'd totally shattered his stereotype about rich woman.

He hugged her closer. "You're a little freaky today. I'm worried I pushed you to move in too fast." She had been stressed all morning, running around making sure everything went smoothly.

She shook her head. "I'm just trying to pick and choose what goes into storage and what goes to your apartment."

"And that particular painting the movers just took downstairs is super important to you?" She'd hovered the entire time the movers dealt with it. He was trying to visualize where the hell they were going to put it. Such strange colors—a combination of greens and blues. Some sort of modern art. It looked like toddlers flung their paintbrushes at it.

She laughed. "Hell, no. I hate that painting. My mother picked it out to go with the equally ugly rug and throw pillows. That monstrosity is definitely not going with us."

"Okaaay." He struggled to pinpoint the source of her stress then.

She rose onto her tiptoes and gave him a quick peck. "It's just valuable. We're going to sell it. It will pay for our kids' college tuition."

He froze, his eyes going wide, his mouth going dry.

She swatted at his chest. "Good grief. Don't have a heart attack. It was just a figure of speech. I didn't mean to imply anything."

He finally found his voice and spun them around, slamming her into the wall. To hell with the movers if they came back. He pinned her hands to her sides and met her gaze. "Oh, sweet girl, you misunderstood my shock. I would be honored to have kids with you. A dream come true. As many as you want."

She smiled. "Then why did you look like you were going to faint?"

"Because I didn't realize your paintings were worth that much."

Her smile spread as she tugged her hands free from his clutches and smoothed them up his chest. "Yeah. I have a few valuable things around here. I didn't buy them. My mother did. But I'll be damned if I'm going to give them back. Too bad. They're mine now. We're going to sell this gaudy shit and save the money for a rainy day."

"Or diapers," he pointed out.

"That too."

"You trying to tell me something?" Now he did panic, but only because he hadn't realized she might be pregnant. Not for a single second. Was this why she agreed to move in with him?

She rolled her eyes again. "No. Seriously. Relax. I've never missed a pill. If and when we have kids, it will be after we've discussed it thoroughly. I would never blindside you with something like that."

He blew out a breath and pressed into her farther, grinding his cock against her belly. He wished the movers were done and they would disappear because he had a sudden urge to dominate his little sub and then fuck her senseless against this wall.

But that wasn't in the plans. "You're sure you're good with the move?"

"I've never been more sure of anything, Rowen." Her hands slid up to wrap around his neck. "I love you. Right now I just want to get everything out of this apartment and be done with it. This is not how I like to spend my Saturdays." She wiggled her eyebrows.

"Be careful, sweet girl. If you don't stop teasing me, I might be inclined to take you in the bedroom and force you to your knees. I don't care what the movers think."

A gorgeous flush covered her cheeks. "Don't make promises like that. We have a lot of work to do." She squeezed his neck to emphasize her words.

That was the last straw. She had teased him enough. If she thought he was kidding, she was in for a surprise. He smoothed his hands up her arms, grabbed her by the wrist, and turned to nearly drag her down the hallway.

Two seconds later, they were in her empty bedroom and he had her flat against the closed door as he turned the lock. "Sassy girl."

She giggled.

He lifted a brow. "Have you been needling me all morning on purpose?" The little minx.

"Maybe?" She tipped her head to one side.

He grabbed the hem of her shirt and yanked it over her head. "How about you get on your knees and wrap your naughty lips around my cock." He pressed on her shoulders to get her to comply.

She lowered to her knees and tipped her head back to smile up at him as she opened his jeans. "Took you long enough."

He growled, threading his fingers in her hair. "How about you stop talking and start sucking. I don't care if the movers knock on the door. You'll suck until I come down your throat, so you might want to hurry it up."

She finally sobered enough to pull his zipper down, pop him free, and wrap her hand around the base of his cock. A moment later her lips were on him.

A moment after that, he lost all ability to remember where they were.

It was possible the movers came back, but if they did, he never knew about it. He was in his element. The woman he loved was on her knees submitting to him. She intended to sell her ugly furniture and move in with him. She apparently even intended to have kids with him.

Life was perfect. He wasn't about to waste it ordering the movers around. They could load the moving van just fine without any help.

AUTHOR'S NOTE

I hope you enjoyed this second book in the Club Zodiac series. Please enjoy a sneak peek of the third book in the series, *Collaring Brooke*. I've included it on the following pages.

COLLARING BROOKE

CLUB ZODIAC (BOOK THREE)

Prologue

The sound was almost worse than the result. It always was. That whistling noise of leather whizzing through the air before it struck its target.

Me.

Brooke covered her ears, tucking her small body in tighter, praying it would end soon.

It wouldn't.

It never did.

Another whoosh of leather. Another slice of pain as it hit her across the back this time.

She bit her lips between her teeth to keep from screaming. Screaming was strictly forbidden. It drew attention from the neighbors. She couldn't imagine how much worse her life would be if anyone called the police.

If she could just be better.

Do better.

Not mess up so often.

It was her fault.

She shouldn't have spilled the coffee.

Her hand had been unsteady. She was hungry. Always hungry. It made her shake. Especially in the morning.

"You stupid girl." The belt hit her across the butt, shocking her with how much worse that next strike hurt.

More reprimands. Seething words hissed out in a low tone so none of the neighbors would hear. "You're nothing. You'll never amount to anything. You can't even pour a cup of coffee without spilling it."

Brooke whimpered, but stopped herself as quickly as possible, hoping she hadn't been heard. She held her breath to keep from making another sound.

"What? You're not going to cry like a big baby this time?" Another whoosh of the belt.

She could anticipate every strike from the sound. She'd been beaten so many times that she knew the timing perfectly. She spread her fingers, tucked her face in closer to the corner of the wall, and prayed it would be over soon.

"Get up."

Brooke didn't dare move. That line was often a trick.

"I said, get up." Louder this time. Closer. "Are you deaf now too?"

Her heart pounded.

"Fine. Then stay in that corner for the rest of the day. You deserve it." Footsteps moved away. The belt was tossed aside, the sound of the buckle hitting the kitchen table soothing. It signified the beating was over.

Brooke didn't allow herself to breathe easy, though. She didn't even move. She wouldn't dare move for the rest of the day.

What time was it?

Morning. Early. It would be a long day.

It had been months since the last time she'd endured a beating like this. She could feel the warm wetness of blood running down her back. It was a familiar sensation. It wasn't usually this bad, but she was used to it. She could even predict from the level of pain alone how long the welts would take to heal.

A door slammed.

Slowly, gradually, she started to breathe again. At least she was alone now. There was peace in her loneliness.

She enjoyed being alone.

No one could hurt her when she was alone.

Chapter One

The first time she saw him she was hauling a bucket of cleaning supplies through the dim lighting of Club Zodiac on her way toward the private rooms that lined the hallway.

Brooke had no idea what his name was, but she assumed he was one of the owners. He had his head down, his fingers flying across the keypad of his cell phone while he sauntered toward the stairs that led to the third floor.

He didn't notice her, but then again she stood stock still watching him. He was not only significantly taller than her, but broad. Enormous. His blond hair was tousled as though he'd either run his hands through it or hadn't combed it at all.

Her heart raced for no good reason. She should not be standing there watching him move. She shouldn't even care enough to glance at him. But she did. She continued to stare after he rounded the corner completely out of sight.

A noise behind her made her spin around so quickly she nearly dropped her supplies. Her face flushed, heat rushing up her cheeks as though she'd been caught stealing or killing puppies or something.

"I'm so sorry." The woman who spoke rushed forward. "I didn't realize anyone was here or I wouldn't have snuck up on you. I didn't mean to scare you to death. Are you okay?" The woman was blond with pale skin. She was not much taller or larger than Brooke.

When she reached for Brooke's arm to gently touch her, Brooke flinched before she could stop herself. She had to take a deep breath before she found her voice. "No worries. I should have heard you. My mind was..." Where was her mind? She had no idea how to finish that statement, so she let it hang.

The blonde held out a hand. "Faith Robbins."

Brooke stared at her hand for a moment before she realized she needed to take it. She shifted her bucket from her right hand to her left awkwardly in order to return the gesture. "Brooke Madden."

"Nice to meet you, Brooke. Are you a member of the club?" she asked innocently.

Brooke's eyes widened. "No. I, uh..." She felt utterly foolish. "I work for the company that cleans the building." She pointed at her bucket. "I was about to do the floors in the hallway." *When I got sidetracked by the giant of a man who should not have been able to penetrate my thick walls.*

Faith smiled, her face also flushing with embarrassment. Why would she feel awkward? "Ah. Then I'm in your way. I just came in to practice while the club is closed. Will it bother you if I work in the main room?" She nodded over Brooke's shoulder.

Brooke glanced behind her at the darkened room that was filled with the craziest most unimaginable equipment she had seen in her life. What the hell was Faith going to do in there to "practice"?

For weeks Brooke had been cleaning this club, and only because she cleaned the entire building, including the business located on the first floor below Zodiac. The first time she'd come in, another team member from the cleaning service had been with her, and thank God because Brooke might have left the place screaming.

She realized Faith was waiting for her to respond. "Oh, no. Of course not. Do what you need to do. I'll work around you. I mean, unless that's a problem. I can come back." That wasn't entirely true. The reality was Brooke was almost done for the day. After mopping this hall, she intended to go home. Exhausted.

Faith hesitated, narrowing her eyes slightly. "You're sure you don't mind? I don't mean to traumatize anyone."

Traumatize anyone? Brooke waved her off with a forced giggle. "Don't worry about me. Do your thing. I'll mop this hallway and get out of your way."

Brooke proceeded to mop the hallway, but her curiosity got the better of her, and she continuously passed by the wide opening that dumped the hallway into the main room. Snooping. Faith turned on several lights, illuminating the large room in a way that made it seem far less ominous. The walls, ceiling, and floor were all painted black, but with a few overhead lights, the odd pieces of furniture scattered around made the place look far less intimidating.

When a loud snapping sound rent through the silence, Brooke jumped out of her skin and rushed around the corner to make sure Faith was okay.

She was still breathing heavily when she came to a halt, finding the blond woman facing a strange bench and flicking a long whip thingy through the air. Another snap came as a shock to Brooke, making her emit a sharp squeal.

She clapped her hand over her mouth, mortified at being caught as Faith turned around.

Faith rushed forward again, still holding the whip. "Shit. I'm sorry. I'm totally making your day miserable time and again." She set the whip down on a chair as she approached. "I'll wait until you're done here before I continue. I forget that most people would be horrified to watch me practice."

Brooke licked her lips. "Practice for what?" She glanced around the room, wondering what the hell actually happened in the club when it was open.

Faith smiled. "You have no knowledge of BDSM, do you?"

"BDSM?" Brooke shook her head, realizing how stupid she

sounded as the acronym seeped in. "I mean, yes. I understand the gist. Bondage and stuff. What are you doing with that leather rope?" She sucked in a sharp breath. "I'm sorry. None of my business."

Faith's brows drew together.

Brooke backed up, nearly stumbling. She was supposed to clean the floors and then leave. The owners of CCS—the number one company for business cleaning in Miami—would frown on her engaging the client. Commercial Cleaning Services, Inc. Their motto was: Less is more. Clean and get out. Don't encourage conversation and give a business any reason to fire them.

"Wait." Faith stepped forward. "I'm the one who should be apologizing. It was rude of me to assume you wouldn't freak out. I forget not everyone is used to seeing someone wield a whip."

"What? Goodness no. I've seen everything," Brooke lied as she waved a hand in front of her face to blow off the strange interaction. "You would not believe what cleaning people witness. Whips. Chains. Whatever." She had no actual idea what she was talking about.

For a second, neither of them said a word, and then Faith cocked her head to the side, a slow smile forming. A moment later, she laughed.

Brooke couldn't help but join her. She laughed so hard, she bent at the waist. She couldn't remember the last time she'd laughed like that. And then she sobered as she realized she'd *never* laughed that hard.

Faith was wiping tears from her eyes as Brooke tried to control her outburst.

How mortifying. She couldn't have said anything more ridiculous. But Faith didn't seem to mind.

Finally, Faith took a deep breath and nodded behind her. "Come on. The least I can do is give you a demonstration so you don't leave here wondering."

Brooke stopped mid-breath, taking another step backward. "Oh, no. I couldn't."

"Why not?" Faith glanced around. "You're curious, right?"

Brooke nodded against her better judgment. *More like horrified, but sure.*

The next thing she knew, Faith took her mop from her hand and leaned it against the wall. "Come on," she repeated in a tone that brooked no argument. She gently took Brooke by the arm and led her across the room toward a bench. "Sit here. Don't move. Just watch."

Brooke felt extremely out of her element jumping up onto the bench thingy to sit while Faith picked up her whip again. She was intrigued. And frightened.

Faith approached, spun the handle of the whip around, and offered it to Brooke. "Here. Check it out. Best place to start. It's just leather woven together. When I fling it through the air, it makes that cracking noise you heard."

The one that made me nearly pee my pants. Brooke's hands were shaking as she examined the whip and then handed it back.

"I'm what they call a Domme."

"You mean like a Dominatrix? A woman?"

"Yep, but people don't really say Dominatrix anymore. Just Domme. I'm a female Domme. The guys don't get to have all the fun. Didn't your mom tell you that you can be anything you want?" she teased.

Brooke gulped. *Not even close...* She rocked back and forth on her butt, tucking her hands under her thighs to keep from revealing more than she wanted. Shifting her gaze to the whip, she leaned back a few inches as if she might be injured by it any second. "What are you practicing?" she asked to change the subject. She also really wanted to watch.

"Precision."

"Uh-huh."

Faith backed up several yards, swung the whip slowly through the air a few times, and then gave it a sharp yank, which recreated that same cracking noise as before.

Brooke yelped, flinching as the tail end of the whip struck a pole.

"Precision," Faith repeated as she turned around. "Don't want to hurt anyone."

"You…you…hit people with that?"

"Yes. But it's not nearly as bad as you'd think. I can alter the intensity so that I leave little to no marks." She winked. "I've been doing this a while."

Brooke's mouth was dry. "I can't imagine how that would not hurt." *I know for a fact it would hurt. Bad. It would leave a welt. Probably blood.* She cringed.

Faith turned back around, lined herself up with the pole, and whipped the tail through the air again, slower this time, with less of a crack. It still hit the pole right where she'd aimed, but not with as much force. Nevertheless, it would hurt.

Faith returned to stand next to Brooke, setting the whip behind her on the bench. "That's a bit advanced. I can show you other toys if you're interested."

Brooke was at a loss for words. Half of her was incredibly curious. The other half wanted to run from the club and never look back. "Maybe you could just explain this to me a bit?" She glanced around. "What all happens in here? People come here, get tied to these benches and things, and beaten? Why would they want to do that?"

Faith smiled. "Damn. It's been a long time since I've explained the inside of a club to a newbie."

Brooke had no idea what that meant, but she said nothing.

Faith glanced around. "Your description oversimplifies things. First of all, nothing happens in Zodiac that isn't safe, sane, and consensual. No one plays without a safeword. No one plays without reading the house rules and signing a waiver."

"Who would consent to letting someone whip them?" *Not me.*

"You'd be surprised. People have all sorts of reasons why they practice masochism." She lifted her gaze. "Masochists are people who enjoy some form of pain with their BDSM."

Brooke's heart was pounding. She glanced at the whip, memories of being struck with a similar object more times than she could count flooding her mind. The pain. The humiliation. The torture.

The strangely peaceful numbness.

As if Faith read her mind, she continued. "Many submissives say they get a release from being spanked or flogged or struck by any number of objects. Like they're absolved from some perceived wrongdoing, real or imagined. It can be freeing."

Brooke continued to stare at the whip Faith had wielded so expertly. Freeing... Something about the idea made her skin tingle. It had been so long since the last time she'd felt that kind of release.

So rarely did she step out of line, even lately. But today she had. She'd felt guilt for the last several hours. Her offense? Falling under the spell of a man. It was wrong. She knew it. And yet, she'd been unable to stop herself. The blond god who was part owner of Zodiac had tempted her.

"You okay?" Faith asked.

Brooke jerked her gaze up to meet Faith's.

"I've said too much. I'm so sorry. I get carried away when it seems like someone wants to learn. I forget not everyone wants to hear about my world. Forgive me."

Brooke slowly nodded her head. "No. Really. It's fine." She licked her dry lips. "Would you show me what it's like?"

ALSO BY BECCA JAMESON

Project DEEP:

Reviving Emily

Reviving Trish

Reviving Dade

Reviving Zeke

Reviving Graham

Reviving Bianca

Reviving Olivia

SEALs in Paradise:

Hot SEAL, Red Wine

Hot SEAL, Australian Nights

Dark Falls:

Dark Nightmares

Club Zodiac:

Training Sasha

Obeying Rowen

Collaring Brooke

Mastering Rayne

Trusting Aaron

Claiming London

The Art of Kink:

Pose

Paint

Sculpt

Arcadian Bears:

Grizzly Mountain

Grizzly Beginning

Grizzly Secret

Grizzly Promise

Grizzly Survival

Grizzly Perfection

Sleeper SEALs:

Saving Zola

Spring Training:

Catching Zia

Catching Lily

Catching Ava

The Underground series:

Force

Clinch

Guard

Submit

Thrust

Torque

Saving Sofia (Kindle World)

Wolf Masters series:

Kara's Wolves

Lindsey's Wolves

Jessica's Wolves

Alyssa's Wolves

Tessa's Wolf

Rebecca's Wolves

Melinda's Wolves

Laurie's Wolves

Amanda's Wolves

Sharon's Wolves

Claiming Her series:

The Rules

The Game

The Prize

Emergence series:

Bound to be Taken

Bound to be Tamed

Bound to be Tested

Bound to be Tempted

The Fight Club series:

Come

Perv

Need

Hers

Want

Lust

Wolf Gatherings series:

Tarnished

Dominated

Completed

Redeemed

Abandoned

Betrayed

Durham Wolves series:

Rescue in the Smokies

Fire in the Smokies

Freedom in the Smokies

Stand Alone Books:

Blind with Love

Guarding the Truth

Out of the Smoke

Abducting His Mate

Three's a Cruise

Wolf Trinity

Frostbitten

A Princess for Cale/A Princess for Cain

ABOUT THE AUTHOR

Becca Jameson is a USA Today best-selling author of over 80 books. She is most well-known for her Wolf Masters series and her Fight Club series. She currently lives in Atlanta, Georgia, with her husband, two grown kids, and the various pets that wander through. She is loving this journey and has dabbled in a variety of genres, including paranormal, sports romance, military, and BDSM.

A total night owl, Becca writes late at night, sequestering herself in her office with a glass of red wine and a bar of dark chocolate, her fingers flying across the keyboard as her characters weave their own stories.

During the day--which never starts before ten in the morning!--she can be found jogging, floating in the pool, or reading in her favorite hammock chair!

...where Alphas dominate...

Becca's Newsletter Sign-up

Contact Becca:
www.beccajameson.com
beccajameson4@aol.com

facebook.com/becca.jameson.18

twitter.com/beccajameson

instagram.com/becca.jameson

bookbub.com/authors/becca-jameson

goodreads.com/beccajameson

amazon.com/author/beccajameson

Made in the USA
Monee, IL
10 September 2022

13705866R10174